# Overtaken

## Valerie Storey

*Dava Books* : *Albuquerque*

Overtaken

Library of Congress Control Number: 2010926719

Published by Dava Books, Albuquerque

ISBN 978-0-9643289-3-8

*How long shall I stay in the world?*
*Why do they not leave my heart in peace?*
*Why do I torment myself so vainly?*
*Shall I stay, shall I go?*

Tao Yuanming (A.D. 372 – A.D. 427)

# 1

I bought the house on a Sunday because it was raining, because I had
nothing better to do, because my painting was going badly, and because my
husband, with whom I had only spent forty-eight hours in the last six
months was coming home for good in three weeks time. I needed somewhere to live other than a damp room in West London with only my
suitcase and unfinished canvases.

"Very sound," the agent said, knocking on paneling, opening and shutting kitchen cabinets. "The house is very sound."

I wandered into the dining room and ran my fingers over the walls
painted a pale robin's egg blue. A warm color, and I listened for the "very
sound" of the house. In the silence of the unoccupied neighborhood, all
the residents seemingly gone on holiday or vanished into the city, I heard
the "very sound." A type of purring. A satisfied hum that rose and fell like
the breathing of a sleeper. I was nearly hypnotized by its rhythm.

"The lease is for ninety-nine years," the agent announced, entering the
room and interrupting my thoughts, startling me.

"Fine," I said. "I'll take it."

The purring seemed louder, gratified. The agent smiled, and I could tell
she heard nothing but her own satisfaction at closing a deal. I couldn't wait
for her to leave. I couldn't wait to be alone with the house, my thoughts,
that sound.

# 2

I met Miles in the London offices of Teague & Bloch, geological engineers, the same morning I took my only piece of decent jewelry out of hock. A golden filigree cuff interwoven with small branches of black coral, it had saved me from eviction more times than I cared to count.

I remember because I wore it to deliver a portrait I had started the year before of Gordon Teague, the company founder. As prestigious as the commission had been, it hadn't come cheap; the price of brushes and paint being the reason for the pawnshop. On the plus side, though, I'd had the advantage of a genial sitter with an uncritical wife, and my work had progressed smoothly. There were, of course, the usual problem areas that always bothered me and that I wanted to change on the spot: a shadow below the left eye, an inaccurate fold of the monogrammed handkerchief jutting out from a finely-tailored Bond Street suit. But overall, the painting was deemed a success, and the balance of my payment was in a heavy, cream-colored envelope at the front desk with an unusually bright receptionist.

"Miles Bergsen, Sara Elliott," she said, introducing me to the man sitting on the corner of her desk. "Miles has just returned from Siberia." She shivered.

Miles and I shook hands. "Hello," I said. His hand felt cold to the touch, but there was warmth underlying his grip. "What were you doing in Siberia?"

"Evaluating tundra and antiquated frozen machinery. You know, things that were abandoned with the collapse of the Soviet Union." He rubbed his hands together like a man anxious to thaw, as if he needed to get the bone chilling cold of the steppes out of his joints and memory.

The secretary smiled again. "You must warm him up," she said to me, laughing at her own weak joke.

"Don't mind Priscilla," Miles said. "She wants me to take her to lunch, but I'd rather go with you."

"I don't know…"

"Please. There's a Greek place in Soho I'd like to try. Priscilla doesn't like to experiment."

Priscilla made a face that told me they were old friends who indulged in this sort of banter every time Miles was in town.

"Go ahead," she said. "You two can discuss art while I deal with the important things, like damaged pipelines and unsigned contracts. Don't let me spoil your fun."

It seemed I had no choice but to fall into their game, if that's what it was. We left together, stopping long enough for me to sign for my check and then wait for Miles to examine a full wall display of geological specimens, from fossilized whale bone to great chunks of opal, tanzanite, and tungsten. I, too, was taken by the colors of the specimens and stones, each as appealing to me as if I were walking into a well-stocked art supply store. My interest in the displays must have attracted Miles in some way, but when it led to a discussion of my bracelet ("Russian, isn't it? It makes you very fierce.") I knew we would be a couple by the end of the week. It wasn't every day I met a man who knew Scythian gold for what it was and then looked at me as if I were every bit as valuable.

When we were married a few days later, I had no idea who was the most surprised: me, Miles, or the intelligent secretary, who wore a navy blue designer dress with a broad-brimmed red hat to the Marylebone ceremony. On Miles's side he had the company director and his wife, the secretary as I mentioned, and an elderly aunt who seemed baffled by her surroundings, and kept poking through her large black, square handbag searching out her railway return ticket. She had traveled down from

Manchester, and while kindly disposed to me, she also seemed to find the entire outing rather bothersome and unnecessary. She gave me a silver picture frame as well as an expensive set of eggplant-colored bedding; a wild, exotic shade I would never have dreamed coming from a seventy-eight-year-old retired biology teacher. Her third gift to me was a box of Miles's childhood mementos: school reports and medals, an aging teddy bear, letters he had written her from college and his more unusual world travels. She handed these over with a conspiratorial air, making me believe she was glad to relieve herself of a past that no longer belonged to her. Miles may have been a blood relation, but now that he was married, he was mine. Life had other, more pressing things to attend to, ladies' golf being one of them, I learned over the champagne and smoked truffles Miles's company had generously supplied for our rather hurried reception. When the party was over, the director and his wife offered to drive Aunt Winifred to Paddington Station, and Miles and I were left to cram an eternity into forty-eight hours. He was to leave on Sunday night for Dubai and this was Friday lunch.

I had no one of my own to invite to lunch or anywhere else for that matter, being the only—and adopted—child of global nomads presently ensconced in Melbourne, Australia, and my one close friend, Noreen Riley, was currently on holiday in Greece with her latest boyfriend, an insurance broker she liked precisely for his predictability. I do not know if she would have approved of Miles. She was killed three days after my wedding in an auto accident. The predictable broker had been indulging in very predictable tourist activities—beer and ouzo on a glaringly hot mid-afternoon; very British, very sudden. When I heard of her death, Miles was already in his new job of project coordinator and drilling engineer. Where, exactly, would be anyone's guess. There could be no phone calls or e-mails, Miles had informed me at the airport, only letters through Teague & Bloch, "security reasons" being the sole explanation.

I was too stunned to question him further and could only watch him leave through the gates, the fear that I would never see him again warring with his promise that someday we would be together forever.

Forever, I thought. Such a short and impractical time.

Of our lone weekend together I remember very little except for never leaving the bedsit and being so focused on discovering my husband that it was as if time had become irrelevant. My hands and body were set on recapturing an ancient language, a Braille or a code I was never sure of having simply forgotten, or perhaps I had never known until now. There was one excursion outside for oranges, wine, and a fruitcake that I bought because of the wrapping of wedding bells and sprays of forget-me-not. It was a sentimental gesture I was hardly aware of and as I ate the cake alone the following week, reading the short note from Noreen's mother, wondering if I should wear my wedding suit to the funeral—a lavender gray I thought would be useful but never imagined its utility would be needed so soon—I ate my cake knowing I suddenly had a huge bank account and a husband who had told me to spend it any way I pleased to "set up house." He was to be home in August, this time until the end of the year, and he was seriously considering traveling much less and taking a long-offered executive position in the London office. There was even the hint that the director was planning to retire and Miles was something of a favorite for the job.

As I sat cross-legged on my futon, licking almond paste from my fingers, I thought of one of the last things Miles had said to me.

"Did you know," he said, teasing the gold cuff up and down my arm, "that Arabic is based on the twenty-eight phases of the moon? Hebrew, on the other hand, is derived from letters of flame."

"And which do you prefer?" I asked. I stared at his mouth as he spoke, willing it to return to my own, terrified I would forget his features, that he would melt away from me in some kind of photographic blur in the way I could no longer remember my parents' faces.

"Neither," he said, oblivious to my fears. "They are the same to me, two halves of the same equation. Lunar and solar energies that could not exist without each other."

"The sun and the moon," I said lightly, drawing his face toward mine. "It sounds greedy. My mother was always telling me off about it. 'You want the sun and the moon, Sara. Nothing is ever enough for you.'"

"The sun and the moon," he repeated. "They're yours."

I kissed him full on the mouth. "I could never want more."

He smiled in the same sleepy way that had first pulled me into his life. As his lips brushed my hair, I let the topic slip away with the rest of the daylight. I did not think of it again for months.

## 3

*This man, this stranger...*

That is what Noreen would have called him, Miles: *"that man you mar-ried."* And I can safely say, no, she would not have approved of Miles, or of the idea of my marrying so suddenly and unexpectedly. Noreen was my best friend, but even she did not know me as well as she might have thought. Marrying in haste was very much me. On the surface: demure, polite, a well-brought-up child. At night I had stolen sugar from the ceramic bowls set out on the long oak tables of our boarding school until I made myself ill.

Those memories were strong during my first lunch with Miles, and I was embarrassed by my hunger for his attention and regard. He listened to me talk about art school and my habit of wandering around London at dawn, sketching the sunrise, anxious to get my colors right.

"Marry me," he had said halfway through a rundown of St. Paul's by moonlight. I thought it was a lark. I saw myself as a coltish schoolgirl, reading a forbidden romance under the sheets with a flashlight. *The handsome hero arrives, stepping from the pages, sweeping me away from overdue science projects and my hatred of calculus.*

I looked into his eyes, a deep green. He has seen things, I thought, things I can't even dream of.

"I want a home," he said. "A place to settle in. A place with a wife and, oh, I don't know, fireplaces and normal hours. No back packs. No sleeping bags. Just a beautiful wife, like you. How about it? What do you say?"

Without allowing myself to think too hard, I whispered, "Yes. Me too. I mean a home and all that." My voice seemed to carry an echo, as if we were alone in a pocket of silence in the middle of that busy, frantic restaurant.

"Then it's settled," Miles agreed. "A home of our own. With just us in it." I could only nod before I polished off the rest of my vegetarian moussaka. It was delicious.

Later, as we stood outside the restaurant, uniquely determined to go through with our crazy decision, Miles kissed me with a slowness that again conjured up that feeling of being in our own private universe. A soft rain coated our hair, our faces; the dampness felt like a magical cloak, concealing us with an invisibility I savored all the while I told myself this was madness, but I wanted it more than life itself. People jostled us on every side, but we held fast in the middle of the footpath.

"Forever," Miles said.

"Forever," I repeated. Office workers, harried shoppers, snooty people with snippy little dogs skirted past us as we clung to each other. I didn't care what they thought. I had him all to myself. The hero had chosen me, just like I knew he would. My mother would have a fit. Her marriage, like everything else about her, was orderly and precise and planned. "Sara," Inge would have said in her soft Swedish-tinged accent, "you will be the death of me."

She said things like that, never meaning them—what mother did?—but I had been a trial to her, I knew. Between her and my adoptive father, Evan Elliott, my parents had given me what could only have been described as an imaginative childhood. As a working couple, they were much sought after as sound and recording engineers, tracking the nuances of bird song and innuendo from continent to continent. One year alone we lived in Bali, Mongolia, and São Paolo. When I was ten, we lived with the Laplanders, following the reindeer, setting up camp and boiling snow for cooking reindeer hide. My mother told me Andersen's stories for the first time that winter, about Little Gerda and the Snow Queen. I don't know who listened more wistfully, my father or me, but I had loved the way

Little Gerda had to rescue Kay on her own, and I was always frightened for her. I wasn't like Little Gerda. I wasn't like Inge. I didn't like being the strong one.

But now at thirty-two, Miles had freed me of ever having to rescue anyone, and after signing a sheaf of papers that made as much sense to me as the pictographs my father painted for his own amusement on the tanned and stretched reindeer hides, I had a house too large to know by room if not by heart.

It seemed extravagant, all that space after my cramped bedsit. But the price had been so ridiculously low. I held Miles's last missive forwarded from Teague & Bloch in my hand, instructing me to choose whatever I wanted. He would love it on sight, he said. Where, why, what—none of that mattered to him as long as I was happy. It was a tall order, too selfless to really be an invitation that inspired confidence. Any other woman would have been delighted to comply. I left the purchase as late as possible, and then wondered how I could have been so nervous and indecisive. It was everything I wanted and it would be our home, the haven Miles had said he wanted.

A part of me had been inclined to act out at the signing, snarky questions about mutilated bodies secretly tucked away between the water heater and the airing cupboard, or perhaps, I asked, human blood sacrifices had desecrated the back patio? But no, the agent assured me straight-faced; there was nothing to hide. Two stories, three large, well-appointed bedrooms, a sitting room with the perfect area for a studio to one side, a kitchen, two bathrooms—one *en suite*—and a solarium dining room. "That's it," she said, "and a bargain at twice the price."

"What about that small closety-thing at the very top?" This last room she had scarcely bothered with, shrugging it off when I pointed out it wasn't on the floor plan. She only opened the door when I insisted.

"It's a locker. Storage. Air ducts. Don't worry, I doubt if you'll be charged extra just because it's not on the plan!" She laughed in exasperation and tied a scarf patterned with scenes of the Eiffel Tower around her throat. But I could tell the room had nothing to do with heat systems or plumbing. Not quite a loft or an attic, it had something nursery-like about it. Or studious. "Strange" was the only adequate description. I recalled dreaming of a similar place during my childhood. A secret, hidden place, like a small train compartment or curio cabinet. A place with sliding panels, inglenooks, built-in shelving, and William Morris wallpaper climbing the walls.

This particular space was quite empty except for an upholstered divan nestled against the wall. A single cashmere shawl woven in a paisley pattern was draped against one end as if someone had left expecting to return. The agent seemed in a hurry for us to leave, but I wanted to sprawl on the divan the second I saw it, an odd compulsion as I have never been a person known to sleep in the afternoon. In Spain I was always restless during the enforced siestas, impatient with a country that fell asleep during the day as if succumbing to some curse or narcotic. I stared at the brightly woven shawl. What time of day had Noreen and her lover been killed? And if it had been late afternoon, and if Greece was as sleepy as Spain, who else had been on the road to hit their car broadside in full daylight?

"Wakey, wakey." The agent waved her pen in front of my eyes.

"Sorry," I said, following her downstairs again.

"You artistic types," she said. "Always in a dream world."

Maybe, I thought. Maybe that's why my mind was in a continual jumble, leaping from one subject to the next. Like how I couldn't stop thinking of the man at Noreen's funeral. Or how hot it had been that day.

Of the three hundred or so mourners, including Noreen's publishing firm from the mailroom boys to the CEO, I noticed one man in particular at the back of the church. He had entered late, hesitated, and then taken a seat to one side not with the others in the pews but on a plain, straight-backed chair totally out of keeping with the rest of the seating.

Although barely spring, the day was unseasonably warm and filled with summer. Sun streamed in from the back of the church, washing all the usual highlights: a mural in the style of Lord Leighton, memorial tablets from the Boer War. Despite the warm weather, the man wore a heavy gray overcoat with a collar of Persian lamb. His black walking stick was topped with an unusually large image of a panther's head that I wished I could examine more closely. Even from a distance its intricacy and quality were unmistakable. He smiled when he noticed my interest, but the service had already begun and I was forced to turn away.

I sat crowded in the front, close to Noreen's family and other friends. Noreen had been a popular acquisitions editor, raising an obscure medical publisher to the dizzying heights of medical thrillers and even a coffee-table art book on the history of dissection that became on overnight success when it was featured in a blockbuster film. Most of the women in attendance had been to school with us at St. Anne's, an Anglican convent that took in girls from ex-pat families. I continued to correspond irregularly with several of them, but Noreen and I were the only ones who had had the nerve to move to London and stay there. In Noreen's case it had been because she was really good at her job; in mine it was due to the fact that I had lived in so many varying degrees of discomfort throughout my unorthodox childhood that I had no qualms about striking out on my own in a large city. Besides, I had a small scholarship to study at the Courtauld, and I could see no other career calling me as strongly as the need to paint.

At some belated stage of the service I realized I'd been daydreaming as usual, and the funeral was over. I filed out the door behind the others in a stupor of silence. There was no coffin. Noreen's parents were free thinkers who had their daughter cremated; her ashes placed in a stoneware jar her youngest sister, an arts major at Dartmouth, made during an earlier semester as a class assignment. Raku blues and golds, it was a fitting holder for my flamboyant friend. We hadn't seen each other in months, but I had saved the postcard from Athens sent just after her arrival there. Suddenly the English sun seemed weak and watery when I thought of Noreen in that blinding Mediterranean heat, the light deflecting off the whitewashed congeries of shops and small houses. I needed a drink.

The man in the formal overcoat again made a fleeting appearance in the corner of my eye, tipped his hat, and without waiting for me to respond, disappeared. Before I could question his presence, I was caught up by my former school friends clamoring for my attention.

"Married!" they shrieked before remembering we were at a funeral. "When?" they whispered in more subdued tones as they grabbed my hand to study the rings more closely: luminescent moonstones in a modern setting Miles had bought from the V&A gift shop. I admit I was rather vain of their weight and sparkle, and unduly proud of my newly-married status, although none of it carried over when I returned to the bedsit, the wedding gifts carefully repacked in their boxes, cards in place, and lined against the wall in readiness for Miles's return and the house he encouraged me to look for and buy.

Now, deed in hand and decorators paid and gone, that house was mine, ours, and Noreen would never have coffee in my brand new kitchen. The smell of commercial paint, carpeting, and furniture was overwhelming, nothing like the pleasurable pine smells I associated with my work. I tried opening windows and doors and felt too vulnerable, too exposed in this neighborhood of young stockbrokers and high-tech wizards. I didn't want to give the impression that because I was an artist I was some party-giving Bohemian who flung her doors open any old time of night to ask the neighbors in for beer and chips. So I closed the doors and suffered, pacing from bathroom to kitchen to the front door in a fruitless attempt to breathe fresh air. Mainly I was just bored.

The eggplant sheets and duvet were on the bed; the silver picture frame captured me in a pose alone at my wedding looking surprised and festive, my rings catching the camera flash. I had never had a photograph of myself on view before. In fact, I had never really liked family snapshots placed around a house, but it seemed a married, house-dwelling thing to do. I'd test it out, I thought, and if I didn't like looking at myself I'd use the frame for pressed flowers or some other daft recreation, something for the bathroom.

I was beginning to feel like a very poor excuse for a suburban new-lywed when a pounding at the back door broke my concentration. The sound was angry, insistent, and I stubbed a toe in my rush to answer it.

A blonde middle-aged woman wearing a tidy button-down shirt and crisp white chinos peered through the glass of my back door. She held a stack of mail that as soon as I unhitched the latch she thrust in my face as if I had caused her some personal insult. Too late I remembered it was afternoon and I was still wearing a wrinkled, not very clean cotton night-gown.

"They're yours," she said, not at all friendly. "I'm sick to death of hav-ing to tell the post office to get it right." The pile was enormous.

"I'm sorry," I said, confused by her animosity and the heavy fumes in the air. "It does seem like a lot." Why had she let it accumulate so?

As if she had heard me, she said, "You're never home."

Not true, I wanted to argue. It seemed I had been a prisoner to deli-very crews for weeks. Then again, I had been out shopping a lot; perhaps our schedules had failed to coincide.

She gave me that hostile look again. "One's from the Middle East." My heart leaped. Miles. She continued to frown, as if I owed her an explana-tion. What did she think? That I was corresponding with terrorists?

"My husband," I said, knowing it was none of her business. Then be-cause Miles would be her neighbor soon, I added, "He's away, working in the Saudi oil fields. He should be home any day now."

She sniffed and turned away, tossing over her shoulder, "You need to talk to the post yourself. I'm not going to be responsible anymore."

I closed the door on her bad humor and sifted through the pile of cata-logs and bills before I found Miles's letter, the one he wasn't supposed to send. The texture of the envelope was the same rich paper I recognized as his company's stationery. I held it close, not wanting to rush. I looked around for a suitable place to read and settled for a chair belonging to the new teak dining table. There I carefully pried open the envelope and removed the single sheet of deckle-edged paper. I read the sparse lines and felt the floor drop:

*Return cancelled; unexpected delay. Remember the sun and the moon.*
*Yours.*

4

He wasn't coming home. Miles wasn't coming back. All that preparation, all my feeble plans for his return were of no use whatsoever. I thought of the numerous and vague "married people" rituals I had imagined us performing together: trips to Sainsbury's to choose the week's groceries; rushing to catch trains and dinner dates with powerful employers and clients; walks on Sundays with visits to antique bookstores and outdoor markets. None of that mattered or applied anymore. Instead, I would be working alone, rarely setting foot in Sainsbury's except for the infrequent carton of milk or clutch of bananas, and there would be little need to rush for dinner. My early-rising clients elected to meet over morning coffee to discuss fees and sitting dates in between video conference calls and checking their e-mail. My evenings suddenly seemed very long and very empty.

The thought of what I would do without Miles had passed through my mind only once before his departure. After that, I had shoved it away, believing my work, shopping, and preparing a home for his return would occupy my every waking hour. The short days we had together had spilled into each other, a montage of taxi rides and rain, hurried drinks quaffed amongst strangers, a heady whirlwind of self-congratulations and the trip to buy Miles a raincoat, the recognition and comfort of knowing we had found each other. Perhaps that easy, intimate rapport should have been my clue that we had grown too close, too comfortable in too short a time. We had used up our entire married life in less than a week. I had been given a fortune in happiness and I had squandered it like a silly teenager.

Night fell, and I sat at the table senseless, all the hours of waiting turned to stone in the pit of my stomach. He wasn't coming home. He hadn't even signed his name.

The house was steeped in darkness when I had the peculiar feeling that someone was watching me. My angry neighbor, no doubt. Reluctantly I rose to close the blinds and pull the drapes, but the feeling persisted. Perhaps it was the gloom of the unknown house, but the image of the man in the pricey overcoat at Noreen's funeral came to mind again. Who was he? Why would I think of him now? The house agent had been right; I did live in a dream world.

For several moments I walked from room to room, only to be re-minded of how much work I had accomplished in a foolish attempt to please Miles. I suddenly longed for the bedsit again, when I remembered the small unused attic room on the uppermost floor. It could only be reached by a back stairway that I had ignored until now.

When I opened the door and stepped inside, I was aware of a subtle breeze despite the lack of windows. I had not entered the room since moving in, and I was certain nothing had been disturbed. Even the paisley shawl remained in place. The divan appeared welcoming and the air smelled clean, free of the synthetic paint fumes and fabric protector wafting through the rest of the house. If anything, there was a faint perfume in the air, lemon perhaps, mixed with rose sachet. I remembered the scent coming from a discarded pomander hidden in a box of old books I'd found while my parents prepared for another journey; Fiji or Macedo-nia, it had all become one to me. The smell had been comforting then as it was now, and after the stuffiness of the downstairs, I was grateful to lie down on the lumpy divan, drawing my feet under my nightgown and pulling the shawl over my shoulders. I closed my eyes and felt, rather than heard the soft purr of the house overtake me.

*Walking up great stone stairs to a vacant, but furnished mansion. On the left a fountain of square-cut stone, the water reflecting a waterfall, magnolias, the sky. The cloying humidity I remembered from New Orleans. A panther laps noiselessly at the water; a dove rustles the tree branches. I can feel the coolness of moss underfoot. The panther turns from the water and follows me inside where I am greeted by costly furnishings, hangings, crystal, an alcove with another cast iron fountain, ivy, books, clothes set out for someone—me?—to wear.*

*We are alone. Beauty and the Beast. The panther will always look after me, protect me, love me. We need nothing else but each other. I can sleep and dream in this house of grandeur and money, my every wish for solitude fulfilled. I do not need to speak to anyone; the panther and I are beyond words. We know, and listen, and hear. He will eat the flesh of animals and I will live off pomegranates and vegetables cooked in exotic spices. My panther, my love, will rescue me from the sordid world of industry and commerce, and here with his books, his violins and vintage wines, we will live forever.*

*Tell me, panther, why me? How did I arrive at this jungle-green forest of hibiscus and noisy parrots, the song of sliding leaves, heavy rains, and small jeweled snakes? Panther, my love, my beast, my everything, where will I wear these silks and old French laces? Where will I put my feet again except in the fur of your blue belly or the finest of Afghani rugs? Every item on this dressing table from perfumes to boar brushes…*

I woke with a start, the shawl falling to the floor as I hovered between sleep and memory; I could still taste the bitter pomegranates on my tongue. I pulled the shawl back over my knees while outside a storm blew strong and menacing; the wind tossing leaves and branches against the one, high-set narrow window. A window. I stared at it, hard. I was certain it had never been there before. Unless I hadn't noticed it. I was beginning to think I saw my world through blinkers.

I shivered with the sense that something was about to happen, something I could not guess at but that I knew would be important, life-changing. The dream had been so real. I wanted to go straight back into it and lose myself in whatever rapture it was offering. I'd always preferred what I couldn't have. As a child first entering St. Anne's, I had for a time wanted to join the community of nuns who taught and cared for us. The idea of renouncing my life for their rituals and private corridors kept me fascinated for several terms until I discerned a very similar order and surrender through my painting. Now, lying upon the divan, the dream fragments still clouding my vision, all those same yearnings for escape rushed back to me.

I forced myself to sit up and realized it was nearly daylight. As I watched the room begin to lighten through the storm clouds, I tried to consider my unhappiness of the previous night in more rational terms. Perhaps the dream was a gift to show me what the imagination can do given half a chance.

It's like this, I told myself: my husband is away working in the oil fields. It's what he does. Schedules get delayed. Plans go awry. In the meantime, I had my books, my painting, and, all right, my boredom. I also had money and food and a generous clothing allowance. I had tea from Fortnum's, and the National Gallery to visit whenever I chose. I was good at what I did. I worked hard to imitate the sheen of satin, the drape of a gown, or the soft cheek of a child straight from a Reynolds' portrait, the skin a tight little peach. I was highly praised for my efforts and the praise was gratifying. So what could I complain of? I may have been troubled last night, but I had to let it pass. Miles's letter hadn't said, "Never coming back." It was just a matter of timing. I would call Teague & Bloch and ask for their advice. To date they had proved courteous and gracious with all my other requests and notes to Miles, even if they could pass on no information of their own.

Anyway, I was wasting time. In a few hours I was due to arrive at the home of a new and important client to conclude the final sketches of her daughter, Courtenay, in her wedding dress. The Hon. Mrs. Thomas Claiburne, Monique to her friends, was a well-known collector; her commission for a life-size portrait in oil of Courtenay as a bride meant more than a fee, it could get me permanent gallery space.

My daily schedule had changed a great deal since leaving the bedsit. I no longer had to gather my sponge bag and towel to creep down to the communal bath and shower at the end of the hall. Instead, I now had my own sumptuous bathroom, replete with candles and oils and fragranced soaps I had bought in preparation for Miles's return. This morning I ignored it all and showered in mindless haste before tugging on a pair of black tights, a short-sleeved gray knit tunic, and boots. Technically it might have been summer, but last night's rain stayed heavy in the sky, and I added a light leather jacket before deciding to wear a new pair of beaded earrings so long they brushed my shoulders. I wasn't used to having money or the things that it could buy. I tilted my head in front of the bathroom mirror and for a moment I felt as if I were back in my dream of panthers and old mansions. My eyes closed as I recalled the heightened sense of detail there had been to everything I touched and breathed. If I stood still I could almost sink down into the dream's velvet enchantment again and stay there. Abruptly I pulled myself back. A dream wasn't where I should be this morning. At the last minute I remembered my gold cuff and wedding rings before I had to run to catch my bus.

Monique and Courtenay were waiting for me in the breakfast room of their Georgian villa planted on the edge of Regent's Park. As I handed the maid my jacket, I gazed at the stately room filled with the work of famous contemporary painters and thought it was no wonder I dreamed of luxury and idleness. Without exception all of my clients lived in houses so similar to each other they could have been the result of one master interior architect. I hoped Miles would think, once he did make it back, that I had given our own home more individuality and style. My efforts had certainly cost enough.

Courtenay was twenty-three but on most days, at least with me, she acted like a spoiled twelve-year-old. I noticed she wasn't wearing her wedding dress. In its place, she sat over her coffee and Italian *Vogue* in a ribbed Henley, a white T-shirt peeking through the open neck, her jeans gently torn at the knee.

"Morning," she mumbled, eyes fixed on the magazine. Her mother was more practiced at receiving tradespeople first thing in the day.

"Sara," Monique said, ringing for the maid to come back. She set aside the elaborate unfinished tapestry draped over her knee to take—then drop—my hand. I caught her eyeing the gold cuff, a move she masked with indifference when she realized I was watching her. She threaded a needle with a heavy strand of garnet wool and gestured with false helplessness toward the bride-to-be. "She refuses to wear the dress today."

I'd been through this scene a dozen times before with an equal number of young society women. "It's fine," I said. "I'm finishing up her face today. The dress can always be worked in later." I didn't bother to add that I rarely needed the sitter to be present when I reached that stage. My trick was to prop the purchased wedding dress across a chair and turn on the lights; it was easy to fake the body that was meant to be inside.

Courtenay ignored us while Monique returned to her embroidery, an Arthurian scene that claimed her full powers of concentration. I waited awkwardly until the maid, Rosa, came to show me into the cleared conservatory that had been my temporary studio for the last four sittings.

Potted begonias and maidenhair fern were clumped against the walls in a haphazard arrangement with my easel and boxes of art supplies. The scarlet and gold-dusted lady's slipper had been shoved into a corner that I thought must have irritated Monique beyond reason, but she hadn't complained, not openly. The portrait, she had declared within my hearing, took precedence over everything else, even the wedding scheduled for November.

I zipped into an old smock I kept in the room and thanked Rosa for the steaming pot of coffee she brought me. I then waited for Courtenay to arrive. I stared out to the lawns wondering why I had never met Monique's husband. Neither had I been introduced to Courtenay's fiancé. It was curious how isolated and distant the three of us were from the men in our lives; an inopportune presage, I thought, for a wedding.

At last Courtenay wandered into the room and settled herself without a word into the scarlet brocade wingchair that was to be the backdrop for her portrait. Her wedding dress was a high-necked ivory taffeta affair taken straight from a picture she had seen of a nineteenth-century Russian bride. It didn't surprise me that she had left off wearing it; the tiers of pearl buttons that went up the side and sleeves must have been a pain on the best of days.

"What do I do now?" she asked.

I shrugged. "Look like you're in love?"

"Like this?" She lifted her face to the light like a Rossetti angel.

I took out a black Conté pencil and flipped to a clean sheet of paper resting on the easel. "You got it."

I stroked in the shape of her lips. The slight flush on her cheeks, her clear, open expression…despite Courtenay's studied disinterest in this whole portrait business, I couldn't help but think that I had never had such a winsome and unselfconscious model in front of me. I strengthened the planes of her throat and collarbone. Apparently the man she was to marry was a successful young lawyer. It seemed all the young women I had painted over the last few years were engaged to the same pool of young professionals, every last one of them branded with that odious epitaph "Successful" with a capital "S." It pleased me that Miles came from a world of hands-on sweat equity.

My pencil glided with the tooth of the paper as I thought of the old ladies I saw cashing their pension checks at the post office, knitted caps pulled over their tight perms and hearing aids. Had they once thought their lives and husbands would be "successful"? Ever since art school I'd lost sleep from the secret fear of joining their ranks. Perhaps that was the key reason I had seized the chance to marry Miles. Security.

Courtenay's pose was beginning to droop.

"Can you straighten your shoulders a tad?" I asked.

Her head jerked back into place. "You sound like my mother." I didn't reply and she hummed tunelessly for a minute then asked out of the blue, "Did your mother make such a fuss about your wedding?"

"She didn't get a chance. My parents live in Australia."

"What the hell do they do in Australia?"

I winced. Girls like Courtenay weren't supposed to say "hell." "Nature programs," I said stiffly. I wasn't in the mood to talk about my parents, but Courtenay just about jumped out of her chair.

"Don't move!" I warned.

She froze in place, but her questions seemed unstoppable.

"What programs? TV? They film for TV?"

"Sound. They're sound engineers. It's pretty awful stuff."

Courtenay shifted her eyes toward me without moving her head and waited for more. I wasn't used to speaking about my family. The words seemed mean and ill-mannered, but I couldn't help how I felt. Things had not been good between us for years.

I stopped to assess my range of pencils and chose a blunt-edged carpenter's pencil for her hair. I could sense she wanted me to say more. I pushed the tip of the pencil into the paper harder than I'd meant to.

"They're into these heart-breaking stories," I said. "You know, the ones where the tiger cubs starve to death after drought, or poachers have killed the mother. They had a big hit one season about newly-hatched turtles waddling out to sea and being picked off one by one first by pelicans, then sharks, and last of all, the tide. DVD sales went through the roof."

I finished off the highlights bouncing from Courtenay's casually swept up hair, knowing that it would all have to be redone for the final portrait. The tiara that went with her wedding dress called for two tightly coiled braids on either side of her head, nothing like this early morning mass of curls and spring-clips.

"I think we're nearly finished here," I said. I picked up my coffee; it was cold.

"Why do they do it?"

"What?"

"Your parents. Those awful sounds."

I had tried not to think about any of this for ages. What would be the point? We disagreed, end of story.

A radio sat on a low table and I reached over to turn it on, thinking some music might squelch any further conversation. The plan worked for a bit until the station I chose switched to an inane classical piece that incessantly repeated a sound like wounded bird calls: *whoop, whoop; whoop, whoop.* It was idiotic; my mother would have loved it. Before I knew what I was doing I turned to slap at the "off" button and managed to knock over a tray of pastels at the same time.

"Damn!" I bent over to salvage what I could before Courtenay leapt from her chair to help me.

She stared at the mess. "Don't they look beautiful, all scattered and crushed like that?"

My mouth formed itself into a tight line. "Beautiful" was not at the top of my list. Courtenay squatted beside me and gingerly collected the crumbling pieces of taupe and burnt umber into her palm. I shooed her away.

"Thanks, but you'll get covered in dust. Here, let me." I was annoyed at the sudden disorder, but the breakage I could live with. "I only use them in bits and pieces anyway," I said more to console myself than Courtenay. "Most of the time I break them on purpose. Why don't you sit down again and I'll be with you in a sec." I thought I should call Rosa for a broom.

Courtenay sat back in her jeans and T-shirt and cleaned her fingers with a damp rag from my easel. "It's cool being an artist," she said. "So creative and purposeful. Romantic."

I thought of Miles and the company decision to keep him abroad, assuming it was Teague & Bloch who called the shots. "Romantic" went right in the same bin as "cool."

"I could list a number of people who would happily take your place at the altar," I said.

"Ha."

I gathered the last of the pastels and sighed. She wasn't the first debutante to make the grand confession that her true heart's desire was a crust of bread and a garret somewhere.

I turned back to my easel and groaned. Courtenay really was a baby. "Okay. Where is it?"

"Where's what?"

I pointed to the blank page facing us. "Umm. Let's see. The sketch? And don't say, 'What sketch?' I have a headache. A big one."

"I didn't touch it."

"Right. And I'm the Dalai Lama."

"If you say so."

I flipped through the newsprint pad. Not a single crayon squiggle. "Courtenay, I meant what I said about having a headache. And this is just, well, stupid."

"I promise you—"

"Who then? Rosa?"

Courtenay looked at me as if I had just lost my mind. I probably had.

I rubbed my temples. "Let's forget it, okay? We'll start over. It was just a sketch." Under my breath I added, "And your mother's paying the bill." I indicated that she should resume her pose and I began to draw again in silence, wondering if the first sketch was somehow wadded up under her Henley.

"I'm not a brat, you know."

"Keep still." When she had stopped shifting around I said, "Maybe you're sitting on it."

She stood up, the chair seat empty. "Not guilty." She sat down again, temper clouding her face. "If this is what marriage does to brain cells, maybe I should bail out right now."

I thought of the barbs I'd intuited over the weeks whenever she mentioned her conservative, and very absent, fiancé. If he was anything like the staid inhabitants of my own "up and coming" neighborhood, maybe Courtenay had a point.

"Though I must admit," Courtenay said with just a splash of acid, "your marriage does have a certain appeal."

"For heaven's sake, why? Miles isn't even in the country." My hand shook as I darkened the curve of her lips.

"Well, there you are."

I stared at her for a long moment, and we both began to laugh, except after a minute I felt uncontrollably close to tears. Images of last night's dream crept back into my memory and I wished I could run back to its fanciful landscape.

"I'm sorry," Courtenay said, the well-bred young woman rising to the surface again. "I suppose that was rude."

I waved off her apology. "I'm fine."

"It's just this wedding," she said, one leg over a chair arm. "Serge doesn't want all this fuss any more than I do, but our parents..."

"Close your eyes and hold your breath." I sprayed fixative over the new drawing. I counted to ten and took a tentative breath of what still smelled toxic, and then closed my sketch tray. Courtenay and her complaints were wearing me out; I needed lunch.

"Why don't we call it a day? I can continue 'Early Twenty-First Century Bride in Russian Wedding Dress' at home."

"Super." She threw me a brief wave and then fled as if I had released her from the classroom. If I had been in any other frame of mind I would have found her haste insulting.

In a way, though, it was good to have her gone, and without her company I was careful to straighten and clean what had served as my studio space. That first sketch was still nowhere in sight. I wiped up the last of the chalk dust; my eyes burning with unshed tears. The sketch had truly disappeared, thanks to Courtenay, and I didn't feel any of her reluctance to be married. More than anything on earth I wanted Miles back where he belonged, with me. If only I knew when that would be.

I took one last look around; I was finished here. I was about to leave when Rosa came in with my jacket. She tsk-tsked at the cold coffee and offered to bring me fresh.

"A sandwich?" she asked when I told her I wasn't thirsty.

I shook my head. "No, thanks." Talking about my parents and thinking of Miles had made me restless. I wanted to walk and make some sense out of the last few hours. I also wanted to call Teague & Bloch, and I regretted my refusal to carry a phone.

"Is Mrs. Claiburne available?"

Rosa nodded toward the door. "The señora, she goes for her hair appointment."

"Oh. May I use the telephone?"

"I will get it for you." She left, and then returned with a zebra-themed phone that had to belong to Courtenay. Rosa left the room again as I was punching in the number.

The phone rang and rang before a recorded message whined: "The offices of Teague & Bloch are closed at present." A long list of possible situations with corresponding numbers to press followed. None of them applied to my situation. The message ended with: "If this is an emergency, please press nine."

I hesitated. An emergency? I pressed the number. And was promptly cut off. I held the phone away from my ear. I didn't have the heart to go through the procedure a second time.

Instead, I went out to the hallway where Rosa was standing politely, her hands folded across her apron. I passed her the phone. "Can you please tell Mrs. Claiburne that I'll be taking my things out by the end of the week? I'll bring a cab. And if you could thank her for the inconvenience to her conservatory. I know it's been difficult."

Rosa took in my words carefully. "It is fine, Missus Bergsen. No problem." She opened the front door. I liked that she had called me "Mrs. Bergsen," bringing me somehow closer to Miles.

Outside it was cool and overcast, a typically wet and dull July day. I started toward my bus stop, and then changed my mind. For a second I considered taking a cab to the other side of town to see if anyone was actually working at Teague & Bloch, but the idea exhausted me before I could give it any real consideration. But I didn't want to go home, not yet. What I really needed to do was clear out my old studio, the one I had kept since my student days and stopped going to when I moved into the house. I had been promising myself that I would take care of that last chore for weeks. Now with a free afternoon and close to the tube station, I thought, just do it. I had spent hours arranging a studio area in my new sitting room and it was high time I used it.

I headed for Baker Street. Once I cleared up all these loose ends, I reasoned, I'd feel more organized and sensible. Sketches wouldn't vanish into thin air and I'd dream of normal things, like—

The street swayed and my knees bent with a familiar, sickening buckle. I drew in a breath. I should never have sprayed that fixative inside the house, I thought. The dangers were clearly posted right there on the label. I leaned down and swallowed air in gulps. I wasn't sick, no, no, just light-headed; the blackouts were not returning. I should have let Rosa make me that sandwich.

A horn blared from somewhere deep in the traffic and the dizzy feel-ing of being pulled out of my body left as quickly as it had arrived. I straightened up and gripped my handbag, tightly. My eyes started to blur when I noticed I was outside a grocer's shop. I nearly fell over again in my rush to buy lunch.

## 5

The rain had cleared and I was feeling better after I'd eaten, boarded and changed trains, and was outside again. The blackouts and dizzy spells had started the year I turned sixteen, and I remained immobilized in a Bournemouth convalescent hospital for the winter while my parents wrote me long letters from Iceland and Estonia. The hospital stay was a string of listless days, my fatigue alleviated only when some of the younger female doctors brought me my first art materials. Since then, I'd wavered between gratitude for finding my vocation and a dogged fear that the dizziness would spoil everything.

Over the years I had learned to be careful: not to move too fast, or twist my neck unthinkingly, actions that could put me in bed for a week. Today it seemed all I needed was food.

Balancing an egg salad sandwich on top of a lidded cup of tea, I used my key to enter the Docklands complex housing the Rafe Hemmings Co-operative Art Space. A non-profit eponymous enterprise funded mostly by grants and donations, the "Hemmings Place" as it was often called, held close to sixty professional and student artists alike at any given time. My history with Rafe started when he came to lecture at my college one summer and I was "lucky" enough to be invited a few months later to share in his well-known studio space. Sharing his bed and tantrums followed almost right away, but even after our break-up my right to use the complex had never been challenged.

The wing rented out to students, and where I kept my studio, was not the best maintained. I noticed rainwater dripping from a broken window onto the dusty floor of the tight area I had staked out as my own. I shivered; the place was downright Arctic. It had been weeks since I'd even thought to change the damp rags along the sills or to slip a tin under the worst of the leaks and now a pool of water filled the corner.

I scrunched up my sandwich paper and added it to a pile of trash I didn't remember leaving.

While I waited for my tea to cool I summed up my belongings: the cheap student easel, the brick and plank shelving holding my reference books, my trays of paint in granulated stages of disuse. There was little that I wanted to keep. Even the brushes that I had clung to since my teenage hospital stay had finally lost their sentimental, and only, appeal. Worn out and moth-eaten, I hadn't used them for years. All the same, I was loath to see them go. I set down my tea and began to box the lot up for the next starving student I imagined would be thankful for my dregs. I could still remember when that was me.

When I was finished, I started in on the layers of rough sketches and practice sheets taped to the walls. Most of them were pictures of Noreen. Quickly, before I could think too much about it, I sealed them into some plastic sleeves I found under the bookcase. I then picked up my box of cast-offs and managed my way downstairs. The beat of a bass guitar thumped through the walls. I kicked the first door I came to because my hands were too full to knock.

"I'm busy!"

I tried to nudge the door open with the box. "It's me, Sara."

"Why didn't you say so?" Peter Wilcox opened his door and ran his fingers through a paint-stained beard. He came as close to a smile as he ever did. "Where've you been?"

"I bought a house."

Peter and I had known each other since art school. It didn't mean we were friends; he detested my society ladies and I had never understood his angry, jarring brushstrokes. He glared suspiciously at the box I carried as if I were about to bequeath some distasteful commission his way. "Did you buy a house or a mortgage? Or a millstone?"

I pushed my way past him. "Does it matter? Anyway, whatever you want to call it means I don't need to be here. I can work at home now."

Peter followed me back into his room, still eyeing the box.

"So I thought I could give you some things," I rattled on. "They're quite horrid. You'll love them." I let the box slide from my arms onto a rickety table. At the end of the table was an oval canvas Rafe and my other teachers would have classified as discordant. Peter's attempt at style set the room spinning again, which was probably the point of the piece. I took a deep breath and focused on the table legs.

"So what have you got, then?" Peter asked. He had never cared about the effect his work had on me.

"Dried paint, old brushes."

Peter croaked out a shaky laugh. "The students will rejoice, no doubt." He poked through the contents. "Seen Rafe's newest?"

"He's been in?"

"Off and on. Does he know you're leaving?'

"I thought he was in Greece."

"He won't like you just taking off."

"I don't see why not. What's it to him, anyway?" As far as I was concerned, Rafe Hemmings was a part of my life that had ceased to exist. I tried to change the subject. "Kind regards to your wife—" I began, when Peter interrupted.

"We could go take a look upstairs if you like," he said. "You know, for old time's sake."

I hesitated just enough for Peter to take the lead.

"Oh, come on." Peter was already out the door. Reluctantly, I followed him, wishing I could just throw my memories of Rafe out with the rest of my rubbish.

We stepped onto a landing where Peter lifted aside a pair of heavy sisal curtains. Technically I knew there was nothing wrong about us entering Rafe's personal space. Most of it was kept open to the co-op's tenants any time of day or night. Students in particular were told to make the gallery of works-in-progress a chief resource. It was only when Rafe was preparing for an important sale or exhibition that the doors were kept bolted and alarmed, with plenty of hand-lettered signs warning potential intruders to stay out, or else. Still, I never could quite get over the feeling that Rafe kept a special set of invisible "No Entry" signs just for me. After we split, we did our best to avoid each other, and so far I hadn't had any reason or opportunity to tell him about Miles.

I looked up at the dirty gray clouds blowing past the industrial skylights. The iron girders framing each window were oppressive and made me want to leave.

"I can only stay a minute," I began when the sheer immensity of Rafe's work stopped me short. Ten meters of canvas stretched across the back wall, every millimeter densely covered with a landscape I instantly recognized with a jolt deeper than anything I could share with Peter. It was the house—the house in my dream.

I shuddered, and walking backwards, retraced my steps toward the door so I could take in the full impact of the work. The maple floorboards creaked beneath my boots. I shivered for a second time when the foghorns from a river barge let loose a long series of groans.

"So what do you think?" Peter folded his arms and leaned against an obsolete soft drink dispenser.

I took a step closer to the canvas, and then stepped away again in a batty minuet Peter observed with a smirk. A drop of moisture gathered between my shoulder blades and fell with a slow trickle down my back. I didn't know what to say. It was definitely the house in my dream, right down to the ivied walls and the glowing eyes of a panther crouched by an old stone fountain.

"It's not like you to be so reticent," Peter commented, arms crossed and head to one side. "Anyway, isn't this what you love? What do they call it? Hyper-something. Hyper-hokey…"

I shook my head. "Oh, shut up," I mumbled. I simply didn't understand how anything could be so exact, as if Rafe had managed to catch my dream somehow, or even stranger, I had dreamed my way into his painting.

I stared at the piece without comprehension, not bothering to worry what Peter might take my silence to mean. I turned away.

Peter sauntered over to join me at the window. "You okay?"

I pushed my hair away from my face and managed a weak smile. Out on the river tourists were busy photographing each other in the mist. "Do you know where, or what, the scene is supposed to be?" I asked.

Peter grimaced. "Can't tell. And it's not Rafe's style, is it? It's a tad too—paint-by-number."

I leaned my forehead on the window glass. We'd had this argument a thousand times in art school. "If you mean tasteless, why don't you just come out and say so?"

"People like paint-by-number," Peter admitted.

"Envious?"

Peter sighed and scratched at his beard. "It's been a rough day."

That was all it was, I told myself, a very rough day. I was tired and my imagination had gone wild. Besides, after a childhood globe-trotting with my culture-loving parents, it was hardly surprising that a fairy tale mansion would one day enter my dreams. They must have taken me to every historical landmark known to humankind. Museums and ancient castles had been hardwired into me. It got so bad that one decisive afternoon I had to rebel by declaring I would fling myself from the next parapet we climbed if they didn't let me "be a child." The next week found me enrolled in St. Anne's.

And yet. There was something distinctly different about the house in the painting than any place I had visited with my parents. If I had seen it on one of our trips, I would have remembered.

Peter turned off the lights and made sure the windows were tightly closed. The room had all the warmth of a refrigerator.

"Thanks for the tour," I said, stooping to leave through the opening Peter made between the curtains.

"Some tour. One bloody painting. He'll make a fortune from it, mark my words."

Back downstairs, in my own studio, I showed Peter my old easel and folding chair. "Want them?" I asked. "They could come in handy."

"Sure, why not?" He grabbed the easel. "Hey, hope it all goes well with the house and new studio."

"Thanks."

He was shambling out the door when I called him back. "Peter?"

"Yeah?"

"Why did you want to show me the painting?"

He shrugged. "Just thought you'd like to see the *masterpiece*."

"And now that I have?"

"You tell me."

I lifted my palms in defeat, speechless again.

"Okay." Peter set the easel down. "When's the last time Rafe's worked on such a huge scale? Or gone in for 'Kinkade on steroids'?"

He had a point. Rafe specialized in surreal scenes interpreted from Greek mythology. His colorful, slap-dash style usually included a background meant to portray his beloved Ismene, the Greek island he had purchased and was now able to retire to for most of the year.

"If I were you," Peter said, tugging at his beard, "I'd want to think about it for awhile, that's all." He leaned forward and squeezed my shoulder. "See you around." The unexpected gesture made me teary-eyed, and I smiled brightly to hide it.

For a few seconds I remained in place listening to his footfalls echo down the stairs. I picked up the plastic sleeves containing my sketches of Noreen and held them to my chest, thinking about Rafe's painting. Peter was right. Rafe had never attempted anything like it, and the style was, much to my chagrin, embarrassingly close to my own. That style was one of the reasons Rafe and I had parted ways; he distrusted my adherence to "commercialism." I had wanted to survive, and if a conventional style meant I could please my clients, I was there, brush in hand, ready to sell my soul.

I clutched the sketches; thinking of Rafe always made me feel bad.

On my way out the door, I dropped a fifty-pound note into the supply kitty. My time here was over. It had to be if I was to come to grips with my real reasons for hating the place, starting with the night I had sketched Noreen while telling her the truth about my last fight with Rafe; that I could never forgive him for thinking being adopted was some kind of crime. Because in my case it was, and I didn't know how it could be fixed.

# 6

The "crime" concerned my birth certificate. It was a fake. A total, absolute fraud created by none other than Evan Elliott, the man who called himself my father. Using the same skill he had once put into his reindeer hide pictographs, he had forged my documentation the month after he and Inge bought me from the villagers in Kamchatka.

"That's right," I'd said to Noreen as she reclined on the floor so I could sketch her long, straight back. "Bought me."

It took me twenty-five years to learn the truth of my questionable adoption, and although I'd told Rafe in a fit of candor, it was one of the few things I hadn't mentioned to Miles. I considered telling him when we applied for our marriage license, but something held me back. Fear, embarrassment, Rafe's negative reaction. There was no way I could explain in the limited time we gave ourselves that when Inge Elliott first saw me I was three years old, dressed in a pink nylon dotted Swiss pinafore and rabbit fur ankle boots, and was suffering from the aftereffects of shock. My only known link to my biological mother, whom the villagers claimed was buried beneath the modest mound they had built for her, was the heavy Scythian gold arm band I refused to let out of my grasp until we reached Juneau, Alaska and Inge convinced me to trade it for a toy polar bear that matched my boots.

Not one word of this story held a drop of memory for me the day Inge let it pour out before lunch one morning during my last visit to Australia. All I could think at the time was that she had either drunk too much of the cooking sherry, or else she had begun to believe her own stories about the Snow Queen and Thumbelina.

Whatever it was she had tried to tell me, half of it in Swedish, I could not believe that I had once been bartered for a knapsack of American dollars, or that Evan would have the audacity to file forged documents with Somerset House and then go on to tell his own parents that I had always been his child. I left Melbourne confused and angry, and it was only when I was unpacking back home in my London bedsit that I found the cuff tucked away at the bottom of my bag with a note from Inge: "Someday you will understand." To date nothing had made that true.

Things only got more muddled when Noreen stopped our sketching session by siding with my parents but agreeing that lying was wrong, so she was forced to tell me she was sleeping with Rafe. I don't want to remember what I said to that, but it strained our friendship to a point that was never truly healed, a fact I brooded over during most of her funeral.

It was late when I got home from the art co-op, but the sun had finally appeared from behind the clouds, filling the sky with strands of dusky gold. My newly-varnished front door reflected the last of that same light, making me pause for a second on the doorstep with a thrill of ownership that continued as I placed my bag and sketches inside the entryway on a side table. As I did so, I couldn't help but reach out and run my hand over the wood, amazed and somewhat humbled by how much had come into my life through Miles. My feelings about Rafe and Noreen's "relationship" seemed petty compared to what I had now.

I went upstairs to change my clothes. The bedroom windows faced the yard behind the house. I had been so preoccupied with the interior that I had neglected the gardens horribly. An abundance of honeysuckle contested with goldenrod and what could only be, despite my lack of horticultural knowledge, weeds. Somehow, though, it managed to be beautiful, the colors of the leaves and branches vibrating in the twilight. I wondered how I had let it become so unruly, and then realized gardening was something I had thought Miles would take care of when he returned.

I tried to imagine what life would be like with Miles in the house ten, twenty, thirty years down the road. The most exciting scene I could invent was a plagiarized Anita Brookner knock-off: me, dressed in elegant casuals, continuing to decorate and rearrange the house in ever-fading shades of gray. Miles pottering around in a mended blazer, a jaunty ascot tied at his throat, incessantly pouring drinks with a heavy hand on the gin, a habit that would make our stolid guests squeal in mock despair, "Oh, Miles! You always put in far too much!" just before they guzzled the liquor down. Me fretting over scuffed floors and running out of crackers.

It was the life many of my clients lived, and it wasn't much to look forward to. Not that I ever supposed I would attain their great wealth or social standing, even if Monique Claiburne was right about my reputation being "on the rise." But there must also have been something in me that wanted the security of belonging somewhere, even to a stranger. Perhaps it all boiled down to a lack of originality, what my art school colleagues and Rafe denounced as my "salability." I had the sudden urge to prove them wrong and lash black paint over my sketches of Courtenay Claiburne. I suspected the result would be closer to her real persona than the delicate society portrait her mother had commissioned to feed her own ego. Then again, I couldn't think of anything more stupid, or pointless as destroying the work I loved.

In lieu of going on a vindictive rampage, I put on my nightgown, leaving the gold cuff on my arm. My biggest problem, I thought, was I hadn't taken a vacation in nearly fifteen years. My trip to Australia four years ago had only depressed me and I had justified staying home after that by telling myself that my itinerant childhood had been one gigantic holiday. More recently I had extended the fantasy by believing my weekend with Miles had been Thailand, the Taj Mahal, and the Pyrenees all rolled into one. But I had been wrong, horribly wrong, and now it seemed that nothing could take this empty loneliness away.

In my bathroom I threw my clothes in the hamper, washed my face, and thought of the room overhead. I had to go back up there; it was the only place I felt I could rest, could hide, could forget…

*It was the man from Noreen's funeral, holding out his hand, beckoning me closer. "Anton," he seemed to say. "My name is Anton Kaminsky." The light flashed from the top of his fabulous walking stick, as if he were sending me a message only I could decipher. I looked down by his feet. The panther sat like a well-trained pet—watching me, I could swear, with human eyes, twin emeralds set against the black ink of its fur. Resistance was pointless. Why lie? I wanted to be here; wanted to know what dwelled behind those closed doors. I ran forward, a child again; and then they were gone, only the sound of purring, faint now, and far away. My breath was uneven, as if I had stepped across a great chasm only to find myself alone. Again.*

The shawl was bunched at my feet, leaving me uncovered as my eyes searched the attic room, expecting somehow to find the man and the panther standing in the corners, about to explain what they wanted from me.

I breathed out and huddled against the cushions of the divan as I re-played the vision. The man—Kaminsky—was the stranger I had seen at Noreen's funeral. How old was he? Where did he come from? There was something world weary and ageless about him that reminded me of the foreign exiles my parents were always befriending in far-flung corners of the globe. We had drunk coffee with Hungarian Jews in Columbia; eaten fig pastries with Viennese Turks in Fiji. Anton Kaminsky could have been any one of them.

Outside, the rain had resumed, spattering the windowpanes with sleet. I could not recall the weather in my dream, but the man, Anton, as I regarded him, wore the same rich, gray overcoat and hat that he had worn at the funeral. I had seen that type of hat in archival photos and films: a banded brim, and deeply folded in the crown. And then there was that curious walking stick with its elaborate handle fashioned from, I was certain, Scythian gold.

I twisted my armband around my wrist, my fingers tracing the loops and whorls of its intricate, inexplicable pattern. Until my mother had given me the piece, I had never heard of either the Scythians or their gold. It was the pawnshop dealer next to Teague & Bloch who had first recognized what I had brought him, sending me to the library and Internet for more information on the nomadic people who had crossed the frozen Eurasian wilderness centuries ago, their pack animals transporting golden treasure made for them by Greek artisans. How I had ended up with such a thing was still a mystery to both the pawn dealer and to me, but it had raised the dealer's respect for my taste by several important financial notches, allowing me during the worst of times to pay my rent, buy art supplies and groceries, and even a pair of chartreuse Italian sandals I had craved in the middle of winter.

I flexed my shoulders and neck. The divan had grown suddenly uncomfortable and the room colder than ever. I wrapped the shawl around my shoulders and decided to return downstairs. Reluctantly, I stood and closed the door behind me.

Downstairs I was met with a quandary. How was I meant to fill in these hours waiting for Miles and not lose my mind? My choices were limited: cook a meal I had no appetite for, or continue to work on Courtenay's portrait. I turned on the television and watched the images as if through broken glass.

The phone woke me at nine. I had been dozing on the couch, intermittently dreaming of Courtenay Claiburne and for some reason, spirals and labyrinths, circles that forced me to go round and round in search of nothing I could name.

When I finally answered the querulous ringing, I didn't recognize the voice on the other end. The faulty connection together with someone asking for "Mrs. Miles" made me think it was a wrong number, but then I realized "Mrs. Miles" was me.

"Yes?" I asked, my heart pounding. "Do you have a message from Miles? From my husband?"

"My name is Granger." The voice faded out then came back louder than ever. Perhaps the caller was on the road, driving.

"Laurie Granger," the caller continued. "Miles and I went to the same school. Years apart, of course. And Venezuela. We were in Venezuela together."

"You were?"

"I can't hear you. Are you there?" Laurie Granger asked.

"Yes, I mean, wait—" I sat up straighter and tried again. "I don't remember Miles mentioning you," I said. "Or Venezuela."

Granger sounded peevish. "What's your name?" he asked.

"Sara."

"Hello, Sara. I'm in town and I thought we'd do London."

"I'm sorry, Miles isn't in town right now, but—"

"Yes, I know. He told me to look you up."

"He did?" I could barely breathe.

Static cut up the line and I thought I heard him say, "I've got Daile with me."

"Daile?"

"My fiancée. How's Sunday?"

Three days away. "If you like—"

"Good. Let's say we come out to your place and take it from there?"

I stammered out what I hoped were understandable directions while I made a mental shopping list. I was out of everything except white wine and chocolate and I thought people with news of Miles deserved something more substantial. Garlic, cheese, bread…it would be the meal of their lives. And there would be news; news of Miles. Perhaps I would be saved from myself after all.

## 7

Granger hung up, the final plan being that he and Daile, who was, apparently "drop-dead gorgeous," would come to the house for lunch. After that the three of us would go on a walking and bus tour of the usual sights finishing with what Granger kept calling "a slap-up dinner" at a "real English pub," whatever that was. I put the phone down and wondered how long Granger had really known Miles. His accent was unusual, but I had heard it before: an Australian-American twang with a dash of pidgin my father kept slipping into the last time I was home. Living with sound engineers had given me a well-trained ear.

Over the next days I kept my head clear and the house clean for the appointed luncheon. As soon as I was satisfied there was nothing more I could do until the actual day of Granger's visit, I concentrated the rest of my attention toward meeting my deadline for Courtenay Claiburne's wedding portrait. The work kept me busy, the veil in particular pleasing me with its bands of shifting color. After several false starts I was able to capture the shimmer of fragile netting and beadwork framing Courtenay's face. I hadn't felt so good for days.

By the time Sunday arrived and the doorbell rang, I had just put the finishing touches on Courtenay's earlobes and had stuffed a loaf of garlic bread in the oven. I still had garlic on my hands when I went to the door to greet my guests.

Seeing the white-haired man in the safari jacket together with his dippy escort in five-inch heels—stilettos—sent a wave of gaiety through me.

Laurie Granger was so obviously "oil and ex-pat" that I knew his story about being friends with Miles had to be true. Daile appeared ageless, somewhere between twenty and forty. I was about to offer her a glass of wine when Granger beat me to it. Taking Daile's blue and gold Eiffel Tower scarf from around her neck, he gave it to me for safekeeping before ushering us "girls" into the lounge. I folded the scarf over the back of a chair, struck by the coincidence of an identical scarf having been worn by the agent who had sold me the house. But before I could ponder the strangeness of the occurrence, Laurie had taken command of my kitchen: checking the oven, pouring wine, chatting me up with an easiness I found unnerving. He seemed to have no end of stories to tell Daile and me, anecdotes that mostly revolved around work crew pranks and missed trains: "Did I tell you about the time I got stuck in Peoria for three weeks? Without my pants?"

It was Daile who had the guts to shut him up. "Honey," she said as he sliced another piece of bread and refilled her glass, "you're boring Sara." She picked at her salad and sent me a red-lipped, low-cut smile. In my severe gray denim skirt, black tights, and long-sleeved T-shirt, I felt like her grandmother.

"Daile's from Texas," Laurie divulged as if that explained everything.

"Is that where you met?" I ventured, wishing I could lead the question back around to Miles. So far the subject of my missing husband hadn't come up once.

Daile nodded. "It was love at first sight."

"With Texas or each other?"

Laurie brushed past my question. "We're on a busman's holiday," he said. "Paris. Rome. Here." He held an olive from the salad up to the light before popping it into his mouth. "Daile took a cookery class in Paris. That's where she got that overpriced scarf." He gave her an indulgent smile I watched coolly from behind my wine glass.

Daile made her pout as babyish as she possibly could. "It's Hermès and you know it's an investment."

Oh, God, it would be Hermès. What if I'd snagged it, or mayonnaised the damn thing? "What was cooking school like?" I asked.

Daile reached for another baguette. "They showed us how to make parfaits and even, um—" She tapped her fingernails on her plate. "Oh, what's that cheesy thing? It's like egg Jell-o in a pie crust."

"Quiche?"

"That's it! Laurie adores it. What about your husband? What does he like to eat?"

"I haven't had much of a chance to find out yet. You see, Miles—"

"But Laurie said—" She stopped when Laurie sent her a signal with the wine bottle.

I held out my glass for a refill. "Laurie said Miles has been ordered to stay away? It's true, he has. In fact, he's been away so long I might as well be a widow!" I laughed without humor. "And don't tell me to try ringing Teague & Bloch. They seem to have an aversion to answering their telephones." I turned to Laurie. "So you see, I was rather hoping you'd have news."

Laurie settled his avuncular grin on me and filled my glass. "Now, don't you worry about a thing," he said. "I expect Mr. Teague will be sending Miles home any day now and you'll be making him full English breakfasts loaded with beans and toast and good old bangers." He patted his stomach, making me worry the pasta salad hadn't been filling enough. "It's been ages since I've had a decent breakfast. Or dinner," he added with a loud belch.

Daile yelped. "Laurie! All that grease and fat.

"Once we're married," she said to me with a coyness that clashed with her skimpy top and plastic earrings, scarlet baubles shaking in disapproval at the thought of Laurie stoking up on cholesterol and calories, "Laurie's going on a strict diet." She looked down her nose. "Like the one you're on. You've kept your figure," she said, although her eyes seemed to ask why the hell I covered it up in prison gray.

Laurie's smile became a mock frown. "You girls worry too much about appearances. It's a disease."

Daile mirrored his frown. "Men." She turned her attention back to me.

"So tell me more about this Miles of yours. What's he like? Is he English, too? Do you see his family?"

"Miles doesn't have much of a family. After his parents were killed he was brought up by his aunt."

"That's right," Laurie said, surprising me. "Aunt Winifred." He took some more of the salad. "Old Miles was rather fond of her, though I don't know why. Tweedy sort. Canasta parties and gin martinis down at the pony club. Not much fun for the little tyke, I suppose." He paused and gave me a look chock-full of melancholy. "Terrible tragedy to lose his parents when he was just a nipper." He blew his nose on a serviette, loudly.

"Terrible," Daile repeated, fluttering her eyelashes nicely and winning a quick one-armed hug from Laurie.

I needed to get away; their cozy domesticity was turning my stomach. I excused myself to run to the bathroom. Once I was behind the closed door I considered how long I could stay there. After three minutes of reapplying my lipstick, counting my towels, and staring out the window, I decided I was being unfair. Daile had never seen Buckingham Palace, and Laurie was in a lather to take her photo on a bearskin. *With a bearskin*, I corrected myself.

I poured cold water on my wrists before splashing my throat with Bal à Versailles. I breathed in the old-fashioned fragrance of powder and musk while I wondered for the umpteenth time that day what I was doing with these people. It's because they love me, I told myself when I heard Daile pounding on the door.

"Are you okay in there?"

"I'm fine," I called out. I checked one last time the fit of the gray denim jean jacket that matched my skirt. "Terrible," I thought. *"Just terrible."*

# 8

Daile had a list: Harrods, Buckingham Palace, the Tower. It was no good trying to point out to her that it had gone four o'clock, we were in the wettest July on record, it was Sunday, and none of the sites were anywhere near the other. In the end the rain alone was enough to convince Daile to go no farther than Mayfair and the top of Curzon Street.

Soaked to the skin, her hair flattened against her scalp and her mascara weeping down her cheeks, the moment Daile saw the candlelight flickering from the entrance to an upmarket wine bar she practically shoved Laurie and me down the narrow stairway. At the bottom we were met by a cellar that was at least warm if not exactly a tourist haven. Daile's relief at being out of the late afternoon downpour was more than palpable. She shrugged out of her glaringly new Burberry and demanded I give her a mirror I didn't have.

"God, that was horrible," she sighed after she did her best to fix her face without the aid of a compact. Her efforts weren't entirely successful; the waiter who took our order looked at her as if he wasn't sure she should be allowed indoors.

She and Laurie played "this little piggy" while I passed the time waiting for our chardonnay and grilled cheese by studying the artwork lining the walls. Just as I expected, an original Rafe Hemmings was prominently showcased behind the bar. Large, messy, and steeped in Rafe's personal mythology, it too was horrible and the reason the drinks cost three times what they could be had for down on the Strand.

Our order arrived and Daile thirstily gulped her wine without any pre-liminaries or small talk. "I think we should just get a bottle each," she said to no one in particular.

Don't get me started, I thought. I'd restricted myself to two glasses at lunch, but now that I was here sipping the crystal cold wine in small, measured doses, I knew I couldn't hold out any longer. I was dying of thirst. Laurie Granger seemed to feel the same way.

"If we can't see the Tower we might as well get blind, sweeping blot-to," he said with a laugh.

Daile bit into the steaming cheese. "Perfect." She chewed contentedly for a minute. "Comfort food. Yummy."

I drained my glass. This was as good a time as any to tackle the ques-tion of Miles.

"What I do know," I said, hoping my words weren't as slurred as they felt, "is that you still haven't told me very much about your friendship with Miles. For instance, when did you see him last?"

Laurie blinked as if it had just occurred to him that I might be a nuis-ance. "I thought I mentioned it."

"No, you haven't."

Daile cut in. "Can we get another round of sandwiches? Ham this time?"

"I don't eat meat," I said too quickly. Daile's face fell and I regretted speaking. "I'm sorry. Get what you want." I resisted telling her ham was just bacon in disguise. Instead, I turned back to Laurie.

"So, when did you see him last?"

"Who?"

"Miles." I tried not to clench my teeth.

Laurie wiped his fingers on the tablecloth. "It was—" He stopped to check his watch. "Two weeks ago."

Two weeks ago—only days before Miles's letter. I kept my voice steady. "And where was that?" Daile gave me such a peculiar look I blushed, hoping I didn't appear as pathetic as she made me feel.

Laurie rubbed his chin, and then suddenly snapped his fingers. "Dubai.

It was Dubai." He turned to Daile. "Wasn't it, Dai-Dai?"

Dai-Dai was in Dubai, too? I could have turned it into a song: *Dai-Dai of Du-bai. Du-bai* was where Miles was meant to be. All was right with the world, tra-la.

"How did he seem to you?" I asked, but just then the lights dimmed even further and a New Age-y soundtrack announced the start of a film screening against the white wall opposite Rafe's painting. I glanced around the bar. The place was far busier than it had been only minutes ago. Perhaps it was known as an independent theater on Sundays. Deep cobalt and watery greens flitted across our hands and faces. Daile set her glass down and turned toward the undulating images of a scuba diver riding on the wings of a giant manta ray.

"Isn't it sexy?" she exclaimed. "Like we're really underwater."

I grudgingly had to concede she was right. The room hushed and I stopped thinking about Miles for a minute as I let myself be carried along with the film. The diver and ray rode an undersea current over the seabed into what could have been infinity.

I felt tears forming in the corners of my eyes. I wanted to say I was sorry for being a bitch and a bore, sorry for judging Daile, sorry for wanting this meeting only to pump her and Laurie for information about Miles. Daile looked so travel weary and spent as she sat with her mouth open, eyes drawn to the underwater ballet on the wall. I glanced back at Laurie. His sunburned ruddiness had been replaced with a white haze in the ripply effect cast off from the film. Five minutes later I could hear a distinct rustling as the bar patrons slowly lost interest in the bottom of the ocean and returned to their drinks and conversations. Even Daile held out her glass for a top-up, but Laurie pointedly ignored her.

"Alrighty, Sara," he said. "It's been quite a treat. But we need to get back to our hotel. Russell Street and all that."

What the "all that" was had me mystified, but I was hankering to be released from their company. I had learned next to nothing about Miles that I hadn't already guessed for myself, and tomorrow's hangover would be colossal.

We gathered our coats and headed back up the stairs. The sky had darkened considerably since we had entered the bar; more rain, I thought. I steeled myself against a sudden gust of wind. "Perhaps we should just take the nearest tube station," I said.

"Fine with me," Laurie agreed. "Daile?"

She grabbed Laurie's arm in response and we began to hurry through the night when something caught Daile's attention. "Oh, look," she said, stopping, nearly pulling Laurie into a headlong fall.

I followed her gaze. "It's an alley."

"But doesn't it look so dark and spooky and Jack-the-Ripper-ish? Somebody could have *died* in there."

Laurie groaned. "She's just crazy about Jack the Ripper." He kissed her on the cheek. "Yanks."

Daile kissed him back. "Don't be a party pooper, Sara," she said when they were finished. "Don't you want to see what's hiding in there? It won't take a minute."

"What for? To see where the restaurants throw their slops?"

"Ha-ha. No, not to see garbage. To see the *ghosts*." She smiled playfully and widened her eyes.

Laurie took her by the arm. "I'll protect you girls," he said. "Tally-ho, then. Let's go see the cabbage leaves."

Daile rewarded him with another kiss and I had no choice but to follow them into a malignant backstreet that offered nothing better than the stink of stale wine and urine. Mayfair certainly had its underbelly. A slice of moon tried to break through the heavy cloudbank, making the rows of seedy buildings appear just as sinister as I believed them to be. Why Daile found them even partially attractive had me flummoxed, and for a minute I tried to see the neglected, cinder-covered stone facades through her eyes. I gave up; the lane was disgusting.

"Are you sure this is where you want to be?"

Daile didn't reply and we went deeper into what was beginning to look more and more like the entrance to a landfill when she unexpectedly seized my wrist. "Hand it over," she snarled.

I laughed. "What?" Daile playing an American gangster was the last thing I expected from our excursion.

"You heard me." Her nails were like pincers. I looked to Laurie to take her away, but he was standing against a bin, idly flicking what I thought was a knife.

I saw the glare of approaching headlights and before I could yell, "Watch out!" I was shoved face first into a filthy wet wall from where I heard the sickening thud of impact I knew had to be either Daile or Granger or both. I twisted around at the same time the car gained speed and drove away, and then there was only Daile and Laurie lying broken and crooked against the oily pavement. Laurie's knife was nowhere to be seen; I thought he might have thrown it.

Cracks of light from the doorways played over Laurie and Daile's expressionless faces, and I felt as if the life had left my own body. My hands deadened and I couldn't move my legs, I couldn't call for help. I couldn't even remember what we were doing here. Nothing made sense. The silence of the street closed around me, absorbing every other sound but the roaring in my ears. If there was any activity or music on the other side of the walls, I heard none of it, only my own fear threatening to force me into what I dumbly supposed was a faint.

I realized I was clutching my handbag in both hands, as though I was about to "hand it over" to Daile, if that's what it was she had wanted. The paralysis in my legs was as bad as the numbness in my brain and I stood there for what seemed like forever until I saw the next pair of headlights and something in me unlocked as I stumbled toward their light.

Someone will help, I thought; someone will make them start breathing again, will pull that hateful nonchalance off their faces. I flagged the car down, feeling like an unwanted extra in a very bad film, and waited as it drew to a standstill a hairsbreadth away from the bodies. Something jejune and forgettable escaped my lips as I rushed to the back passenger door. A Rolls. I didn't stop to think what it was doing here, filling the alley with its bulk.

I peered through the tinted windows and hoped whoever was inside wouldn't hold me responsible: *What did you mean by dragging two foreigners into an alley? With a knife? Why didn't you dissuade them? Go for help?*

My knees shaking, I wrestled with the door handle until it released, opening the door with a slight hiss. I looked inside. An animal noise of recognition made me want to back away.

The man I called "Anton" gazed up at me as though we had arranged to meet.

Anton, I repeated to myself. The man from Noreen's funeral. The man in my dreamscape; the man with the panther.

"Get in," he said.

I leaned on the door for support and struggled to make my voice calm and adult. "Please, you don't understand. There's been an accident."

"I understand," he said. "Now you must get in the car." On the seat beside him lay a small, unframed religious painting. The words *sixteenth-century Spanish* filtered through my mind.

I jumped when a hand behind me came to rest on my shoulder. Anton's chauffeur had crept up and was urging me to sit down on the seat beside his employer. Anton moved the painting to a place between the door and a highly polished attaché case. I noticed his hands were encased in kid gloves the color of freshly turned earth.

"Hurry, Sara," Anton said. "We are losing time."

"But what about—?" I turned back to the street where Daile and Granger were neatly placed against a wall, their hands upon their chests like medieval effigies, making them comical, and a burst of hysteria escaped my throat. I looked at Anton and without thinking collapsed onto the proffered seat and then nearly slid to the floor. The woman in the painting sent me a mocking sneer of scornful piety, her red slash of mouth twitching on the verge of a very secular ecstasy.

"Are we going to the police?" I asked.

Anton reached across me to shut the door. In the over-rich interior, the dark viscid painting could have been smeared with blood for all I knew, and this time I really was going to be sick, but Anton passed me a handkerchief braced with lemon and ice.

"Hold this to your face," he said, not unkindly. "Your lip is bleeding."

"But—"

The car nosed its way forward.

"But nothing," he said. "Your friends are dead. There is nothing more we can do here."

We picked up speed. "They're not my friends." I thought the nausea would overpower me.

The Rolls pulled away from the alley and merged with the stream of taxis and evening traffic siphoning down into the heart of the city.

"We have to tell someone." I attempted another look out the window, but Anton had his hand on my waist and I couldn't move. He held a finger to my lip, grazing the place where it was cut. Through the pain I heard a sound so close to the bone I tried to mention it. "That sound…like purring."

Anton smiled, knowingly, I thought, and I dropped his handkerchief into my lap as the edges of my world went black. *Black as fur*, I remembered thinking just as the car turned a corner and Anton let me fall into total darkness.

## 9

*We dream in sunlight; I rest my arm across blue-black fur, my fingers ruffling, plying into its softness, pinching folds of skin around loose neck muscles. The sun brings out a faint dusty smell: clay, grass, warm animal. I must leave soon. I have stayed too long as it is.*

I woke to the sound of water cascading past the open windows of a room I called mine. For all I knew, I could be anywhere, a thousand leagues away from London or as close as the house next door. Nothing made sense. I drifted into memory, back into the night I arrived, memories that were vague and lucid in turns: Laurie and Daile like broken figures of stone; the suffocating car ride; snatches of conversation; a view of high walls and iron gates; a recollection of Anton coming to my room, holding my hand, informing me I was now in the care of a tall, elegant woman who moved like a dancer but who was in reality my maid.

"Her name is Jeanne-Marie and she will look after you," he had said, his voice like the river beyond the windows, falling and pushing over itself through the night. I remembered saying I didn't need a maid, but Anton only smiled and said he would be back at the end of the week. He had business to conduct, he said. I was so tired I could not form the questions teasing the back of my mind. Simple things, like, why was I here? And, wasn't this all part of an elaborate dream I would leave once the light hit my bed?

Miles, I had thought. How would he find me here?

I slept, it seemed, for weeks.

But now I was fully awake, not in my own house in London where I expected to be, but still in the large and splendidly furnished room Anton had given me that first night.

Morning sun streamed into the room as I watched Jeanne-Marie arrange, then rearrange, the bottles on my dressing table. Cut glass atomizers caught the light from the inlaid gold and silver brushes like sparks from her fingertips. After a while I couldn't bear to watch her working there any longer without speaking. I struggled to sit up.

"No," she said, rushing to my side. "Lie still." She pushed me back against the pillows. Her hands were cool, as though they had been in water.

"I'm fine," I said. "I need to get up." She gave me a long, appraising look, and I said more firmly, "I want to get up."

"When I am finished." She returned to her dusting.

I stayed in bed. Perhaps I had been ill. More than anything I wanted to be alone.

"Please." My voice felt rusty. How long since I had last spoken? I lifted a hand to my hair and brought away a scattering of silk and velvet violets. Jeanne-Marie turned at the sound of my astonishment.

"What are these?" I held the flowers out to her, thinking they might vanish if I clasped too tightly.

"They were in your hair when you arrived. Don't you remember?"

"They couldn't have been. I was with Laurie and Daile." The horror of that night flooded back to me, but Jeanne-Marie paid no attention to the quaver in my voice.

I reached back up to touch hundreds of the petals woven into my hair. Such small, absurd things. I knew they could not have been in my hair that night; I had never worn flowers, real or artificial, not even as a child. Inge and Evan had believed flowers stayed on the stalk. Anything else was foolishness, and harmful to the environment. Wherever we went, we had stepped carefully.

Jeanne-Marie returned to the bed with a violet robe that matched the flowers. I balked when she held the robe out to me. "We are not very formal while Monsieur is away," she said. "There is no need to dress."

I didn't care what the customs were here; I wanted my clothes. "Where is the bathroom?"

"Through that door," she replied, indicating an alcove to my right. "Shall I help you?"

Stiffly, I swung my legs over the side of the bed, embarrassed at my weakness and inability to move. "I can get there on my own," I said. Jeanne-Marie came to me with the robe all the same. I waved her away and clumsily shrugged into the sleeves myself. I gritted my teeth; I would do this without help.

The bathroom was enormous. From high above me, stained glass windows dripped rainbows of color into a bath the size of a sarcophagus. Along the walls, shelves carried vases and urns of the sort I had seen only in museums and behind glass. Mosaic starfish defined in lapis and gold tiles floated across the floor.

"Madame?" Jeanne-Marie called out. "Are you all right?" I cringed. Daile had asked me the same thing only moments before we had left for our "walk." It might have been another lifetime, it felt so long ago. I pressed my face into a towel that smelled of the lemon scent I remembered from Anton's handkerchief. A memory of pleasure coursed through me, its strength at odds with Daile's nasal prattle.

"Madame?"

I laid the towel beside the sink. "I'm fine," I said through the door. "I'm on my way out."

My reflection in a mirrored cabinet stopped me. Rather than the pallor of illness, my skin glowed. My eyes were radiant; the thought of a fever passed through my mind.

I returned to the bedroom and Jeanne-Marie led me to the dressing table. I sat down, and her face softened.

"That is correct," she said. "Please to lean back."

I did as she requested and she plucked the flowers from my hair as if they had been no more than small twigs I'd collected after a walk in the woods. A breeze blew in through the open windows, rattling the leaves outside, and I shivered in my thin robe, thinking of the river.

"You are frightened?" She tossed the last of the flowers into a small net bag she closed with a smart pull on the ribbon drawstrings.

"Why am I here?" I asked. Jeanne-Marie laughed. Brazenly she helped herself to one of the rouge pots scattered amongst the other cosmetics on the table.

"We are not imprisoning you," she said.

"That's not what I meant." I groped for the right words to describe my predicament. "It's just that I need to get back," I said. "I've got clients and work and things to do. Besides, I'm expecting my husband home any day now." When Jeanne-Marie remained silent, I added, "I don't even know the man who brought me here."

Jeanne-Marie daubed the rouge onto her cheeks, leaving two doll-like circles that suited her. "Ah, chèrie," she sighed, angling her head to catch the light, "you would feel like a pinned butterfly to hear how much he knows about you."

A cross between a protest and a sob stuck in my throat. Jeanne-Marie turned me around and studied me full-face. "Listen to me," she said. "What happens here is up to you. Just be aware that you are not the first, nor will you be the last."

A lock of dark hair fell from her otherwise unyielding chignon. We stared at each other in silence, the sound of the wind and the water a low pulse framing our separate thoughts. She pushed her hair back into place.

"You are free to use the house as your own," she said, "except for one place. Monsieur, amongst many other talents, is a gardener. His greenhouses grow rare and exotic plants that must not be disturbed. Only his man, Grégoire, is allowed to enter. Do you understand?"

My spirit sank. It didn't take much to figure out why I couldn't go into the greenhouses. From witnessing a hit-and-run I'd gone to being the houseguest of a drug king. I looked around the room again. Whatever he was dealing paid him well.

Jeanne-Marie left the mirror and stepped lightly to the door. She pulled it open, revealing a high-ceilinged and heavily paneled corridor beyond. She turned back to me from the doorway. "To ensure that you will do as I say," she said, "Monsieur has left you a pet."

I froze when the huge animal entered the room, gliding on its paws past Jeanne-Marie's skirt. She laughed when she saw my expression. "He is harmless. A big kitten. He will play with you."

As if to demonstrate the truth of her words, the panther padded toward where I sat, and then as delicately as a housecat, laid its heavy feral head in my lap. Words escaped me as I placed my hand, tentatively at first, on fur, ears, and lastly on the thick crimson collar around its throat. Hanging from a ring of beaten gold was a medallion. I knew the design as soon as I felt it. The swirls and embellishments were so precise they could have made the companion piece to my armband; the one Evan and Inge had found in my hand nearly thirty years ago. None of this is real, I thought. None of it.

Beneath my touch, the beast began to purr, the rumble from its throat vibrating through my entire body. Startled, I took my hand away. It was that sound again, the sound in the house and in Anton's car, as vital to me as I my own heartbeat. I shut my eyes and floated away.

# 10

I was freezing. Every muscle and joint ached as if I had been the one to be mowed down in that grisly back alley.

I lay on my side surrounded by the dense weeds of my sorely untended garden; any memory of how I had got there, or why I was in so much pain, had gone, along with my jacket and shoes. A strip of light along the horizon told me it was morning. But which morning? Mud and grease streaked my gray denim skirt. My black leggings were laddered down both calves. My handbag had broken open; lipstick, keys, and wallet scattered across the gravel.

I touched my face. Wet, dirty, but no blood that I could find. Fighting the stiffness in my knees, I stood and gathered what I could of my belongings. My keys were beside an old length of hose, and I entered the house through the kitchen.

The remains of my lunch with Laurie and Daile were still fresh. The pasta salad glistened with oil; the unscraped plates had yet to crust over. I sniffed a full-ish glass of wine; it was perfectly drinkable and I swallowed the contents before I sank onto a chair, too tired and too frightened to call for help.

In the distance I could hear the rumble of a car engine. Monday? It had to be Monday morning. I held the empty wine glass by the stem so tightly it was a miracle it didn't snap in two. Shower, I thought. Get out of these clothes, wash my hair. Maybe after I'd dressed there would be a news report and I could find out what had happened to Laurie and Daile.

I started for the stairs only to stop. Neatly folded over the banisters, Daile's Eiffel Tower scarf waited for her to return and reclaim it. Had she not been wearing it? And I thought I'd put it on a chair. I took the fabric between my fingers, the gritty scrape of the cheap East European acetate hissing "fake Hermès." What other lies had the pair told me? I looked down at my torn stockings and skirt. Perhaps they could be considered evidence, proof of an "intentional accident," one I had witnessed and failed to report. I should burn them, I thought; the clothing and the scarf.

Going up the stairs, I stepped out of the clothes as I climbed, wrapping each piece more and more tightly around Daile's scarf until I reached my bedroom. There I stuffed everything into an old plastic shopping bag. I looked around for some place to hide the bag, anywhere but my closet or hamper. The bundle seemed tainted, horrible to me. I left it in the middle of the room while I went to shower.

When the hot water ran out and the sky was fully light, exposing, it seemed, all my past faults and misdeeds, I thought of something Miles had asked on our last afternoon together.

"What is the worst thing you have ever done?"

My face flamed red, and I was grateful for the darkness of the room. "I stole something and let someone else take the blame."

"Tell me," he said.

"It was in India," I replied. I had gone, I said, to the first movie my parents had taken me to see, a story from the *Mahabharata*. The village headman had set up a sheet for a screen with a reel-to-reel projector. I sat with the other children, self-conscious in my khaki shorts and white shirt my mother had purchased from the Army & Navy store the summer before. Even after a year, the clothing was still too big for me. In the dark I kept sneaking glances at the other little girls on either side of me, as bright as tiny Christmas trees in that barren landscape. Watermelon, saffron, amethyst; sparkly nose rings, translucent glass bangles on their thin wrists. Their feet rang with tiny bells as they danced and cheered for the virile monkey king, Hanuman, whose every thought was so charged with devotion even his fur arranged itself into mystical Sanskrit letters: *Rama,*

*Rama, Rama.* Mesmerized, I watched the actor playing Hanuman, his eyes piercing the night despite the spotty texture of the film and the flapping of the sheet when the wind kicked up.

Like me, the boys were more simply dressed, their shorts and shirts echoing my own drab clothing. Except for the kohl lining their eyelids as a barrier against the earlier sun, we were identical. My short black hair had been cropped to above my ears, and in the absence of sun block I had turned a healthy brown. Stick arms and legs stuck out of the hardwearing serviceable uniform Inge had chosen for me, and my heart longed for the silk and embroidered cottons of those village girls. I remembered the wind on the back of my neck and wishing for a long braid of shiny hair. Inge insisted those braids were full of lice, as dangerous as the cobras hidden in our foodstuffs and unguarded tents.

When the film was over and Hanuman had reunited Rama with Sita, there was only a small interval filled with the sound of the men spitting betel to the dust, and the women coaxing babies back to sleep before the next film began.

While the adults conversed and the village children ignored me, I wandered through the small groups of vendors and peddlers, some selling *pan*, others the long shiny ropes of orange *jelabies* and coconut custards. The bangle seller had his cart parked nearby and he had left it unattended when he became engrossed with the working of the projector. I found myself drawn to the colors of his wares—always the colors—the glass studded in gold paint, or covered in fish scales of patterned mirrors. I thirsted for their icy brilliance on that hot, dry night, the wind blowing sand against my bare arms and legs. Everything in that village was so dry, I thought, imagining I could taste the colors on my tongue: greens with the zing of lime ice, blues like alpine glaciers. At first I had only wanted to touch their liquid chill, but within seconds I couldn't help myself from taking as many as I could and putting them in the pockets of my khaki shorts.

Later, after I had returned to my seat and "King Solomon's Mines" was about to start playing, the peddler noticed the bangles were gone. How he could tot up their loss so quickly turned me to stone, and the cry went out that he had been robbed. My heart froze as the man ranted and the parents shook their children down. Thanks to my parents, I was never even a suspect.

At last a boy who had been accused of stealing *pan* the week before was seized as the most likely culprit. His cries and pleas for mercy fell onto the dusty ground and he was beaten within the proverbial inch of his life. Justice meted out, the film began to roll.

The bangles remained in my pocket as light as a kiss and as heavy as thirty pieces of silver. I couldn't bring myself to cry when I threw them down the latrine on my way to bed. No shame could match my horror as I thought of that hungry child kicked and cursed because of my greed.

"Do you know what happened to him?" Miles asked as I lay sweating awake beside him, the sheets tangled and twisted under my back.

"We left the village the next day. My parents mentioned none of it. Perhaps they thought I hadn't seen the beating."

"It's over now," Miles said. "I wouldn't dwell on what can't be changed."

"But what if it could be?" I persisted. "What if I could go back and confess, or never take the damn bangles in the first place? What then?"

He pulled me close against his side. "If we could repair all of our mistakes, what would prevent us from making more of them in the future?"

"Is this a mistake?"

"What?"

"Marrying so quickly."

"Do you feel mistaken?"

"No."

Miles laughed and stroked my hair. "Then you have your answer."

Yes, I had my answer. We turned to each other and within minutes I had forgotten why I had ever asked.

# 11

*The phone; ringing, ringing, ringing.* I rubbed my eyes, my forehead. How long had I been asleep this time? I picked up the receiver; Monique Claiburne's voice bit the line like a spring-loaded trap.

"You never came to collect your belongings," she said.

Oh, Lord, I thought. I was meant to pick everything up from her house on Friday. I'd let it slip while I shopped and cooked for Laurie and Daile's lunch date.

"I'm sorry," I said, inventing excuses. "I haven't been well." The back of my nightgown felt clammy.

"Miss Elliott," Monique said. "I paid a deposit of fifteen hundred pounds toward my daughter's wedding portrait and for you to keep to a strict deadline."

"Bergsen," I muttered. "It's Mrs. Bergsen and I'll meet the deadline." I looked at a digital wall clock I'd never set to the right time.

"I don't think you will meet this or any other deadline. I'd like to request a refund. The commission is cancelled."

I felt as if I'd been slapped; I had to sit down. "I know it's been difficult to have my things at your house, but the painting will be delivered on time. That's the important part, don't you think?"

Monique didn't reply and I estimated how long it would take me to dress and grab a taxi if I started now. I could brush my hair in the cab. "If it's okay with you," I said, "I'll be at your house within the hour."

"It's not convenient," Monique snapped. "I've packed your boxes. A driver will deliver them to you this afternoon. I've added his expenses to your bill."

Bill? What bill? Monique owed *me*.

"I have no desire to view or exhibit your work, Miss Elliott."

"Bergsen," I shouted, but she had already cut me off.

I replaced the phone on the hook with a curse. I'd never lost a commission before, especially not one as important as this. Monique Claiburne's opinion mattered. I wiped my eyes with my hem. For years my work had been my touchstone, my life, and now, like everything else, it was slipping away from me faster than sand through my fingers.

The drained, disabled feeling I'd had before I went to bed returned. My teeth hurt, my scalp ached, my eyes burned. Maybe I really was coming down with the flu. I dragged myself into the lounge and fell asleep for a second time that day.

The noise of the van bringing my art supplies forced me awake again. I opened the door a crack, wide enough to talk to the driver, and told him to put everything on the steps. He looked as if he wanted something for his trouble, so I ran upstairs for my handbag, but when I returned he was gone, leaving in his place a collection of badly packed and dented cardboard boxes. My easel, I noticed with fury, was broken.

I opened the door fully to bring the stuff inside, not caring about my disheveled, slept-in look. My pristine neighbor stood some distance away, watering her window plants. I ignored her and lugged the boxes inside one by one. Once they were piled in the hallway I stepped on the easel and nearly broke my foot.

Forget Monique, I thought recklessly. I had money, Miles's money. But money wasn't the point. Monique could take her damn check and eat it for all I cared. What I was deeply sorry to lose was the work, the art. I loved what I did, and each new picture still intrigued and challenged me. I wanted to paint Courtenay; but nobody was going to talk to me like I was a child, or a thief. I thought of the boy in India. Heat rose to my cheeks. I needed a drink.

Minutes later, sipping a glass of white wine and still in my nightgown, I decided I wasn't ill at all but suffering from being caged up in a stuffy house. In my room at Anton's, I recalled, the windows had been kept open to the sound of a river rushing past. I had felt surrounded and protected by a more natural, gentler world. I shook my head. Stop it, I told myself. There is no "room at Anton's." There is no "Anton."

I opened my own very real back window only to be greeted by a sticky humidity filled with a fine soot that settled on my face and hair. A pneumatic drill on the next street over heralded the start of yet another renovation project. Noise and dirt forced me to close the house up again. Immediately the rooms seemed overstuffed, overcrowded. Nothing felt right. I couldn't breathe; the glare had only worsened my headache. What to do? I circled the pile of damaged art materials like a shark, tried to ring Teague & Bloch, and then threw myself down on the couch with a wail of despair. Why couldn't Miles just come home?

I flipped on the television and waited impatiently through a news brief about an upcoming solar eclipse. No mention of a double homicide or a hit-and-run involving a pair of tourists knocked down like bowling pins. Perhaps these accidents happened every day. Or perhaps, I thought more cynically, the "accident" had never happened. I pressed the "mute" button.

I rotated my empty wine glass in my hands. My imagination was running away with itself. Wasn't that the diagnosis when the blackouts started up at St. Anne's? "Too sensitive. Highly-strung," the doctors said. Inge had agreed. And when painting was suggested as a possible outlet and solution, she had been the first to approve the opportunity for me to get better.

I stared at the soundless television, thinking Inge had been right; there was, and had always been, one solution. I had to get back to work. To hell with Monique Claiburne. I would paint Courtenay for free and present her with the finished portrait as a wedding gift.

Besides, it wasn't as if I didn't have other clients. If this was Monday and I had only lost about twelve hours or so, I had a portrait to deliver in the morning, a commission I had finished several months ago. Before moving into the house, I had kept it along the wall of my bedsit. Now it sat drying in the second spare bedroom.

I had to get up; had to keep going. I slid off the couch and ran upstairs to where I had put my ruined clothing along with Daile's scarf.

Three sneezes later I was outside tending a small fire in a metal bin perilously close to the weeds. Smoke rose from the bin and coated me in the same dusty soot that had come through my windows that morning. I tried watering the fire with the only hose I could find, an unusable piece of rubber with a good-sized crack across the middle. The stupid thing leaked more water than I could squirt from the corroded nozzle.

"There's a ban on burning," my neighbor called to me over a fence from three houses down.

"Not much more to go," I shouted back. I poked at my jacket with a long-handled stainless steel soup ladle I had yet to use for anything as homey as soup. I watched the bowl blacken in the flames.

My neighbor shrugged. "Next time you might like to get dressed. I'd hate to see you have an accident."

I blushed and kept my face toward the fire. I was in the same ratty nightgown I had been wearing the first time we'd met. I wanted to mutter, "I did launder it," but when I looked up she was gone. A final lick of flame consumed the last of my gray skirt just as I knocked the bin over with the hose. The copper grommets from my ruined clothing winked up at me from the embers, and for the hundredth time I wondered if I could be implicated in Laurie and Daile's deaths in some way. I plucked the Eiffel Tower scarf free of the fire, a mad gesture, I knew, but I couldn't bring myself to part with it. The scarf wrapped around my hand, I squeezed the defective hose and sprayed what water I could over weeds and ashes alike, soaking my nightgown in the process until it clung to my skin.

Back inside, my hair dripping, I returned to the TV. Still nothing. I turned it off and wandered from room to room, paintbrush in hand. I looked at my surroundings as I imagined Miles might see them, then through Anton's eyes. It doesn't matter what Anton might think, I told myself, incredulous that I would continue to regard him as more than a dream figure. Anton, the chateau, the panther—they were a mirage. This, I told myself, my hands on the walls, is a real house; a house for Miles. The dishes are for Miles. The couch is for Miles. Yet there was something so modern and faceless about my purchases I found myself hating them. What had once seemed useful and charming, sensible and elegant, now struck me as cheap and garish.

I needed to get outside again. Buy a newspaper, milk, anything to take me away. I threw on my oldest clothes, wiped the soot from my face, and fled.

Out on the street, I made myself walk at a more normal pace and rhythm. It's all right, I repeated with each step. Everything's going to be fine. Fine and dandy. I passed the prevailing landmarks of gated gardens, the small post office, a sandstone church surrounded by a destitute cemetery soon to be plowed under to make room for a new block of flats. I was about to cross the street to the Indian grocer where I bought most of my household goods, when I stopped, one foot on the curb, the other about to be crushed by a motorcyclist who swerved just in time to scream out a rush of obscenities.

On the other side of the street, directly across from me and wearing what seemed like a parka and hunting boots, Miles held a door open for Courtenay Claiburne.

The door was no different from any others lining the street, leading nowhere special. But Miles I would know anywhere. Ditto for Courtenay. I couldn't move.

*Miles in London with Courtenay entering a brown brick building.* I couldn't put the image into any kind of sensible order. Hysteria bubbled up in my throat and I back-tracked into the shadows cast by an awning outside a fruit and vegetable shop. I wanted to race home and slash her portrait with my fingernails. Sweat soaked through my shirt as I inspected a sampling of pomegranates while a thousand unrelated possibilities sped through my mind. Should I go after them? And once I confronted them, then what was I supposed to do?

The shock of seeing them together took me so off guard I could barely remain standing. I continued to study the shiny waxed fruit, feeling as if I had done something unspeakably oafish by seeing my own husband, a

husband meant to be in a Saudi oil field. And why was he wearing a parka
and boots in this heat?

What was I meant to do? Follow them? Make a scene? A couple holding hands jostled my elbow when they reached over me for bok choy and
apples. I windmilled back to the curb where I stared at the nondescript
facades across the street.

My feet refused to go any farther. Courtenay's sleek summer shift
made me want to cover up my tacky paint-covered jeans and worn black T-
shirt. The traffic lights changed and I realized I held a pomegranate in my
hand; I must have taken it from the fruit stand. It fell with a thud to the
pavement when I was suddenly pushed along with the throng of pedestrians crossing the street. Worried I would lose track of Miles, I went with
them until I was safely across, and then hurried to the door I had seen him
enter. Feeling ridiculous, I rattled the handle; it was locked. I scanned the
list of handwritten names labeling the bells and buzzers. Nothing was
readable. Foreign names and alphabets swam before my eyes filling with
angry tears. Why was he here? What was going on?

As if I were in yet another of my improbable dreams, I entered the
Indian store and grabbed a liter of milk, a bar of Cadbury's Fruit & Nut,
and a travel magazine I chose because the cover featured a backdrop of
snow and glistening trees, icicles hanging from their branches. *"Secrets of
Kamchatka"* tore across the sky like a meteor.

A girl in a sari carrying a toddler repeated something: I was in the middle of the aisle. "Sorry," I mumbled. "Sorry, sorry."

I paid for my purchases, fumbling for my change, and then ran the rest
of the way home, my head pounding with each slap of my sandals against
the footpath. Everywhere there seemed to be noise: back hoes digging up
the cemetery, horns blaring, traffic grinding and crunching through the
confined streets. The noise followed me all the way to my front door and
inside, managing to keep up a constant echo that buried any breath of that
subtle purring sound I craved as I staggered to the kitchen and slumped
into a chair. After a minute it stopped, and I swiveled my chair, reached
into a cupboard, and found an unopened bottle of vodka. Adding ice

seemed too great an effort. So did finding a glass.

What was Miles doing? And why with Courtenay? The questions went round and round my head, worse than the warm vodka. Why did I even care? I opened the travel magazine and realized it was upside down. The story on Kamchatka might have been written in Russian for all the sense it made to me.

What was it Miles gave me that I needed so much? I tossed the magazine to the floor. My answer shamed me. I had had his attention. He had listened to me. Me, the child of sound engineers who had instructed me to spend my life in silence while all I had wanted was to hear my own words float upon the air. Back when we had traveled as a unit in our lean-tos and canvas tents, there had been no requests for a recording of a child's British-accented voice interrupting the honk of low-flying geese or inserting itself between the pauses of African bullfrog calls. "Ssh" had been one of the first sounds I remembered Inge forming in my ear.

I picked up the magazine and stared at the wintry cover. *"Ssh."*

When I met Miles I had a lifetime of words to release and Miles was an avid listener. But my barrage of words and images had prevented me from hearing any of his own stories—I had no idea who he was.

The sun slipped behind a bevy of clouds as I drank the last of the vodka. When the bottle was dangerously close to empty and I had eaten the rest of the chocolate, I was astounded to find I could walk. I opened the milk I had bought. Sour. I poured the full liter down the sink and promptly passed out.

# 12

*In my dream I saw a row of brides, their faces as impassive as mannequins. Most noticeably, there were no grooms. Perhaps the women were on their way to becoming nuns, or worse, it occurred to me in a panic of fear and sweat, they were on their way to be executed, or sacrificed.*

*Seeing them dressed in white with full veils and decorous neck-high bodices, I sensed something drugged and tragic about their promenade against a stark landscape of industrial bleakness. The skeletons of abandoned oil refineries loomed black and threatening against the leaden sky. I wanted to call out and warn them that they were marching to their slaughter, that nothing good would come of their macabre parade. They moved so slowly I had time to study their gowns: empire waists, some with hoods, others ruffled and trimmed in lace. I didn't want to think of those fine fabrics soaked in blood and tossed in the dirt.*

*I tried to form the words that could sound out a loud enough warning, but it was useless. One by one the brides passed over the meridian while the storm clouds gathered and the air became so thick and heavy with fog and pollution I thought we would all die anyway. It was, I found, easier to lie in my makeshift grave, the spiders and rubbery earthworms crawling over my hands and face, comforting me with their aliveness and lack of concern for the world.*

I woke on the stairs with a jolt, feeling the wet clay covering my legs, smelling the twisted plant roots, hearing the steady rustle of the brides' long skirts rasping against the damp pavement. I thought of their satin shoes, blunt-toed and oil-stained, peeping out from under their modest hemlines. My own wedding had been nondescript and businesslike. There had been no time to plan out an elaborate ceremony, and a frou-frou confection of a dress had seemed like a silly and exorbitant gesture.

I stood and went to make myself a cup of coffee, when I realized I wasn't wearing my rings. Then I remembered they were tucked into a small side drawer of my new pine dresser. I had put them there with my gold cuff before I went to burn my clothes only hours ago. For a brief instant I imagined one of the bride's cold hands reaching out to me, and all I could think was how free her long fingers were in their bare and unencumbered state. My rings, like the cuff, were heavy to wear, oppressive on the worst days. But Miles had wanted to spoil me. After we had bought the rings, there was still more he wanted to give me.

"I have something for you," he'd said. We had stopped outside the entrance to St. James's Park. Squirrels dived from the trees while families took photos of the sky and each other, and because we looked so happy, of us.

I leaned into Miles's shoulder, the padded twill of his jacket solid and comforting to my cheek. He seemed so real, so utterly stable and confident; the kind of man I had ceased to believe could exist in this day and age. I inhaled what smelled like crushed carnations, spice and sun, a geranium sharpness underlying each breath.

"Aren't you just a bit curious?" he asked when I continued to stand with my eyes closed, my arms wrapped loosely around his waist.

"You've given me so much already," I murmured. It was true. My rings were stunning. And there had been all sorts of other small but significant things: theater programs, a sudden bouquet of violets and white hyacinths, a chocolate orange because I had mentioned loving them as a child. What more could I want? Especially when I learned of the bank account trans-ferred to my name.

"This is different," Miles said. "It's—" He stopped and looked toward the trees. I followed his eyes and saw nothing unusual. Yet he continued to stare after I lifted his lapels and shook him back to attention.

"It's?" I prompted.

He glanced back down at me. "It's what I would say to you if I had the words." He reached into his pocket and brought out a paper box that he put into my hand.

"Open it when I'm gone," he said. "On the day you feel most alone."

"That's silly. I want to open it now."

He pretended to take it back and I grabbed his hand. "Promise you'll wait," he said.

I held his gaze with my own. Was he asking that I wait to open the box, or more pointedly, that I wait for him to return? My mood became more serious. "I promise," I said. Gently he released his hold on the gift and I weighed it in my palm.

"Give me a clue," I said. "Jewelry?"

He kept up his air of mystery. "You'll see."

I hated secrets, hated "wait-and-see." I always wanted to know "what was what," wanting my answer *now*. It drove my parents crazy, but I couldn't stand the suspense of waiting to open Christmas or birthday gifts a minute longer than I had to. I put the small box in my handbag. Our wedding was to be in two days time and suddenly I couldn't bear to wait for anything. I felt hamstrung by the weak sunlight fighting the cover of dense cloud, the smell of diesel wafting from Pall Mall, the sturdy feel of my shoes on the walkway.

But I showed none of this to Miles, and when he suggested a late tea in a quiet arcade he knew, I could only nod and let myself be led by the hand like a child.

The box was upstairs in a drawer with my rings and armband. True to my word, I had not opened it. Yet.

The stiff wrapping paper peeled away without tearing. Beneath its folds, a battered cardboard box with a list of Asian characters penciled on one side seemed nothing special. I used my thumbnail to separate the tape holding the lid in place, and opened the box without difficulty.

A bracelet nearly identical to the one I already owned glinted in the light from the window. The heft of it alone told me it was real and not a modern copy. Stunned, I removed the piece from the box and placed it

around my right wrist, uncertain how to accept the gift after what I had
seen that afternoon.

I held my arm to the light. Instead of the black coral branching between the swirls and intricacies decorating my other cuff, rough-cut amber
studded the band now glowing like honey against my skin. Together they
made a pair; one light, one dark, both Scythian, both magical and older
than I could imagine. "Remember the sun and moon," Miles had said. So
why had he chosen to forget?

I returned to the kitchen. There was another bottle of vodka conveniently wedged at the back of my freezer. The coffee could wait.

# 13

My head pounded as a car cut in front of me and I hit the horn button, hard. Aspirin hadn't taken the edge off my hangover and I worried my makeup was too anemic. I would have done anything to stay in bed. My arms ached to the point where I had decided to leave off my rings and the matching cuffs, or that was the excuse I gave myself. The truth was that after a night of drinking and thinking about Miles and Courtenay, I didn't want the jewelry anywhere near me.

I also didn't know how much longer I could brave what was fast becoming a hellish drive out to the Hansard estate, a Tudor manor house a good forty minutes outside of London. My rental car reeked of tobacco and I couldn't get the windows to work properly. I had only taken the vehicle because the back seats folded down flat enough to accommodate what was my largest commission to date.

I wove in and out of the traffic, my stomach recoiling at the thought of the sherry and cake that would be cut and waiting for me as it had been on each of my previous visits with Benita Hansard. Despite last night's vodka, I would have to accept the refreshments, even if I was sick on the carpet. A Cuban refugee married to a powerful industrialist, Benita was the consummate hostess; she would be hurt and suspicious if I refused her hospitality.

I exited the motorway and drove in silence down a provincial single lane road, hoping no one was approaching from the other direction. Once I had lived for these home visits. They were part of my life plan: house, marriage, career; I had thought I wanted all of them, that they would bring me, what? Now all I wanted was to find a hole and die.

I pulled into a petrol station and checked on the canvas. Wrapped in layers of bunting and bubble wrap, the portrait of Benita's late sons hadn't moved. The two teenage boys, brought back to a tenuous life through a palette of earth tones broken only by their matching navy-striped fisherman's jerseys, had drowned four years ago in a freak accident peculiar to their class and money: a careless incident combining speedboats and fishing line. The younger, Alessandro, had nearly been decapitated, an image Benita could not remove from her psyche. More than once I had had to warn her from smearing the penciled contours of his throat when I brought my sketches to her for approval.

I restarted the rental car and drove until I pulled into Benita's circular driveway. Just as I'd expected, Benita was waiting for me, probably since dawn. She had her front door open before I'd finished parking beside a thicket of untamed rose bushes.

"Sara!" Benita exclaimed, running to hug me. Molting *Cardinal Richelieu* showered maroon petals at my feet as if I were a visiting VIP. Benita peered over my shoulder, her grip tight. "It is ready, no?"

"I think you'll be pleased."

Together we carried the huge package inside to the drawing room where Benita had cleared some floor space. "As you can see," she said, "no frame." Benita had been waiting for the carved gilt frame ordered from a local craftsman for over a year. His fitful procrastination had given her a calendar's worth of sleepless nights that she proceeded to relay to me yet again.

"He is slow," she complained. "Always an excuse. Not like you," she added. I smiled my thanks and wished she could pass that information on to Monique Claiburne.

We placed the painting in front of the fireplace. Benita stepped back as I unwrapped the protective layers, my stomach clenched with that skip of apprehension I always felt just as I pulled away the last of the muslin sheets. I stood waiting in a knot of agony until she finally smiled.

"It is just right," she said. "Just as they were. My boys."

She turned lovingly to me. "You see into the soul, Sara."

I blushed. I didn't want to appear insensitive to the compliment, but "see into the soul"? After the last few hours I was beginning to think I couldn't see anything beyond my own nose.

Benita drew me toward a deeply padded couch the same color as her roses bunched around the room in huge yellow ginger jars. The anticipated cake and sherry sat ready for us on a tea tray. For the first time since I had met her, Benita seemed to have made a truce with the past. Her brow was less furrowed than usual, and she poured the sherry into two griffin-etched glasses with a carefree hand.

She extended her glass. "To the painting. To my sons. And to your talent. Thank you."

I didn't know what to say. I looked at the cake and realized I was hungry. The sherry slid down my throat as Benita chatted about her only remaining child, a daughter living in Sweden. "Isn't that where your mother is from?" she asked.

"She left when she was eighteen to be an *au pair* for a family in Oxford. That's where she met my father. 'Just like in a fairy tale,' she always said." Something in my voice made Benita put her plate down.

"Tell me what is wrong, Sara."

"Nothing's wrong. Everything's great."

Benita looked into my eyes as if she were the one to "see into the soul."

"Is it your husband?"

I nearly laughed. My husband, I thought. Not to mention Courtenay Claiburne, or his two "friends" being killed, or hallucinations so real I was losing work on a daily basis. My husband. I coughed and finished my sherry. "Yes," I said. "I am somewhat worried about him."

"When do you expect him back?"

"I don't know."

Benita returned her gaze to the portrait. Carefully, I set my empty glass upon a table inlaid with ivory signs of the zodiac. I cleared my throat again and the words tumbled out before I could stop them.

"To be honest," I said in too much of a rush, "I think he is back."

Benita faced me. "What do you mean? How could he be home without telling you?"

I shrugged. How indeed? I studied the pattern of rose leaves on my cake plate. As a rule I didn't like to discuss my personal life with my clients, it seemed so gauche and unprofessional. Announcing my wedding was about as far as I was willing to go. Now it appeared I would have to tell them about my upcoming divorce.

"Talk to me," Benita said. She sounded more like my mother than a client.

"I saw him."

"Where?"

"I went to buy milk." I stopped, embarrassed. It was all so mundane. Why couldn't I have been out shopping for apricots dusted with hashish, or jellied eels in tarragon sauce? Something with a more compelling back-story. But Benita was waiting. "He was with another woman," I said. "A girl, I should say."

"Someone you know?"

"Yes. Her name is Courtenay Claiburne."

Benita leaned back in her chair and pursed her lips. "So. Monique's daughter."

I must have looked dumbfounded, and she added, "Everyone knows the Claiburnes. Courtenay is engaged to be married. Douglas and I are on the guest list."

"Until yesterday I was painting her portrait."

"What happened yesterday?"

"Monique sent me packing."

Benita tilted her head. "No."

"She cancelled the portrait."

Benita considered this last piece of information. "That is too bad." I had nothing more of my own to add, and she said, "You know, it may not have been your husband you saw. Forgive me for saying this, but you were not together for very long. The memory plays tricks." She gestured to the painting. "One of the reasons I wanted this picture was I had started to forget my sons' faces. A terrible thing to admit, but true."

I understood what she was saying, I felt the same way about my parents and even Noreen, but there was no way I could forget the way Miles walked or tossed his head back when he laughed. And I knew Courtenay in the way I knew all my clients after repeatedly sketching them. I had seen Miles and Courtenay together, end of story. My head started to ache again and I keeled over, bringing Benita to my side. "What is it?" she asked.

It was the dizziness. I shouldn't have drunk the sherry.

"Come," she said. "You are tired and I think also overworked. I insist you rest in my room."

"No, really, I couldn't." A shattering wave of nausea belied my feeble protest.

Benita placed her hand on my forehead and I thought of Jeanne-Marie. "Can you try to stand?" she asked. I leaned on her arm for a second, my legs as weak as cotton wool beneath me.

"Good. This way," she said, all business. "Just up these stairs, like so." She guided me toward the staircase, helping me up slowly until we came to her bedroom. The same intense clarets and vermilions she loved in her garden and drawing room were prominent up here as well, but I was too weak to appreciate any of it.

"I'm sorry," I started to say, when she shook her head.

"Sara, please. No apologies. Anyone can tell you are worn out. You young women burn the candle at both ends. Lie down right here." She patted the bed. I obeyed without further hesitation, and she unfolded a soft knitted throw over me before she went to her bathroom for a cold cloth. When she came back and placed it over my eyes and forehead. I did not want to cry, but when she whispered, "I have left a small basin here on the floor," I felt the tears escape from under my lids.

"There, there," she said. "Stay for as long as you need. I will be downstairs." She patted my hand before tiptoeing out of the room. I had never felt so mortified in my life. Nor as coddled. The shaded room, the cold cloth, and the comforting, childish feel of the blanket were already having the desired effect of making the nausea pass. I rolled over onto my side. Just a while, I thought, my eyes growing heavier with each breath. *Just a few short minutes.*

*He wanted to go home. He staggered along the sea edge, following the ragged shore. In the distance, he could recognize the shape of Anton's outline. The beach was littered with ice and amber, mounds of drying seaweed. The sun was strong but the air cut like glass. The cold had reached through the layers of his parka right to his bones; wind corralled the hardened sand into mounds that crunched beneath his feet. He was dying, and he knew it. He had lost what had once protected him: the seal pelts, his coral amulets, the gold nuggets. He fell to the ground only to awake to Anton standing over him, his walking stick poised ready to strike.*

# 14

I lurched awake, a sadness so thick over me slow tears fell from my eyes before I knew they were there. I brushed them away, salty and strangely cold. Miles, I thought. What was happening to him; to me?

I dried my eyes and sat up, the blanket pulled under my chin as I felt around the floor with my foot for my shoes. In the corner I could see Benita's nightstand laden with books. The amount was impressive in itself, but the titles, an unusual miscellany for bedtime reading, intrigued me more: Fulcanelli's *Mysteries of the Cathedrals*, some metaphysical volumes on the esoteric meaning of color, and topping them all, *A History of the Scythians, Their Disappearance and Revival.* I had read a similar book while searching for clues on my first gold cuff. I didn't think Benita would mind if I leafed through the pages before returning downstairs.

I left the throw on the bed and carried the book to a window where I opened the curtains a fraction to let in more light. On my lap the book fell open to the middle. I skimmed the pages, passing over the oft-quoted accounts left by Herodotus, the ones describing the Scythians as blood-thirsty barbarians intent on rape and pillage with each leg of their nomadic existence.

The next chapter was more interesting—it discounted everything Herodotus had to say. According to the book's author, modern scholarship had re-evaluated the historian, deeming his prejudices as typical for an unsympathetic scholar of his day, a man suspicious of any culture foreign to his own.

After scanning several pages on the history of the Scythian burial sites, or kurgans, found in Pazyryk and Tuva, and the pilfering that had destroyed them since before the time of Catherine the Great, I came to a section that suddenly switched topics and sidestepped into the significance of amber. Immediately my thoughts returned to my new cuff and my dream of Miles. I had seen him on a beach positively glowing with gobs of the stuff.

The well-thumbed pages were illustrated with old black and white landscape photography taken in the early days of the camera. The silvery photos showed a stark, frozen beach covered in shiny sea-tumbled pebbles I now thought had to be pellets of amber. The pieces were everywhere, lying in piles between stacks of drying seaweed and strings of salted cod. The scenes on the pages were identical to the beach I had just seen Miles struggling to cross before Anton lifted that elegant stick to strike him on the head.

I closed the book; it had been a while since I'd had the time to sit and read. I also realized I was feeling much better; time to be thinking of going home. I stood and fixed my hair in the mirror, tucked in my shirt, and retied my shoes. Some minor adjustments to my skirt and I was ready to return to the drawing room.

I carried the book on the Scythians as well as three others downstairs with me. As I crossed the entry hall I could hear Benita on the phone. When I appeared at the door, she looked up, placed her hand over the mouthpiece and smiled.

"You look good," she said. "I'll just be a minute here. Please take a seat." She waved me toward a chair and then resumed her conversation with what sounded like a caterer.

"That's right. Three cases of the merlot and cancel the prawns. I don't care what he says; they're bad for my husband's digestion. Yes. Excellent. Thank you."

She put the phone down on the same table that had earlier held the sherry and cake. In their place was an Art Nouveau coffee set.

I held up the books. "I hope you don't think I've been snooping," I said, "but these looked so fascinating. I'd like to borrow them."

"The books on color." She seemed delighted by my choice. "They were worth every penny. I ordered them from a man who travels to Paris." She smiled. "You may take them and any others you like. I've read the ones you are holding more than twice."

"Thanks."

She checked the coffee pot. "So you are a student of alchemy, too?" she asked.

"Alchemy?"

"You have *Mysteries of the Cathedrals* there, by Fulcanelli."

"Oh. I didn't look that closely at all of them," I admitted. I must have added Fulcanelli to the pile by accident.

Benita nodded and poured the coffee into cups.

"Have you read many books on…alchemy?"

"More than I should let on," Benita said with a wry laugh. She brought me my coffee and waited while I poured in a splash of cream. "My husband thinks my interest in the subject more than unbalanced. I think he considers me what you would call a 'crackpot.'"

She returned to her own seat, her face pensive again. "But," she added, "when my sons were killed, I had to know if there was a reason for their loss. It was so senseless to me. Sanctioned wisdom said I should consult with my priest, pray more, attend mass every day."

"Did it help?"

Benita stirred her coffee. "Not in the least. That is when I stopped going to church and instead began to investigate the hermetic sciences. I began to read the myths and legends from around the world regarding the origins of such things as good and evil, dark and light. Sound and color." She paused and sipped her coffee, weighing her next words carefully.

"As I read through these topics," she said, "I knew that somehow Alessandro and Carlo were safe, and that they had returned to a source that was infinite and more powerful than anything the church taught. A place," she declared firmly, "without punishment for so-called sin."

She shook her head. "As though my boys had lived long enough to even know the meaning of such an abhorrent and sad word."

I listened to her with a mixture of faint understanding and deep skepticism. My adoptive mother, Inge, had gone through a similar search at one time in our travels together, reading everything she could find on metaphysics and the paranormal, seeking out-of-the-way shamans and healers when she had the opportunity, which was rare. My father thought she'd gone nuts.

"My mother was once obsessed with mythology," I said. For some reason I added, "I think she wanted to learn more about me." I suddenly relived an episode in a shaman's tent where she had held me tightly while an old woman with a face like a dried walnut stared into my eyes and sang a song that sounded like bending saw blades.

Benita's face was a study in controlled curiosity.

"Because of the way she found me, I guess," I replied to her silent question. "In Kamchatka."

"That explains your jewelry," she said, glancing at my bare arms.

"I didn't wear it today. Too heavy."

Benita continued to stare at my arms, and I said, "Miles gave me another one. Another cuff. I only got it yesterday. Opened the box, I mean."

"Does it compare to the bracelet you have?"

"It's thicker, with less carving. I think it's made with amber."

Benita took in this information and then set her cup on its saucer with a scraping sound.

"I have been thinking," she said. "This business with your husband is not good for you. You must contact his firm."

"Teague & Bloch?" I shook my head. "I've tried. No one answers the phone. It's all just voice mails and emergency numbers that don't work."

"What about the police?"

"Rather drastic, don't you think? I'd feel like an idiot."

"Then you must go to his company yourself."

I imagined what it would be like approaching Teague & Bloch after all this time, cap in hand, asking for my errant husband. Just the thought of the secretary in her red hat and ironic smile made me shudder.

Benita glanced at her own wrist. A platinum Rolex alerted her to the time, but she seemed reluctant to send me home, so I did it for her.

"I've imposed myself for way too long," I said, getting to my feet.

"But are you sure you can drive?" she asked. "It is so late and the traffic is so bad…"

"I'm fine."

She stood and walked to a desk tucked into a corner, and then returned with the balance of my fee as well as a wrapped bouquet of the *Cardinal Richelieu*.

"The portrait is beautiful," she said. She gave me one of those quick, staccato European embraces that always left me breathless and addled over the correct way to return it. I held the roses to my face to cover my ineptitude.

"Don't worry about the Claiburnes," she added as we walked out the front door and down to the rental car. "Monique is—" She paused. "Impulsive. In fact, I will tell you a little secret." She opened the car door for me, and said, "I first met Monique at one of my 'metaphysical' meetings I attended in London. It was a diverse group, made up of people from many walks of life: lawyers, school teachers, artists and writers. Monique stood out from the others. She was, shall we say, more passionate. She had opinions and she was not afraid to express them, no matter whose toes she stepped on. I suppose that's what makes her such an excellent patron of the arts. She is vocal in her loyalties, sadistic in her criticism, and unfaithful to her husband.

"But Courtenay is not her mother. She is not the type of girl to go after other women's husbands. She has, I believe, seen too much of her own mother's behavior to follow in her footsteps." She looked me in the eye and patted my arm. "Once you've spoken with—what are they called? Teague & Bloch? They will tell you there is a sensible reason for what it is you saw.

"Ask them," she repeated as I started the engine. I tried to look like I believed she was right about Teague & Bloch, waving and smiling in a show of optimism while I nearly drove into her rose bushes. I liked Benita, and after today I regarded her as a genuine friend, but I couldn't go to Teague & Bloch. I couldn't.

Not in a million years, I thought, attemping to cut through what seemed like a ten-year traffic backlog along the motorway. Yet as I waited for my car to move, I questioned my earlier reluctance. If I was to know the truth, the real truth about Miles, I had to start acting like an adult and go to Teague & Bloch as Benita advised me to do.

A break in the traffic let me slide into the lane I needed and I was able to pick up some speed while I wavered between cowardice and taking the bull by the horns. After driving past a particularly revolting new housing complex that had gone up in the last year, I made my decision. I would do it. Ask Teague & Bloch.

Their building was only a five-minute walk away from the parking garage where I needed to drop off the car. I figured that after I'd paid my bill and stopped in at the chemist's for more aspirin and a tube of mascara, I would have a good hour before they closed for the day.

I timed it right. My errands complete, I drank dolefully from a bottle of over-priced Italian mineral water as I walked to the corner, wondering if my excuse of wanting to check up on the CEO's portrait would hold. I passed the Burger King, the barricaded jeweler's, and the temp agency that seemed to have more jobs advertised in their windows than they had space for. Teague & Bloch was on the other side. I tossed my water bottle away before I pushed through the revolving doors, took the lift to the third floor, and realized I had made a horrendous mistake.

The office was gone. Kaput. Not even arguing with the graphic designers upstairs, a team of conventionally hip and computer savvy young people who insisted there had never been a company called "Teague & Bloch, Geological Engineers, Ltd." could bring them back. Teague & Bloch were delusion and hearsay, as ephemeral as Benita's alchemical studies.

"But that's preposterous," I said. "They've been here for years. My husband works for them. I painted the CEO's portrait!"

A girl with a shaved head and what looked like a bone through her nose rolled her eyes. "We've been here for over a year," she said, her scorn focused on the bouquet of *Cardinal Richelieu* at my chest. "Perhaps you should try meditation."

I refrained from slapping her and instead raced back out to the marble foyer where only weeks ago there had been the full display cases of tungsten and fire opals. Except for the Art Deco brass light fixtures and an ottoman I remembered being part of the butter yellow Danish furniture, not a trace of Teague & Bloch remained. Everything else had been removed: the portrait, the filing cabinets, the efficient secretary. I scanned the floors for a dropped business card or an old invoice, but the rooms had been vacuumed clean. The clatter of my heels hit the floors with a hollow sound that hurt my ears. By the time I had checked each room a fourth time, the nasty design team upstairs had left for home.

Defeated, I took the lift back down to the street where I watched the wind kick the dust into swirls of cigarette butts and hamburger wrappers. Leaves the same burnt color as the sky blew past my shoes. I breathed in and choked on the smog-ridden twilight before I turned away in despair.

Maybe the angry bald girl was right; I should try meditation. Or maybe she'd said "medication"?

I set out for home but could only go a few steps before I had to stop outside a small park and sit down. I hunched over my bag filled with Benita's books. Once I locked the door behind me, I worried, I might never step outside the house again. Compared to my earlier fears of recurring blackouts and dizzy spells, my current condition was a thousand times worse. This time I was losing my mind, not just my nerve. As the sky glowered above me I wished that Miles and I had never met. And then it struck me. Perhaps we never had.

I left the roses on the bench.

## 15

I was walking down the street at night. Which street, what night; don't ask. Cars rushed by, their headlights reflected in oily puddles that splashed mud and water over my legs and skirt. I didn't care; I just kept walking past a hundred shop windows that all looked the same. With each step forward, the night became colder and more miserable. My feet were wet; my hair stuck plastered to my head, dripping rain down the back of my collar and sliding down my back; Benita's books stabbed me in the ribs. Where I was going or why I was walking held no meaning except for the vague notion that it was the only way I could stay alive.

Over and over I thought of that first lunch with Miles, of his proposal and how right it felt; how right that my life should belong to him. I remembered leaving the restaurant and how, after that first kiss, he had hailed a taxi to take him back to his club, but he continued to hold onto my hand through the open window.

"Dinner," he said.

"Formal? Casual? What should I wear?" The cab moved away from the curb before I heard his answer.

I went to Selfridges that very afternoon and purchased a black velvet dress I had wanted for weeks. At the last minute I told the clerk to throw in a necklace of fake aquamarines that were advertised on sale. Back at the bedsit when I fitted the dress against my body, the synthetic stones shining in the lamplight, I didn't care how bad a decision it was to marry a stranger. I didn't care about right or wrong. All I knew was I wanted him.

When Miles picked me up that evening the dress was the perfect choice; a sign, I thought, that I could already read him, that we were both on the same page.

We went to a private dining room reserved for us in a hotel before we went to a late showing of a new play that only ran at midnight. The characters were dressed as allegories taken from a Restoration masque. Their somewhat ribald, stylized speeches were simply a backdrop to my own thoughts as I sat close to Miles, my hand in his. "Tomorrow," he whispered as Autumn battled with Virtue and Spring, "we'll buy the rings." I thrilled at the words and let his hand move to the back of my knee where his fingertips explored the black lace of my stocking. I shivered in the semi-dark and knew that we would always be a couple, no matter how far Miles traveled apart from me. We were together and there was nothing that could separate us. The small matter of Dubai loomed ahead, but he promised it would be his final trip as he could not bear to lose me now that I was found.

Now, very lost and grievously alone, I wrapped my arms around my wet jacket and scuttled away from the cars mistaking me for one of the nameless, faceless prostitutes trawling behind me. I signaled a cab. It was time to find my way home and plan the rest of my life.

Order. I craved order like a drug, I thought, burrowing into a terry dressing gown. My hair washed, my nails scrubbed, I sat at the burnished teak dining table and lit a scented candle. Bayberry suffused the room as I placed a glass of wine on my left and a basket for catching paper on my right. My neighbor's complaints must have been heard. Sometime during the day more than a fortnight's worth of unopened mail had been delivered to my door.

I divided it into three piles: bills, advertising, and personal correspondence. So far, so good. The phone and the electricity amounts appeared reasonable. I had used neither service excessively and I was still within the limits for avoiding any extra charges or cut-offs. A bill for a gardening service that had never appeared went into the basket, as did an installment on a stereo system I no longer wanted. I had purchased it for Miles with the idea that he would like music in the evenings, a suburban and dismal fantasy when I considered I didn't even know his tastes. He could have liked industrial punk and Cambodian reggae for all I knew. I swallowed what was left of my wine and decided I would swap it for something more practical, a tanning bed, for instance.

The bills paid and put away, I next went through the junk. Dog food specials, cheap rail holidays, offers for computer lessons. I gathered up the pile of fliers, tore each one to bits, and dropped everything into the basket. I stared at what was left. Three hand-addressed envelopes.

The first was from my mother. I held it to the candlelight, realizing it was also the first she had written me since I had given her my new address.

I opened and read the lengthy note slowly. She congratulated me on the purchase of the house; she knew the area and even remembered walking there with my father before I was born (*found, bought, stolen,* I mentally corrected her upright handwriting). She asked if Miles had returned home yet, but if not, she knew I could cope: *"Don't you remember when you were six and we lived in the Sudan? A cobra came into your room while you were dressing for breakfast. You did not move, in fact you pacified the snake, Amah said. Afterwards you did not cry like other children would have. No, you said you were very, very hungry and wanted tinned papaya and cornflakes. Pappa got them for you right away."*

No, I thought, refolding the paper. I couldn't remember.

The second note turned out to be an advertisement from a dry cleaner. I tore it to shreds. But the third, a simple monogrammed card from one of my school friends who had been at Noreen's funeral, an event that seemed a lifetime away now, held my attention. Pamela "Twitty" Lansbury would be in London for a week; could we meet? I looked at the date and realized tomorrow would be her last day in town. I glanced through the rest of her message; she wanted to wish me every happiness on the occasion of my marriage, something she hadn't found the chance—or the words—to say at the church.

Could we meet? My first impulse was to reply, Good God, no, but then I thought of my mother's story about the cobra. Twitty Lansbury was about the farthest thing there was from a poisonous snake, but right now I saw any meeting with anyone as the equivalent of petting a pit viper. Which meant I had to do it.

I phoned Twitty's hotel. If it wasn't too short of notice, I told her voice mail, I would meet her tomorrow outside the Royal Academy. As I put the phone down, the taste of tinned papaya filled my mouth. Perhaps on some level I did remember.

"I'd love for you to read it," Pamela gushed for what had to be the tenth time over leek pie and a salad of spindly organic lettuces. She was referring to some manuscript she'd been writing *for ages* and had planned to send to Noreen for help

"But why me?" I asked. "I don't know a thing about publishing."

"But you have such good taste. Noreen always said so."

I frowned and pushed my plate away, my leeks uneaten. "Twitty" hadn't changed a whit since school. White-blonde hair held away from her face with a black plastic Alice band, baby-puke yellow cashmere twin set and an outmoded strand of graduated cultured pearls; it was the same outfit she'd worn on parents' days and tea with the vicar.

"I'm an artist. Noreen was the grammar girl." I refilled my wine glass from the carafe we had ordered. I was drinking far too much and I knew it. I stared at the lettuces on Twitty's plate; they were identical to the tiny squids littering the fishing docks on Corfu. Rafe Hemmings had pointed them out to me during our one and only "working holiday" together, the one where it was obvious our relationship wasn't going anywhere.

Pamela followed my eyes and nervously poked at her salad with a fork. "Do you see something?" she asked, spearing a mushroom slice.

"Your lettuce. It looks like squid."

"Ick."

I smiled in a way I hoped would appear bright and cheerful as opposed to drunk and lopsided. "Besides, I don't have time to read."

"Huh?"

"To read your book."

"I just need someone to tell me if it's any good." Pamela eyed a cherry tomato wedge with suspicion before she moved it to one side. "Don't you ever want someone to validate your work?"

I shook my head. "No," I lied. "I don't need a second opinion to tell me my career is over." I laughed loud enough for Pamela to glance over at the other diners.

"You've never spoken like that before."

I turned in search of our waiter; the carafe was nearly empty. "Always a first time."

"Noreen thought you were a genius."

"I sincerely doubt that." Twitty did ramble on. Where had all the waiters gone?

"It's the truth," she said, the crease between her eyebrows suggesting her patience with me was thinning. I pulled myself together and set aside the flippant mood I had assumed for no one's benefit but my own.

"I'm sorry," I said. "But I don't think I ever heard Noreen say that she thought I was a 'genius.' In fact," I added somewhat angrily, "it was rather the other way around."

Twitty took a sip of water. "She envied you."

I shook my head.

"That's why she wanted to chuck in the editing and get married."

"What?"

Twitty shrugged. "She was in love."

"With the insurance broker?"

"That's not who I mean. Whom I mean," she said, demonstrating why we had given her the nickname "Twitty." She perched her elbows on the table and lowered her voice, a piece of grated carrot stuck to her gum. "I shouldn't tell you this," she said as if she were about to leak an issue of national security, "but I don't think it matters now, what with you being married yourself and—"

I cut her off. "Tell me what?"

"Noreen wanted to marry Rafe Hemmings. In fact, she was just about to when, you know, the accident. That's why she was in Greece."

I gave up any hope of refilling the carafe and let Pamela's words sink in. "She was in love with Rafe?" I asked, trying to see Rafe as anyone's husband. "But that's impossible. It was just a—fling. She didn't love him. Nobody loves Rafe."

"He doesn't sound very nice," Pamela agreed.

"Why are you telling me this?"

Pamela squirmed. "Well, you know, you and Rafe."

"But now it's me and Miles. And Noreen is dead. Dead," I repeated. My voice must have screeched up several decibels because I felt as if the entire restaurant had gone silent either to warn me or to listen all the more closely. I watched Pamela fold her serviette like we had been taught in school. When she was finished, the look she gave me held more kindness than censure. "I'm sorry you've been left on your own," she said.

"Not as sorry as me," I said, wondering if I had any white wine left in the fridge back home.

She held the serviette as if seeking strength from a lifetime of etiquette and quality tableware. It didn't seem to be working. With a sigh that was close to a whimper she said, "So are you going to be in town for the eclipse?"

"Pardon?"

"The eclipse. It's been on the news. A full solar eclipse. It's going to be here soon."

"You're joking, right? One minute you're telling me my so-called greatest admirer was going to marry my scummy ex- and the next you're asking me about a damn solar eclipse?"

Pamela blushed but she held her ground. "You never used to be this mean," she said, a catch in her voice.

Now it was my own face flaming. "God, Pam, I'm sorry, but I feel like I'm having a conversation from a nightmare. Because you're right, I am lonely, I'm losing my mind, I think I'm seeing things…and yes, the eclipse sounds very super-duper…I did hear about it…and I'd really, really love to read your book if I could just find more time, but…"

I stopped. The flow of words sounded insane to my own ears.

"You need a break," she said, looking away. "You should come up to the Lakes sometime. I know Mummy would love to see you."

"Thanks," I said. "I'll think about it," I added in a tone implying I'd rather eat dirt. One look at Twitty's face and I thought I should. Eat dirt.

She blinked back the tears. "I have some shopping to do," she said. "Take care of yourself, Sara." She gave my hand a damp, affectionate squeeze, and while she promised to let me know the next time she was in town, I knew she would do her utmost to avoid another meeting, at least in this current lifetime.

I remained at the table surrounded by the ruins of our half-eaten lunch; I could just imagine her running back to her hotel and telling "Mummy" all about the way Sara was falling apart and drinking too much and it was no wonder her husband didn't want to come home. My final vision of Twitty's pleated skirt swinging over her boxy hips as she fled my company was enough to make me reach for my empty glass. That's when I saw she had left her manuscript.

Our waiter brought me the check. "At your leisure, miss," he murmured before floating away again. Thanks, Twitty.

My eyes focused on the unbound, dog-eared pages of Twitty's "book." The stack of typed pages was thin; hardly the great British novel she had crowed about during lunch. I pulled out my credit card, recalling that Twitty had always been prone to exaggeration. The waiter took my card, and then returned with my receipt. I added a guilt-sized tip to cover my noisy behavior. When he started to leer I stowed Twitty's meager pages under my arm and left.

Back at the house, the rest of the afternoon and night dragged slowly. I couldn't stop thinking about what Twitty had said about Noreen and Rafe: *Noreen had wanted to marry Rafe.* Well, well. And it was my fault. I had as good as thrown them together when I opted out of a party at the Japanese embassy.

Noreen's medical publishing company had hoped to print a special edition on the rituals of *seppuku* without appearing sensational. They thought if they could lure both Western and Japanese scholars on the subject, as well as some bigwigs from the art world, the book could sail to the top of the bestseller charts. As a highly-ranked post-modernist mucke-ty-muck who also spoke a smattering of Japanese, Rafe was on the guest list, but by this stage we were incommunicado.

Noreen lived too far away from the embassy to go home after her work day, so she had changed clothes at the bedsit, something she often did whenever her company needed her to entertain in the evenings. Just before she was about to leave, she fluffed her hair in the mirror hanging over my sink, then made a face. "I feel so naked," she complained. I straightened the wide-sleeved faux kimono she wore over a skirt. A stand of plum trees across her back shimmered against copper silk.

"You're covered from neck to toe. What do you want, a *burka*?"

"I meant jewelry." She held out her bare arms. Her nails had been painted in a shade that matched the plum trees.

"Close your eyes," I said. I went to my miniscule closet, took out a flowered hat box and after peeling away the tissue paper and a package of family photos, I lifted out the child-sized rabbit skin boots Inge had sent in the mail. I put them to my cheeks, willing the brindled fur to remind me of something I still couldn't place.

"Okay, eyes open," I said, taking the gold armband from the box.

Noreen's eyelids parted. Seeing what I offered her, she shook her head. "Oh, no. I couldn't."

I continued to hold the piece out to her. "Why not?"

"It's too valuable."

At the time I didn't know anything about its value, just that Inge had passed it along with a scrap of paper that explained nothing. I placed the cuff over Noreen's wrist. Excess became her. The swirls and beaten gold looked regal against her skin.

"I'll bring it back in the morning," she promised.

"No rush," I said before she left in a cloud of hairspray and Chanel. Three weeks later the cuff was returned by messenger. *"Sorry,"* the accompanying card read. *"Too much work. Dinner soon. N."*

"Too much work" lasted until we both forgot about breakfast, lunch, or dinner. I poked at Twitty's manuscript on the floor with my foot. As a writer, maybe she was just a born liar at heart, and I shouldn't believe a word of what she said. On the other hand, I knew if I had taken the manuscript I had a duty to read it. Instead I shoved myself off the couch, and in a burst of enthusiasm resumed my work on Courtenay's portrait. I gave myself two more hours before bed and decided I would paint the high collar of her wedding dress.

The collar went badly. I could not get that lustrous antique look I was striving for and the dress looked like it had been purchased in some discount after-Christmas blowout sale. I threw my brush down in vexation. I needed to eat; a glass of wine sounded better.

I went to the fridge and poured a small amount into a glass. The unfamiliar bottle of chilled white tasted of snowcaps and berries. I didn't remember buying it, but it must have once been attractive to me placed next to the feta, the purple olives with their hard stones, and a whole-wheat crust I probably would never bake. Things I had bought to re-create my impromptu meals with Miles: mushroom pâté, pastries with honey and lingonberry jam; cheeses studded with cloves and dried persimmons. I let my thoughts drift back as I stood before the open refrigerator, my hand lightly resting on the door. I rocked back and forth on my feet as I listened to the hum of the motor, a soft echo of a purr. Cold air blew against my face, and I decided against any more of the wine. I closed the door and ran up the stairs two at a time. It was almost midnight.

# 16

*The statue at the head of the fountain; square cut stone; the reflection of the trees and sky on the water. The panther laps noiselessly, his fur stirred by the breezes overhead. A dove rustles the tree branches. The luxurious coolness of the loggia wafts over my skin. The panther sniffs, nuzzles the ground, paws every blade of grass. I have returned.*

I turned my eyes from the panther and leaned back in my rattan deck chair as Anton's car pulled up beside the fountain. It was the same vehicle, a Rolls-Royce, which he had appeared in the night Laurie Granger and Daile were killed. Sunlight bathed the car in subtle shades of pearl and granite that had been hidden from me the first time I had run toward its unmistakable winged mascot.

Except for his driver, a tall silent man distinguished only by his utter lack of expression, Anton was alone in the car. Yet even from where I sat, I could somehow sense where he had been: Paris and crowds. There was an aura of artists, dancers in the Moulin Rouge, street waifs and flower sellers. The Paris of Rimbaud and Jane Avril clung to him like the undertones of an exclusive cologne. Entranced, I could have sworn I heard music.

I stood and stretched, a batik sarong tied under my arms and around my hips. The car slowed and stopped. Anton's driver marched to the back of the car. He handed Anton his walking stick, then waited for him to step out and move away before he reoccupied his place in the driver's seat.

When the car drove off, Anton beckoned with the stick for me to join him on the lawn. I did so, somewhat self-consciously, feeling the panther's stare follow me as I crossed the grass to meet Anton beside a coppice of wide-spreading oak trees and azalea. Just before I reached him, the light hit the stick's gold ferrule, sending a flash that blinded me for a second, and I had to avert my eyes.

"So you found your way back," he said once I stood by his side.

"Yes." I wanted to say more, to tell him that I didn't understand the "how," but the "why" was obvious. I needed refuge, but the words to explain myself would not come.

"And you are happy here?"

"Yes," I repeated. As an afterthought I added, perhaps wrongly, "Who wouldn't be?"

Amusement played around the corners of Anton's mouth. "You would be surprised how many have not enjoyed their stay," he said.

For some reason I felt a touch of jealousy at hearing of those "others," whoever they were. "I have never been treated so well," I offered.

In response, Anton led me down a grassy path toward what I called "the woods," a forested and shadowy place I had not yet ventured to enter on my own.

We entered a patch of sunlight filtering through the branches and I lifted my face to its warmth. Anton broke his stride and turned to observe me. His intense gaze suddenly embarrassed me, and I felt strangely undressed in my flimsy sarong and bare feet. I couldn't remember choosing the garment, but I was wearing it when I awoke in the deck chair.

I looked into Anton's eyes, deep stony pools that allowed nothing in. I would never be able to explore even the shallows of that darkness. More importantly, I wasn't sure I wanted to.

"Come," Anton said, taking my hand. "There is something I wish to show you." I started, remembering Miles had said a similar phrase the day he placed the gift box in my hand, but Anton paid no attention. Instead, we went deeper into the woods where the grass became a mossy walkway bordered by foxgloves and bluebells. Instinctively my hand went to my hair; no violets this time, real or artificial. I was—disappointed.

We continued to walk, the verdancy of the foliage a tangible presence;

one more aspect, I thought, of Anton's magical ability to draw me in layer by layer without question. The woods began to clear and we came to a set of marble steps cut into the hillside. The bottommost slabs were placed in a horseshoe pattern, indicating the start of an intricate puzzle formed of thick boxwood hedges.

"A maze," I exclaimed. What else could have fit Anton's enigmatic existence?

But he was shaking his head. "A labyrinth," he corrected. "There is a difference. A maze is designed to confuse. A labyrinth is for meditation. It has a clear beginning and a certain end."

Meditation. That word again. I ventured closer to the edge. The grass sparkled beneath my feet in a sudden burst of sunlight. From within the labyrinth an identical, mystical light sent a stream of fireworks to a lake on the other side. A lone swan glided across the surface, a steamy mist curling upward in its wake. When the light sparked yet again, I realized its source was a huge silver globe resting on a tall pillar.

"A mortgage ball," Anton said to my unspoken question.

I'd heard of the old custom of placing a mirrored ball in a prominent place to proclaim the end of a debt. Still, it seemed an odd thing to find in this of all places.

"For the estate?" I asked, waving my hand toward the labyrinth, the woods, and the house beyond.

Anton came up behind me and ran a finger down the back of my neck. His lips were at the edge of my shoulder.

"For everything," he said into my skin.

I spun around, the imprint of his near-kiss still burning into my skin. Yet his eyes showed no emotion.

"But if you are asking how long have I lived here, well, then," he said. "Let's just say it has been a very long time."

Anton lifted the hair from the nape of my neck. "The important thing is that the house and all that surrounds it is for you."

Words escaped me.

He fastened an antique jewel around my throat, blue wings of Horus surrounding a pear-shaped blue diamond. I couldn't help but stroke the outstretched wings.

"It belonged to a dancer," he said. "A young woman in Diaghilev's ballet. She was killed in the Revolution." He placed two blue diamond earrings shaped like two fallen tears into my hand. "These also were hers."

I struggled to speak, my mind uncomprehending, unbelieving. Anton pulled me closer. "Do you ask why you are here? What it is we have to give each other?"

"You know I do." I looked into his eyes, unable to tell if they were black or the darkest brown, but the story in them was so without life it chilled me to the core.

"Why are you afraid?" he asked.

I couldn't get the words out, although I knew I was afraid that if I went to Anton, I would be giving up Miles. I wasn't sure I wanted that.

"Sara?"

"My husband, he gave me jewelry too," I whispered. I felt his displeasure fall over me. "Scythian gold," I said. "Like your walking stick and that medallion the panther wears." I returned to studying the labyrinth. A stone bench like an altar sat within the center. A shank of cold went through me in spite of the heat. "Is that what connects us all?"

"That is for you to decide," he said in a voice that belied the tension I felt in his every breath. He smiled briefly. "One day you will choose," he said. He glanced toward the sky. "I am going back to the house. Follow when you are ready." He started to walk away, and then he stopped, his back to me.

"Yes?"

Without turning, he said, "You have much to ascertain, Sara. You have run to me, as it should be. But you are resisting. Nonetheless, one day, you will give in to me."

"I don't even know who you are, or what this place is. Why shouldn't I resist?"

He prodded the grass with his walking stick. "I shall see you at dinner."

I watched him leave, only to be startled out of my reverie when I heard the sound of beating wings. I looked toward the lake. The panther stood with its feet hidden in the rushes along the bank while the swan hacked across the sky. The sound of its honking call burst across the emptiness of the deserted labyrinth, and I thought the panther caught my eye as if to warn, or to threaten me. My hands went back to the jewel around my throat, and I wondered what I would wear with it to dinner.

The choice had already been made for me. On my bed was a dress of russet organza. The full skirts shimmered with all the colors of a maple forest in October, reminding me that this unexpected breath of summer would soon be over.

In the adjoining bathroom, I washed in a deep pewter bowl, sponging the water over my face, shoulders, and feet as if nothing else in the world mattered. When I was finished, I slipped into the dress, loving the way the tight flame-colored bodice set off my new tan. I was about to add Anton's gift of the diamonds when I noticed on my dresser there were more jewels: a marquise cut emerald, a pigeon's egg ruby the size of a baby's fist, a choker of shark tooth topaz. I experimented with each of the pieces. The emerald's green fire burned against the golden browns shooting through the opaline fabric of my gown. The ruby shimmered like an exquisite heartbeat. After trying them all, I chose the topaz, the barbarity of its jagged design appealing the most to me.

I tied my hair back with an onyx ribbon, and then stood in front of the mirror where I could only marvel at my Renaissance transformation and sensibilities. How had my usual wardrobe of black leggings and gray cardigans been replaced with the palette of a Medici, making me feel like a duchess on her way to attend a harvest ball?

My face glowed from the afternoon sun. I put on the topaz earrings and decided to go without shoes and makeup as I had done all day. The polished parquet of my room and the hallway leading to the grained marble staircase was delightful underfoot; I wanted the feel of it to stay with me for the rest of the night. As I sailed downstairs in my outrageous, beautiful dress as light as clouds at sunset, I thought that nothing in my life had felt

the way that cool floor did at twilight against the soles of my feet. I could
have flown over the banisters; I could have died of happiness as I rushed
to the dining room and the thought of Anton waiting for me.

I opened the tall doors and he was there as I expected. The table
looked as inviting as his extended hand, asking me to join him. All the
foods I loved: exotic fruits, small compotes, soft cheeses rolled in diced
pine nuts, were arranged in pyramids reflecting the merest halo of candlelight. Although it was well past nine, it was still daylight outside, and the
candles were more for show than anything else.

I sat in a chair to Anton's right and he poured an unlabelled *vinho verde*
into my glass. I was about to drink when he asked, "And what of your
husband?"

I replaced my glass next to my plate. "He has left me."

"How do you know?"

"I know."

A sound like a growl came from the unlit fireplace and drew my gaze
to the panther lying upon a mat before the hearth. Anton smiled and began
to eat.

I hesitated before picking up my glass again, reminding myself that I
was dressed like a queen, having dinner with a man who wanted to give me
the world. I looked back to the panther, its steady breathing calm again and
so like the sound of my house in London that I stopped to listen before I
returned to the array of delicacies Anton had selected for me. After a while
even the purring stopped and all I could hear was the clink of our knives
and forks as we continued to eat.

The rest of our meal was completed in silence, but my thoughts were
anything but quiet. Anton was as removed from me as the panther, and
while I appreciated the respite, I also longed for him to speak.

"Are you sorry?" he eventually asked.

"Sorry?"

"To have returned."

The question panicked me. "Sorry" had nothing to do with it. "Curiosity," maybe. Or "escape." Even "boredom" may have sent me here. But

mostly I knew it was sheer terror, terror that Miles had betrayed me and that I had made a fool of myself.

"I don't know why I am here," I said. "But I know that I am glad of it. And without my husband, I am free to experience it.

"We were only married forty-eight hours," I said. "My grandmother would have thought it scandalous. Perverse. But it's over now, and I am here for some strange reason."

*Oh, the shame of it*, Evan's devout and devoted late mother would have said had she known. The shame of not being wanted, and by a man who might as well be dead. Everything I had dreaded had come true, I thought, right down to no longer being able to remember his face.

The room felt very warm as Anton waited for me to continue. I rearranged my skirts and welcomed the breeze they fanned over my legs.

"You belong here," he said. "My home is yours, if you so choose." A slight smile emphasized his words.

I nodded. In the back of my mind I had always believed this to be true, and the thought troubled me. I glanced around the palatial room. To live, I thought, only for pleasure, as Anton did. I was tempted, and yet also embarrassed, a flaw in me that stemmed, I thought, from my adoption and my birth mother. Why couldn't I be more like Inge? Like Evan? Strong and decisive?

For most of my adult life I had thought painting society portraits would turn me into the kind of person who could take portfolios to galleries and drink bad wine with well-heeled clients. But it was difficult for me to do those things. It's why I had accepted Miles so easily. I was not the person I pretended to be in my dress as fine as a spider's web and as extravagant as an opium dream. Only a person as weak as me would believe she was dressed in airy silk with an enchanted panther by her side.

The evening beyond the French doors to the terrace was so exquisite I could have wept at the irony. Here I was, seemingly coveted and adored and all I could think of was mental illness and Miles having left me. Yet I would have given jewels, panther, and anything else Anton was offering, only to have him back. To return to those forty-eight hours.

It was more than the wine making me tired and drunk with my own unhappiness. I wanted to tear the topaz choker from my neck. Anton reached over and stopped my hand before I could break and lose it, talking all the while in a soothing undertone that led me away from the table and outside with him to the terrace and the river. His words calmed and reassured me, as if I were a backward child he was coaxing toward reason. By the time we were at the river, its waters slowly meandering past manicured banks, the caprice of my mood had passed as suddenly as it had come upon me.

I lifted my hem and stepped into the moonlit water. Standing there, the clear sandy bottom mirroring ribbons of white cloud above and my ankles outlined by the lucent ripples of darting fish, I didn't think about Miles. Instead, I watched Anton make smoke rings. The tamarind scent of his cigar mingled with the clean river smells: jasmine, night-blooming honeysuckle. Years ago I had stood with my father on just such a river:

*"Listen." Evan held the microphone very still, the low beam of his flashlight illuminating an area just large enough to encircle his notebook.*

*The river frogs started singing again, a series of baritone guffaws interspersed with high-pitched squeaks and twangs—a symphony of dissonant but pleasant notes melting into a harmonious hum I never wanted to stop.*

*"How many are there?" I whispered.*

*"Hundreds. There must be more than thirty species of bullfrog alone out there."*

*I crouched between the cattails and tried to imagine thirty different kinds of frog. From day one in the field, my parents had taught me to respect every living thing. But where my father encouraged me to seek beauty, Inge insisted on precaution. Her well-stocked first-aid kit took precedence even over our food. Insect repellent, calamine lotion, the frightening snakebite kit of rubber tourniquet and sharpened razor blades. I crept closer to my father. The thought of the razor was enough to keep me out of harm's way, the cure seeming so much worse than the bite. As early as five I had learned to avoid the things that could save my life.*

"I'm ready to go back now," I said. Consent, pleasure, vindication; all of these came, then went, over Anton's face. He reached for my hand.

"No rings," he said.

"No. I haven't worn them since—" How long had it been since I had hidden them in their watered silk case? I shrugged. That life was behind me, replaced with Hapsburg settings and rose petals between my sheets.

I stayed with Anton on the riverbank where we observed the moonlight playing on the water while his cigar released slow smoke trails, the tip burning orange. Out of nowhere, a small boat appeared, traveling downstream. It floated toward us and when it was close to where we stood, Anton dragged it up onto the sand. He held the boat steady for me and as I took my place, I saw the panther appear through the trees, his blue-black fur all but hiding him until I saw the heat of his eyes. He stood there until the current caught the boat and we began to drift among clusters of waxy lotus petals.

I settled against the cushions and watched the trees slide by, their purple leaves silhouetted against the moon-bright sky. Every now and then I heard the quick slap of fish feeding, their quicksilver bodies leaping to the surface and then diving back again into the water. Owls swooped breathlessly across the sky while Anton smoked the rest of his cigar.

My decision to stay was right. The house in London with my stacked canvases, new sweaters from Peter Jones, shiny pots and pans could fall to the center of the earth for all they mattered now. I was leaving my clean, plastic wife-in-exile life and would never go back. I had made my choice. If I became dead to the world where husbands lied and where people could be run over and killed without a second thought, then I no longer cared.

The boat continued to drift toward morning. The life that awaited me at sunrise had to be better than living some pinched routine as Miles's "ex."

"Where do you go?" I asked, breaking into Anton's thoughts.

"Hmm?"

"When you leave me. Where do you go?"

I sat up and Anton tossed the end of his cigar onto the floor of the boat before he crushed out the embers with his shoe.

"To the past," he said quietly, still twisting the blackened ash beneath his foot. "I visit the past."

Something in his voice told me he wasn't speaking figuratively.

"Do you find what you're looking for?"

Daylight broke over the trees and the boat came to rest beside a low dock built of piled river stones. He stood, balancing on his feet with a practiced gracefulness, and tied the boat to a railing. When he was finished, he turned to help me ashore. "I found you, didn't I?"

"What do I have to do with your past?"

"That is the story, isn't it?"

## 17

Back in my room, someone had turned down the bed and partially closed the windows; Jeanne-Marie, I thought.

I was exhausted; my dress felt too big, the jewels hurt my ears. I went to the elaborate dressing table to remove them. As I did so, I found myself examining the bottles that covered the reflective surface: names and foreign brands I had never heard of. One bottle stood out from the others in its simplicity. I picked it up and immediately liked the way it fit into my palm. The full weight of it was strangely satisfying as I removed the lid and fingered the chained stopper keeping the contents from spilling. I was about to investigate further, when I sensed Jeanne-Marie step up behind me. I glanced into the dimly lit mirror. Her face gleamed in the candlelight. She put her hands on my shoulders and kneaded them before she gestured to the bottle.

"Do you know what this is?" she asked.

I shook my head. "No." I waited for her to take away her hands but she remained possessively in place. "I don't recognize any of these labels."

She massaged the back of my neck. "They are not sold in England. Not now. They are very expensive."

The caress of her hand was making me feel both sleepy and uncomfortable, and I twisted somewhat ungraciously from her grasp. "So what *is* in the bottle?"

"Ether."

I knocked her hand and the bottle dropped to the floor. Why was ether in my room? Was that how Anton had spirited me into his car the night Laurie and Daile were killed? I thought of paint fumes and turpentine and couldn't stop myself from crinkling my nose.

Jeanne-Marie laughed as she retrieved the bottle from where it had rolled under the bed. "What did you think?" she asked, crawling out into the middle of the room. "That we were going to drug and enslave you?"

That was exactly what I thought. "Ether hasn't been used for years." I flushed, cringing at my primness. The expression on my face only made her laugh harder. She stood and uncoiled the ribbon from my hair.

"Such a child," Jeanne-Marie replied, spreading my hair across my shoulders. I stared unbelieving into the mirror. Surely my hair had not been this long when I first came to the house. How much time had gone by? But Jeanne-Marie had left for the bathroom.

"If I cannot convince you," she said when she returned with a stack of hot towels, "then you will have to decide for yourself." She handed me a steaming towel with a shrug.

Decide, decide. Everyone wanted me to make a decision. "But why would I do something as idiotic as use ether?"

"You ask so many questions." She unhooked my dress and the shimmery fabric fell from me like a spurned carapace. "The ether will help you to sleep," she said, gathering the dress from the floor and placing it over her arm. "Is there anything else you will need tonight?"

I held a damp towel to my face, releasing the scented steam. "No, thank you."

"Then I shall leave you." She tapped the bottle of ether with a single mulberry-colored fingernail. "*Bonsoir.*" She was gone before I could reply.

I used the last of the towels and then, for what seemed like hours, I held the blue bottle tight in my hand, wary of its contents, yet curious if what Jeanne-Marie had said was true.

Would I sleep? Or would I enjoy it much more than I should? I pulled the short chain from its mooring. What seemed to be the very essence of ice rose up and out of the tiny cylinder.

I let a drop fall on my hand, and then, without a second thought, I poured what remained of the bottle into my palm until it overflowed down my wrist.

For the rest of the night I strayed in and out of sleep, my arms thrashing, my legs kicking out at phantoms. Somewhere in the back of my head I heard the constant sound of rocks smashing against each other: sea glass, mah jong tiles, river pebbles rolling and spinning and tumbling through a fast moving stream of unwanted memories. I dreamed of being with Miles in an office at Teague & Bloch, the room tight as a Chinese puzzle box. It was raining and I kept saying to Miles, "I'm too weak to lie, to not tell the truth. Lying takes more imagination than I can control." Throughout the dream Miles said nothing until Courtenay Claiburne came to fetch him in her wedding dress, and I was left with indecipherable maps and geological texts that ran together into that sound of stones again, followed by the sweetest of purrs, and none of it mattered as much as my need to be left alone, and to sleep.

When the dreams finally left me, it was as if the night had never happened, and I awoke to a breakfast tray of coffee and cinnamon sprinkled brioche. As soon as I could, I dressed in yet another of the filmy sarongs that packed my closets, and decided to paint the panther.

Jeanne-Marie had told me that except for the greenhouses, the rest of the chateau and surrounding estate was mine to investigate. Today I took her at her word; I set off to find art supplies. At first the size, and solitude, of the rooms that made up the main house were intimidating, but after I had walked through the galleries and sculpture-filled halls, I came to a series of storerooms. Inside, behind sliding cupboard doors and set on oiled and well-dusted shelves, I found palettes, brushes, and finely planed boards quite suitable for painting. Placed between rolls of unbleached fabric were small caskets containing pigments marked and dated from the time of Caravaggio and even Botticelli. Cerise, umber, and powdered lapis waited, it seemed, for me alone to use. On an upper shelf, a marble and glass mortar and pestle stood beside bottles of cloudy Venetian oil I supposed were to bind the colors. I hadn't made my own paints since art school, and I looked forward to the slow and tedious work of grinding and mixing the antique pastilles. Just before I left the room, I took some sheets of gold leaf, thinking I could use them for the panther's collar and eyes, and if I had the patience, for a decorative border.

The panther was where I had seen him the night before in the dining room. Lying on one of the heirloom carpets, he seemed to blend into the cambered patterns of celestial gardens and encoded Sufic wisdom. He paid me no attention when I concocted an easel from a planter. Instead, I watched him disappear before my eyes as his paw merged into an Arabes-que and his tail became the tendril of a climbing vine. If not for the stentorian purr from his open mouth, I might have lost him altogether.

The sound carried my hand and I started to sketch with a perceptible light-headedness, a feeling I couldn't decide was a result of the purring, the ether, or from the old oils I had chosen to mix with my paints. When I began to brush the colors onto the wooden board, my euphoria became a more serious pleasure as I followed the curves of the sleeping animal's back and the line of that sinuous tail. As I painted, I was reminded of how much I needed the simple act of mark making, trailing my pencil or brush across paper or canvas, and now wood.

Three-quarters through the picture I put my brushes down. The panther was still asleep, and I had always liked to leave a section of my work unfinished. While I scrutinized the piece, Anton entered the room with a quiet cough. I dipped a brush into a Meissen jug of solvent, putting more energy into the task than was necessary.

"I shall hang this in the gallery," he said.

"It isn't dry."

"When it is dry, then."

I cleaned my brushes in silence, too shy to argue further. The panther rolled over and Anton went to a chair by the windows. He sat down, intent on watching me as I worked. "Where did you go to school?" he asked.

"Art school? Or when I was a child?" I wiped my hands on a linen handkerchief; Anton's monogram was stitched into the corner.

Anton tilted his head toward the painting. "I suppose," he said, "I am interested to know how a young woman, a modern young woman, comes to paint in such an old-world style. Or with such flair."

I turned the painting to the wall. "I certainly didn't learn it at college," I said. "In fact, I was the only person there who liked glazing, chiaroscuro, correct proportions. Hopelessly out of date." I recalled the night Rafe Hemmings had accused me of wandering too far behind the times: "Get with the program, Sara," he had laughed when I'd refused to paint a canvas black and then sign his name to it, his idea of an art lesson.

"So why did you persist?"

I shrugged. "It suits me."

He seemed to want more, and I volunteered, "I spent a lot of time as a child sitting alone, told to be quiet. My parents were sound engineers, and we traveled to some rather remote areas. I didn't have anything else to do but sit and watch. It made me aware of detail."

Anton took a hand-rolled cigarette from an enameled case. "Remote areas such as Kamchatka?"

I couldn't breathe. "Why do you ask?" From where I stood, I watched the panther turn restlessly, chasing some dream gazelle or giraffe.

"I was there once on business and it is, as you say, remote."

I had no reply to this and Anton smoothly changed the subject back to art school. "This opinion of your work being outdated. Did your teachers share this view?"

"Some of them," I replied, thinking again of Rafe.

"The ones who did like what I was doing weren't very encouraging," I said. "They were convinced I would fail, and that got me worried. I wanted money for my work," I added, half to myself. "I wanted to succeed. Who wouldn't?"

The words of our headmistress at St. Anne's the year I returned from the hospital with my new paint box and brushes still made me want to rebel: *"Art is an unstable occupation, Sara. There is no room for daydreamers and misfits at St. Anne's. If you choose to keep a hobby, please make sure it does not interfere with your academic studies."*

From that moment on I determined to make a living from art, even if it was only from "boring" portraits.

Anton might have been reading my thoughts. "But in your heart?" he asked. "What did you feel there?"

"In my heart I thought the stuff my classmates painted was not only lazy, it was offensive. Especially because," I said, warming to my subject, "I've come to love painting children in satin party frocks, and brides dressed up as Gainsborough duchesses. I think they're...stunning."

Anton motioned for me to sit beside him. I did so and he took my clenched fist in his hand. I hadn't realized how angry I'd felt until Anton slowly opened my palm. He followed the arteries of dried paint with his unlit cigarette.

"I agree," he said, moving the cigarette in a circle over my skin that made my eyes feel as heavy as the ether had. "Women and children are stunning." When he released my hand, the look in his eyes was unreadable.

Whatever it was that I had said to Anton, it had enough of an effect to make him change the seasons. In what had been the midst of summer, Anton called on winter, and inextricably, it arrived. Perhaps my answers to his enigmatic questions had disappointed him somehow and the weather expressed his emotions, but when a hush descended over the estate during my solitary lunch, I knew the muffled light and sudden quiet could only mean snow.

I watched it fall from the warmth of my rooms, the unexpected flakes reminding me of those I had cut from spangled tissue paper as a child, clumsy with the scissors but overjoyed to have Inge exclaim my work was beautiful. She decorated every available space of our hotel rooms with their fluttery sparkle in the same way the snow now covered the statues lining the estate, layer by layer, until they were dressed entirely in white.

When I had the nerve to go back downstairs, I found Anton reading Gibbon by the library fire, the door ajar and inviting. The panther had joined him and dreamed expansively, the deep rumble of its sleeping breath punctuated by sighs of voluptuous contentment. A log cracked and sparked as I entered the room on high-heeled carmine slippers.

Anton turned a page, and I asked, "How did this happen?"

He looked up from his book. "Do you dislike the cold?"

I stifled the urge to laugh. "No, but you have to admit it's strange. What do you use? Some hidden snow machine? Or do you really have power over the elements?"

"Neither." Anton closed his book with a snap. "Would you like some drawing materials?"

I took a chair. "Are you trying to keep me occupied or amused?"

"Both." Anton went to a high cabinet near the fire and pulled open a drawer filled with bound sketchbooks. He searched through them and then brought me a marbled volume along with several archaic bottles of ink and a variety of aged pens. I watched him arrange everything on a portable table he set ceremoniously before me.

"There," he said. I didn't move and he returned to his own chair and book.

"*Rise and Fall*," I noted, the title stamped along the spine.

"Have you read it?"

"Too many footnotes."

"There are always footnotes to history," he said, eyes still fixed on the book. "It is the job of the historian, or the artist," he added, "to amass and interpret them in order to tell as many sides of a story as possible."

"Is that why you want me to draw?"

"I want to keep your work."

I looked at the art materials. Despite having spent the morning painting, I knew I couldn't resist their seduction for long. Anton allowed himself an imperceptible smile, and resumed reading. I began to sketch the scene before me on thin sheets of what felt like vellum, the sepia ink spreading from a nib with just the right amount of "catch." The sound of the nib scratching across the pages pervaded me with a rhythm I turned into crosshatched fur and flame. The intensified languor of my work as I sketched out the panther's ears and tail for a second time that day, followed by a study of Anton's neat hands holding his book, nearly sent me to a place as fervid as that provided by the ether.

I stayed under the spell of the moment and the warmth of the fire while Anton turned pages, the panther sighed, and I continued to draw as if dreaming. I only stopped when Anton rang a glass bell by his side and the panther opened its eyes to watch me. The snow, I saw, had reached the height of the windowsills.

Jeanne-Marie answered Anton's summons. "Cognac," he said to her. "And the furs."

Jeanne-Marie ducked her head, throwing a sly look in my direction at the same time. Minutes later she returned with a tray and two cut crystal glasses arranged around a decanter and a plate of wine biscuits. She left the room again and when she came back her arms were piled high with the furs, a pair of black gloves balanced on top.

"Are we going out?" I asked Anton, gesturing to the apparel Jeanne-Marie had placed on an ottoman.

Anton walked over and took my sketchbook from the table. "Jeanne-Marie, I believe, has packed for you." He turned to her, his eyebrow lifted, and she nodded.

"*Oui.*"

Anton riffled through my pages of drawings. "Drink up," he said. "It will be a long drive."

I poured myself a glass of the cognac and nibbled at a biscuit as Jeanne-Marie tidied and closed up the library. When she had finished she said, "Hurry, now. There is not much time left to dress." She indicated that I was to go with her upstairs.

In my room she handed me a dress of black cashmere. "Where are we going?" I asked.

"I am not going anywhere." She helped me into the dress and I counted as she buttoned the front and neck to my throat with thirty-eight amethysts encircled with six times as many freshwater pearls.

Jeanne-Marie tightened her lips. The long sleeves of my dress had the same amethyst buttons as the neck. Criss-crossing from wrist to elbow, she worked the gemstones nimbly into buttonholes, a frown of concentration creasing her forehead. I thought of Courtenay Claiburne's wedding gown.

"I do not leave the grounds," she said part-way through her task.

"What is beyond these gates is not my concern."

She turned me around so she could button the other sleeve. I waited until she finished, when I then exchanged the slippers for a pair of gray suede boots. I straightened my skirt in the mirror and she passed me a blue bottle similar to the one I had emptied the night before. I closed my fingers around the glass without saying a word. Jeanne-Marie avoided my eyes, her attention focused instead on hanging my robe inside the armoire. I tucked the bottle of ether into a pocket and returned downstairs.

Wearing his usual suit, but now with the addition of a burgundy overcoat, Anton lounged beside the panther, waiting for me. I entered the hallway and he acknowledged my presence with an appreciative nod, then passed a tooled leather collar over the panther's head, the gold medallion hanging from it shining in the last of the daylight. He then helped me into the furs.

Bundled in layers of sable, I wondered at the ethics of wearing them, but Anton only offered me his arm, and together with the panther we walked down the front steps into the cold. At the sight of the snow's glittering expanse I broke away and had to dip my hands into the mounds of fallen powder. *It's real*, I thought, tasting the ice crystals on my tongue. I was about to throw a snowball when Anton's driver, Grégoire, appeared with the car, ready to take us wherever Anton desired us to go.

I blew the snow from my hands before I entered the car, sliding onto the backseat and wrapping the cloak around my knees. Anton sat beside me while Grégoire resumed his place in the driver's seat and turned the car toward the road leading away from the estate and the last of the daylight. The panther settled across our feet and I marveled at how natural his presence had become to me. But then, I thought, that was the way of dreams.

As we drove forward, Anton took my gloved hand and brushed away the moisture leftover from the snow. I entered a realm of forgetfulness as I listened to the car tires crunching the frosted road.

I dozed spasmodically. Each time I opened my eyes I saw a muted dawn appear for a brief minute before retreating again behind the wintry sky, all sense of time extinguished. It seemed we were traveling for days on end, until at last we passed through a pair of open gates set beneath a scrollwork legend or motto of some kind.

Anton stirred, arousing the panther. "Do you read Latin?" he asked.

"Not a word. What does it say?" I sat up and tugged at the cloak that had fallen between us.

"Believe."

The gates were embellished with a cast iron motif that when closed would give the appearance of a crescent moon fitting into the side of a full-rayed sun. "Believe in what?"

"Nothing," Anton replied. "Believe in nothing."

# 18

*"Believe in nothing."* The words cracked the air like falling icicles. I searched Anton's eyes for an explanation, but he had turned away from me to somewhere of his own, his gaze directed out the window to the snow. Like everything else so far, his words left me with nothing but another misshapen puzzle piece in a disordered universe.

We drove away from the sun and moon gates down a wide tree-lined drive, the bare tree limbs holding cakes of compacted snow. Dawn had turned to midnight, and a row of burning torches guided us to an outdoor stairway. Scattered across the snowy lawns, other vehicles the equal and more of the Rolls sat with what seemed a vast number of elaborate sleighs. We left the car when it was parked beside them, and then made our way up the stairs to a grand, open entrance, the panther right behind us. The strains of a full orchestra competing with a chorus of raucous laughter met us from inside the cavernous galleries,

"What is this place?" I murmured, but Anton only held more tightly to my arm.

Liveried footmen appeared from the sidelines and as soon as we went through the doors they removed our outer clothing. I handed them my gloves and immediately I was shown to a hallway of dressing rooms commandeered for the evening.

Here, a maid informed me, ushering me to the ornate mirrors and ruched vanities, I was to leave my boots and dress. In their place I was given a mask of iridescent feathers and a Tuscan red shift folded into a

thousand Fortuny pleats, a Delphos. The dress was straight out of a
Sotheby's catalog, worth more money than I wanted to think about. And
tonight it was mine.

But first I had to cope with the gazillion buttons closing the dress I
wore. Without Jeanne-Marie, I would have to start in on the job of
undressing myself unaided. I tried to unbutton my left sleeve while I heard
what sounded like women's voices coming from the adjoining alcoves and
privacy screens. I did my best to listen, hoping I could somehow learn
more about what this place or event was supposed to be. The voices ran
together in a meaningless buzz, gossipy and smug, annoyed and impatient
in turns until I heard one that made my fingers tighten around one of the
tiny amethysts: *Courtenay Claiburne.*

"It was Sara, Mother. I swear it was her."

"Who would have invited her?"

"But—"

"Courtenay, please." *Monique and Courtenay.*

My face the color of the Fortuny gown, I struggled all the harder with
the interminable rows of finicky buttons I longed to rip off.

Could they really be here? Embarrassment hastened my progress with
the buttons, and in minutes I had the black dress off and the new gown
tied provocatively in place.

The mask would help disguise me, I thought; at least enough to hide
me from the Claiburnes in the unfortunate event that we should run into
each other. I wriggled my toes; instead of my boots I now had inadequate
silver sandals. When I emerged from the dressing room, bare shouldered
and anxious to avoid the Claiburnes, I was as glad of the mask as I was of
the huge roaring fireplaces filling the reception rooms with a near summer
and much-needed heat.

Anton was waiting for me outside the main salon where I could see
spinning, dancing couples, many of the women also dressed in feathery
masks and diaphanous sheets of baroque fabrics like my own. I scanned
the room for any sign of Monique or Courtenay, but the masks made
recognition impossible.

"Expecting someone?" Anton asked.

"The Prince of Darkness?"

"We'll have to see what we can do." Anton, now in a black tailcoat, pulled a startling mask of white owl feathers over his face and led me into the ballroom where the panther was the center of attraction.

"Should he be with so many people?" I whispered.

Smack in the midst of what had to be more than a hundred masked dancers, the beast seemed to bristle with a power that was new to me. We entered the room to join his coterie, each member decked out in a full spectrum of colors culled from forests and jungles, deserts and seascapes. We had become a rare menagerie, a veritable feast for the panther's most dangerous fantasies.

As if to prove me right, the panther shot an obliging paw toward a woman disguised as a toucan. Undaunted, she sliced her wing past his nose. The crowd laughed and cheered while the panther rolled and pawed the ground, a large and playful kitten, making the women bray out in false alarm as they dodged his claws, claws that could shear the delicate hairs right from their arms.

I leaned in to Anton. "You should make them stop," I said, but he only shook his head and I held my breath as I waited for the first blood to flow.

It came in the next second. The panther struck out at a "pheasant" that pushed too close, a whirling dervish of a woman who grabbed at his tail, that heavy, sensitive tail that suddenly whipped out like a lethal black rope. The initial screams of mock terror quickly turned to frightened sobbing as her bright dress seeped red. No one moved and her screams convulsed to silent, horrified gasps, the last stages of shock.

It seemed as if the room itself stopped breathing before the woman's cries ended and faded away. Then, manically, the orchestra began to play again, while the woman lay on the floor alone and with no one to help her.

All during this terrible scene or play, Anton had stood by my side, rigid and remote, but now he strode toward the panther, his hand raised as if for silence. The orchestra stopped in the middle of a bar, and the crowd parted to let Anton pass. The panther locked eyes with Anton and stepped back a pace as if to lunge, but he was no match for his master. Instead of falling prey, Anton grabbed the creature by the collar and subdued him with a single touch as if he were no more than the overgrown kitten he had first appeared to be. The cat rolled onto its back, stretching the length of its spine, then rolled back again to lick Anton's hand with a quick and affectionate nuzzling. The onlookers turned away, bored, and Anton led the beast back to me.

"You must look after him now," Anton said, a smile in his voice.

The panther pushed into my legs, head against my thigh. I could not believe any of what I had just witnessed: a deviant pantomime to amuse— who? Not me. Was this the sort of entertainment my wealthy clients indulged in after hours and behind closed doors? Then I remembered: *"Believe nothing."*

The panther continued to push me forward until I was in Anton's arms. He smiled down at me then signaled the orchestra to resume playing before he led me across the floor into a waltz.

We danced, slowly at first, my feet artless and unsure. But as the music became louder and faster, the steps came to me as if I had known them from birth. When had I last danced like this? In truth, I couldn't remember ever having danced at all. I looked out across the floor to the others gyrating past us, their thoughts closed to me behind their feathers and masks as the tempo increased. Perhaps the faster they danced, I thought, the easier it was to forget what it was they were running from.

"What of the woman?" I asked, my feet flying across the floor. I searched the room for her bloodstained dress in the same way I had continued to search for Courtenay and Monique. "Was any of that real? Is she alive?"

We were close to the doors. Beneath the moon the snow had turned to a sea of incandescent ice. From the height of the ballroom the haphazardly parked cars and sleighs seemed no more than toys. A sensation of worry crept under my skin.

"Don't you care about anyone?" I whispered into Anton's collar. I lifted my head, but his eyes remained distant.

"I care about you," he said as he spun me around the floor, past the orchestra and back to where the panther reclined. Black fur reflected the flames of the fireplace.

Anton held me hard against his chest. Unexpectedly, I found myself enjoying the comfort and possessiveness of his embrace. "Whether this is a dream or madness," he said, "none of it matters. Tonight you are at a masked ball, a world of unspoken desires and emotions. All of this is for you, Sara. All of it. Is it not what you have always wanted? Always craved?"

His words captivated me, and I forgot the injured woman just as I forgot Monique and Courtenay and the improbability of my surroundings. For Anton and this one moment I would forget anything that he asked me to: the sun, the moon, even Miles.

"It is the life you were born to," Anton said. "The life that was stolen from you."

Alarmed, I pulled back. How much did he know about me? Did he know that my birth mother lay in some unmarked grave in a Russian forest? I looked into his eyes and saw only my own reflection.

"Stolen? How?" I asked, too many questions racing through my mind, each as erratic and disconnected as the partygoers swirling around us.

He shook his head and led me from the dance floor to an empty hallway far from the scores of laughing, twirling dancers. I thought it was to find a modicum of privacy in which to answer me. But there, in the murkiness of the dwindling candlelight, he only pressed a kiss to my hand before we headed upstairs, leaving the rest of my questions along with the rest of party.

The upper floors, swathed in secrecy, seemed to extend endlessly as Anton led me with his voice to the rooms that were to be mine for the night. As we walked the halls, he spoke as never before, telling me he had given his time over to the near-sacred search for art and books.

"We each have an infatuation," he said, his arm around my waist. "And mine is to explore that which is hidden." Astrology, kabbalah, gemetria, he had delved into each one. I was reminded of Benita Hansard and her proclaimed studies in alchemy. There seemed to be a connection of some sort trying to make itself known, but Anton took no notice of my wandering attention. He continued to speak, saying there was much more to his fixation than dusting off archaic philosophies and languages, however. There was the beauty of the material world as well, the thrill in discovering secret stores of jewels and fabrics, treasures long forgotten by time and history. And he wanted to share them—with me.

"Your position in my household, Sara, will be unequaled. Clothes, antiquities; travel to any destination you choose."

I listened as I used to listen to Inge putting me to bed with another story, my mind awake as the images took shape and substance upon the canvas of my inner vision.

I was still focused on those long-ago tales when we entered what was to be my suite of rooms. Anton removed from his coat a blue bottle and a handkerchief. Carefully, he measured out a dose of ether he then handed to me like a gift.

"Here," he said. "Not too much."

Heedlessly, greedily, I accepted the gift and fell onto the curtained bed, imagining as I did so that I could hear the rush of metal wings beating the air. The wings seemed attached to fierce devic faces that crowded out my other thoughts until I could think of nothing else, and Anton's voice fought to rise above the melee.

Whether he truly stayed with me, or for how long a time, I will never know, but the words I thought I heard him speak, so hypnotic and terrible, filled me with an unspeakable longing that I never wanted to end.

The surge of pleasure heightened my sense of wrongdoing, yet I could not stop listening. I thought that what Miles had once told me was true; that all language was derived from a universal source of light and dark, and the words we spoke were the ones that shaped us. As I floated with the ether, I knew I was choosing the dark, but it was the place that was the most like me.

I began to tremble as I felt that darkness take over, and I traveled farther and farther away from what sounded like Anton's voice trying to grab me back. I turned to my side; beneath the bedclothes my toes touched fur. A tail twitched; flanks rippled with restless sleep. I knew I should shriek out, call for help; yet it was all I could do not to spread my fingers and run them down the panther's ribcage, inviting him to tear out at me like he had attacked the woman on the dance floor. *Enchantment.*

*A long frozen beach. Gulls wheeled overhead; their cries lost in the crash of the surf. Amber pellets shone out among the gray and black pebbles scattered as far as the eye could see along the deserted coast. The waves were his sole compass in their regular push and pull, back and forth, foaming white, breaking into clear crystal as they rushed forward to spread at his feet, clean and invigorating. He scooped up a handful of the freezing water and let it slide down his fingers. He remembered having a fever; tossing and turning. He was hungry. The wind blew through his shaggy hair and beard. It had been days since he had last washed or seen his face.*

*He carried on following the beach in what he thought was a northerly direction. The ribs from an ancient hull protruded from the sand. Except for it and the birds, there was nothing in his line of vision but for the rocks and the sea when suddenly, there seemed to be someone up ahead, desperately waving his arms. Miles used his hand to shield his eyes from the glare. He stopped in his tracks. The other man approached and Miles could make out gray hair and beard, a skullcap, a chaplet of wooden rosary beads swinging from his belt. His garments were edged in shiny thick fur, sable, no doubt. The man waved again.*

*His first thought was that the man was a priest. How ironic. Here on a beach far from anywhere he'd rather be he would meet a priest.*

*"Father."*

*His assumption was correct. The priest walked up to him and Miles realized the man was pulling a work sled packed with burlap sacks, dried fish, and seal pelts.*

*"Heavenly Father," the priest said, crossing himself. "How do you come to be here? Have you been shipwrecked? Where is the rest of your party?"*

*The dried fish were more dazzling than amber. It was all he could do not to seize the sled and devour the scaly wafers of herring there and then.*

*"There are no others," he said, shoving down his hunger. "There was no wreck."*

*The priest regarded him with curiosity, and Miles found his own eyes straying back to the strings of dried fish. He felt the saliva rise on his tongue. The priest followed his line of sight and smiled again. "You must join me for breakfast," he said. "Come. After we have eaten you can tell me your story."*

*Automatically, Miles reached out to take the sled, but the priest waved him away.*

*"Save your strength," he said. "The work is mine." He moved forward and continued up the beach until they came to an incline in the rock. The path was worn smooth and slippery from the sea, leaving only the most treacherous of footholds.*

*"If you will be so kind," the priest said, "you could help me hoist this load up the hill a bit."*

*Miles took the back of the pallet. It was heavier than it looked. Together he and the old man struggled to heave its bounty up and over the rocks, the wind threatening their every step. When they reached the top, Miles was sweating inside his parka. His hands were shaking and he felt the blood drain dizzily from his head and ears. The weakness reminded him he had just risen from his sickbed.*

*"You are ill," the priest stated bluntly. He indicated that Miles should rest before they went forward. Wearily, Miles lay back on the sharp tussocks of sea grass. He could feel the priest's eyes on him.*

*"Very ill," the old man repeated needlessly.*

*Miles agreed; the effort to live was too much. The sun felt good on his cheeks, the smell of the sea was like coming home. It was a decent way to die. If he wanted, the old priest could pray for his soul, that is, if he had one left. But the priest wasn't about to perform any last rites, let alone permit him to die without a fight. Instead, he poured what tasted like brandy into Miles's mouth, sending him bolt upright; the heat of the liquor burning his lips.*

*"What the hell?" He spluttered and choked, catching his breath.*

*The priest wiped his mouth with the sleeve of his cassock. "Good," he said. "You will live. Praise God."*

Anton and the panther were gone. My head throbbed and the sun spewed into what had once been an opulent, but now very shabby, room. Outside, the winged devas of the night before had been replaced with demented peacocks, and I wondered if the seasons had yet again changed while I had slept. *Dreaming of Miles. Dying.*

I rubbed my hands over my face and leaned across the foot of the bed. The red pleated dress lay heaped on the floor, so crushed and stained I decided to leave it where it was. An extra sheet had been flung over a chair, and I wrapped myself in it while I surveyed the scene outside my window. As I had thought, the snow was gone, replaced once again by summer. I had no idea what I should do next; neither Anton nor the panther were anywhere to be seen. The peacocks screeched and I decided to go downstairs. *Miles. On a beach, lost.*

The lower half of the house was worse. The grand chevroned and gilded salons were littered with trash: confetti, uncorked champagne bottles, parrot feathers, even a banana peel. I opened a pair of sashed windows, letting in the early morning breezes still fraught with yesterday's cold. *Where was he?*

The wind stirred the draperies, releasing a musty smell. I turned back to the ruined ballroom and saw that the elaborate tapestries now appeared tired and threadbare by daylight. Last night they had been antique. Today they were simply old. I sat on a worn armchair and let my fingers rove across the tarnished floral brocade. It was restful to be alone; I needed to think.

Anton had answered none of my questions regarding this place, or why he had brought me here. Perhaps there were no answers. Perhaps I had chosen, as they say, the wrong path, and now, as protected and desired as Anton claimed me to be, I was still on the brink of insanity, without a cure in sight.

I looked at the mess around me, idly shredding a streamer draped through the branches of a glass chandelier. The frayed end hung over my shoulder like Ariadne's thread, eager to guide me out of the labyrinth. But to where? Where was I meant to go? Back to London, painting pictures nobody wanted? Back to waiting for Miles?

Miles. The dream of him by the sea still made me cold. It was the second time I'd dreamed of him on that beach. His clothes were the same ones he had on when I saw him with Courtenay.

Courtenay. I had no proof she and Monique were a part of this group, just as I had no proof I had seen Courtenay with Miles. I had no proof of anything, not even of this empty room I thought I sat in.

I left my chair to go out the open doors. As I walked barefoot on the grass, the feel of the lawn still spongy from its layer of melted snow, I wished for something cold and bracing to clear my head. Icy lemon vodka; ether. The feeling of being trapped clamped down on me.

*Miles. On a beach. Dying.*

# 19

All I remember of the journey back was the sound of Anton writing on a Napoleonic lap desk while the panther slept across our feet. The fields bordering the deserted road were rutted with melting snow, revealing grass and wildflowers the closer we approached the estate. Not once did Anton attempt to speak to me; it was as if the night before had never happened.

As soon as we arrived, Anton took the panther and retreated to his library, closing the door behind him. I let Jeanne-Marie run a bath for me. Later, while I sat in the cooling water, I heard the Rolls taking him away again. When I asked Jeanne-Marie where he had gone, and for how long, she could only say, "Monsieur travels for business. He is a collector and must go, I suppose, to where there are things to collect." She shrugged in that maddening way of hers.

"But what am I supposed to do while he's gone?" I asked Jeanne-Marie as she fussed with my laundry. The thought of the empty days ahead filled me with despair, and my thoughts turned back to my life and house in London.

"Walk, play with the panther. You have found the instruments for painting. Surely that is very nice for you."

"Why can't I go to the greenhouses?"

"Because you may not."

"What's in there?"

She frowned. "Garden tools. Rare plants and special soils. As I have told you, Monsieur is a collector. Plants are another of his collections."

"How long have you worked here?"

"Long enough," she said tersely, "to know the rules."

"Rules?" From where I lay in the bath, I watched her movements. There was nothing malicious or hostile about the woman. If anything, she had only shown me kindness, more like an older cousin or sister than a servant. In some regards she reminded me of the senior girls at St. Anne's, the ones always offering to help us write our school reports or show us how to climb onto the roof without being seen.

I drained the water from the tub. When I returned to the bedroom I went straight to the dressing table. Jeanne-Marie disregarded my wet hair dripping onto the full array of bottles and cosmetics. Furtively, I scanned the display for anything resembling a bottle of ether.

Giving me a towel, she said, "The other girl wanted to go to the greenhouses, too."

"The one before me?" I tried to keep my voice light. Damn, where was she keeping it?

She waved a wide-toothed comb through the air. "The other girl," she said dreamily, as if to embark on a long and satisfying tale. "She did not have hair like yours. Her hair was red, and it went like so." She flipped her hand away from her head. "It was very difficult to manage."

Before I could stop her she pulled the comb through my hair which she then expertly plaited into a braid that hung down my back. I turned my head in the mirror. I could never have managed such a thing on my own.

"So what happened to her, this 'other girl'?" I exchanged my towel for one of the batik sarongs.

Jeanne-Marie scooped up my laundry, draping it over her arm. "She left when the painter came to finish her portrait."

"What painter? Do you mean a portrait artist? Like me?"

"No, chèrie. Nothing like you. He was a spleenish man. Monsieur did not care for him. He and the girl left as soon as they could."

I thought about what she said, pushing away the idea that the "other girl" was Noreen; and the painter, Rafe. Thousands of girls had red hair and most of the artists I knew were unlikable. I sorted through the perfumes and nearly cried out when I saw a blue-tinted bottle.

"Is there anything else you will need?" Jeanne-Marie asked.

My hand trembled as I lifted the cap to what smelled like oil of cloves. "Need? No, I don't think so."

"You might like to visit the library. Monsieur has many old and smelly books you can read," she said as if books were the worst things she could think of. She took the bottle of clove oil from me. "This is for toothache," she said, replacing the cap. "If you want a perfume, I would suggest this one." She opened a bottle that released a citrus scent. "The South Seas, no?" she asked, referring to my sarong.

I dabbed the cologne behind my ears and neck. When I lifted my head, she was gone and I was free. The ether, I saw, was right by my hand.

The library was locked. I thought of the things Jeanne-Marie suggested I do to fill my time. I was too tired to paint, which only left walking.

The way to the greenhouses followed a gravel path accented by marble statuary: nymphs and ravaged goddesses that I had last seen covered in snow. Now their sculpted torsos and vapid faces were as dry as the ground I walked upon. By the time I reached the oversized glass buildings, their flying buttresses rising from the ground like prehistoric skeletons, the sun was lowering, casting a haze over the glass. I stopped to listen; there was a dreamy, unreal quality to the silence that unnerved me.

For all of Jeanne-Marie's insistence that I stay away from the greenhouses, the buildings, now that I had found them, were like so much else on the estate: unguarded and without any kind of human activity. From where I stood studying them, hidden by the towering trees, I was reminded of my days in the convalescent hospital. Most of the patients had been too ill or apathetic to go outside, and I had been free, like now, to wander the grounds alone. I recalled the special brand of lethargy those walks had instilled in me afterwards, and my hand went to the bottle of ether tied into my sarong. Anton's secrets, such as they were, could never be as heavy, or as dull, as my own.

Seen from close up, the enormity of the greenhouses was even greater than I had imagined, but when I peered into the first set of steamy windows and saw the usual collections of ferns and orchids, rows of plants identical to those in Monique Claiburne's urban conservatory, there was nothing unusual or particularly inviting about the set-up. At the farthest end, giant palms supporting a variety of hanging succulents reached the full three-storied height of the structure. A white iron elevated walkway ran the length and breadth of the upper floor, allowing access to the topmost fronds. The rare and alien species Anton cultivated were certainly not grown here.

Two smaller wings flanked the back of the building behind the palms, ending in two vine-covered pergolas. The first annex had opaque windows of frosted glass that cut off any view or obvious entry. I decided to walk to the end of the second building. There I noticed the windows were well above eye level, but oddly, the main doors had been left open. I worried that someone might be working inside, but when I entered, there was no one, and instead of the neatly labeled rows of seedlings and fragile plants I expected to see, there was only a field of grass laid bare to the sky. In the center stood a marble plinth or altar such as the one Anton kept in the labyrinth.

I kept moving forward until I came close enough to run my hands over the vines and beasts carved into the marble, the designs nearly identical to my armbands and the head of Anton's walking stick. Right away I noticed the top slab was crooked, as if it had been pushed aside and then left. I doubted my own strength to make the gap any wider, yet when I shoved the marble, it moved quite easily, so easily that I was able to understand why Anton had made up the story about seeds and endangered flora. The red mane could only have belonged to one other person, "the other girl." The copper and plum kimono I would know anywhere.

I stared at the mass of hair upon the crumpled silk. A shadow fell across me, and I looked up, petrified of being seen. It was the lone swan from the lake, the shade from its wings as menacing as if Anton had suddenly found me here. I watched it sail onward, my hands chafing to reach inside the marble cavity and touch the items, to even pull a handful of locks free from that generous bundle. Yet I knew I could take none of it.

So these were the gardener's secrets. Along the back wall, summer fruit grew heavy on a trellised vine, a gem-like collection of grapes and gooseberries glazed by the setting sun. Had Noreen come here to taste those fruits? Did she take long solitary walks as I now did, her hair blown free by the wind and her lips and tongue dyed with the sweet, syrupy juices? What had brought her to this place? And why had she never told me? All of a sudden the fruits seemed deadly, and I could not bear the sight of them.

The sun had nearly set when I pushed the marble slab back into an approximation of its original angled position. One last look and my nerves gave in. What had I found? My heart pounding, my vision skewed, I hurriedly retraced my path out of the arena-like building, past the other two greenhouses and then, without further warning, I began to run.

I ran the entire way back to the western-facing terraces, winded and panting from the exertion as I stumbled up the flagstones to where Jeanne-Marie sat waiting for me. I spotted a jug on a table surrounded by clay cups. Whatever the jug held I wanted and I poured a full cup which I swallowed down in gulps. Gin and tonic. I wanted to drown in it.

"*Mon Dieu!*" Jeanne-Marie exclaimed when I set the cup down and slumped into a chaise lounge. The scratchy sailcloth cushions felt good and weathered, wholesome after my discovery. Jeanne-Marie stood and poured me another drink.

"Tell me about the other girl."

"What do you want to know?"

"Everything. Why she came here, how she knew Anton. Why she really cut her hair."

Jeanne-Marie said nothing, turning her attention instead to watering the urns trailing masses of ivy and rosebuds down their sides. She had rolled the long sleeves to her uniform to the elbow; I had never seen how strong and brown her arms were.

"It was Noreen, wasn't it?" I asked as she refilled the watering can from a spigot set in the wall. "Noreen Riley. My friend."

She set the can down. "What if it was?" That shrug again.

"I just saw her hair. Her hair," I repeated. I pointed with my cup to the nearly invisible roofs of the greenhouses.

Jeanne-Marie studied me for a second before she spoke. "It is true," she said. "She did not like the effort of caring for it any longer. The brush, it would not go smooth."

"Did you force her?"

Jeanne-Marie broke into a high laughter that caused a flock of birds to shake themselves out of the trees.

"Force her? You are so—" She could not get the words out. "Your face!" She doubled over then straightened herself out of her laughter. The look she gave me was disdainful. "We cut her hair. That is all. It was not my choice. She wanted the hair gone."

She made her hands into scissors and chopped at the air. "She was still very beautiful," she added.

Yes, I thought; Noreen would have been beautiful in a duffel bag.

"Why did you keep it?"

"Monsieur, he is a collector, no?"

"He told me he collected art, not women's hair."

Jeanne-Marie finished watering the plants. "I will be in the kitchen if you need to find me," she said. Before she left, though, she squared her shoulders and looked me fully in the face.

"You should not have disobeyed," she said. "Monsieur will not be pleased when he finds you have gone behind his back."

"He shouldn't leave me alone like this."

"You are not alone."

"I feel alone."

Jeanne-Marie shook her head at the same time I caught a glimpse of white in the sky. The swan was returning to the lake. I wondered how long it, too, could survive away from others of its kind.

Back in my room, I untied the ether from where I had carried it in my sarong as a sort of talisman; against what, I wasn't sure, but I needed to know it was near.

I cradled the bottle in my lap and remembered with sadness the night

Noreen had come to the studio wearing her new, short hairstyle.

It was the week before Christmas when the whole of London left off work in favor of celebrating the season with endless office parties and boozy lunches. Noreen's firm was no exception and I hadn't heard from her in days. I myself was rushing to make three deadlines, all portraits commissioned as holiday gifts. The four-year-old twins had been a breeze, but the other two, prize dachshunds named "Pixie" and "Pooh" weren't really what I wanted to add to my *curricula vitae*.

I was in the studio debating whether to add a sprig of holly to Pixie's left ear when Noreen blew in unannounced from the cold. I couldn't help but see that her hair had been shorn to the nape as she tried to pull a couple of strands into the illusion of a longer style.

"It's horrible, isn't it?"

"Not in the least." I put down my brush and walked a full circle around her, examining the cut from all sides. "My mother used to keep my hair short when I was little. Easier to look after, I guess." Actually, Noreen's cut wasn't too bad, rather stylish and modern, in fact. "When did you get it done?"

"Maybe it will grow," she said without conviction. She started to remove her coat and then changed her mind and slipped back into it again. The bar heater was totally useless. I pushed back the sleeves to the three jumpers I wore against the cold and went back to my painting. Noreen looked over my shoulder. "I didn't know you painted dogs." She watched me with unusually close attention. "I broke up with Rafe."

That made me pause. "So you cut your hair?" I never could get the hang of so-called feminine logic.

"So I told him he was a has-been."

"Bet he loved that."

Noreen shivered despite her heavy coat. "I don't know why I went out with him in the first place."

"He is a wacko," I agreed. I kept my eyes on Pixie's ears. The Noreen and Rafe thing was a topic I wanted to avoid.

"Psychotic, you mean."

I added an unnecessary highlight to Pixie's right eye. Rafe's definition of "psychotic" would be painting dog portraits days before Christmas.

"I think you should move out of the studio," Noreen said.

"And go where?" I turned and couldn't stop myself from staring at Noreen's new cut. Short hair had given her a rawness, a vulnerability I had encountered in some of the patients in the hospital when they took their first wobbly steps out of bed. Without the protection of her hair, Noreen had that same itchy discomfiture, a gawkiness the Noreen who bustled through town in picture hats and thrifted Zandra Rhodes would never have shown.

"What's happened?" I asked, not at all certain I wanted to know, but after my initial anger over learning of Noreen's involvement with Rafe, I had decided I wanted to keep my friend rather than quarrel over an ex-lover.

Noreen didn't answer my questions. Instead, she reached into her briefcase and handed me a plain manila envelope. "Merry Christmas."

I didn't have her gift ready. It was still unwrapped back at the bedsit, waiting for our usual splash-out Christmas Eve dinner. I took the envelope. "I don't have yours with me," I said. "I was going to give it to you when we met for dinner."

"Oh, God, Sara, I'm so sorry." Her hand went to the back of her neck. "I forgot to tell you. I can't make it. I hope you don't mind."

In the background I could hear the laughter of the other studio artists opening yet another cheap bottle of Beaujolais. The co-op was no more immune to the Christmas spirit than the rest of the city.

I should have been disappointed at Noreen's news, but in truth lack of money and time had depleted me over the past weeks, and I felt like spending the holiday in bed with a book. But it wasn't like Noreen to break tradition, or a date. I wanted to ask more without seeming to pry, but she was already heading for the door.

"I have to go," she said. "Sorry about the rush."

"See you in the New Year?"

"New Year."

We hugged, and then she whispered, "You'll think about moving, won't you?"

"Noreen, if there's anything you feel I ought to know…"

She covered her hair with a beige beret. "You just need some place classier by now. Time to move up."

I didn't think for an instant Noreen cared if I painted on the street or in the basement of Marks & Sparks, but when I promised her I'd consider finding another studio, she left with what appeared to be a smile.

I closed my door and picked up the package she'd left for me, telling myself I wouldn't peek until Christmas, a promise that lasted all of two seconds. I gave it a shake; something heavy rattled around the inside and fell out when the unglued flap gave way. The key to Rafe's house in Greece. In another life it had been mine, right down to the lizard key ring I'd bought at the airport in Australia when I last visited my parents. I tossed it to the table in disgust, uncertain who annoyed me the most: Noreen or Rafe.

A piece of origami paper stuck out from the envelope. Folded into quarters, it appeared to be a note, one that I later thought Noreen could not possibly have read or even seen, but one that now, as I considered my discovery in Anton's forbidden greenhouse, made a lot more sense:

> *Noreen, in exchange for your glorious gift.*
> *I am waiting for you.*
> *R.H.*

## 20

I sprawled across my bed and watched the night descend over the treetops. Sleep was futile, and as much as the ether attracted me, it also frightened me. But after several minutes of restless indecision, I poured the contents from the bottle I had saved onto a piece of Irish linen from the wardrobe and inhaled deeply. I hoped the fluid sense of well-being would help me to concentrate as I pieced together the connection between Noreen, Rafe, and Anton. I couldn't stop thinking of Noreen when we were friends at school, silly things like her love of éclairs; the time during fourth form geography when Twitty Lansbury was nabbed with a cheat sheet and Noreen took the blame; Noreen and me sneaking out of swimming practice to buy sundaes behind the changing sheds. Random details that meant nothing and everything to our friendship ran through my mind only to blur into dead ends that left me bereft and edgy. The ether's effect and the desire to know how Noreen knew Anton through Rafe ate away at me until I had to get up.

I put on a robe and relied on my intuition to guide me through the locked and darkened house. As I made my way forward, I was engulfed by a sense of trespass worsened by my earlier, forbidden entry into the greenhouse. Yet when I came to the library with its numerous recesses and carrels, I had the feeling that Anton wanted me to be here, just as he had meant for me to see the greenhouses, no matter what Jeanne-Marie said to the contrary.

I tightened my robe at the waist and entered the room, noticing at the same time a fine dust or sand covering the floor. Perhaps, I thought, someone had been walking by the river and had brought the sand inside; or without Anton, Jeanne-Marie had let the housekeeping slide.

I went to the oak-shelved bookcases, not knowing what I hoped to find. The ether made the shelves appear to sway back and forth as I reached toward the surfeit of books, the majority in languages I couldn't read despite my peripatetic childhood. Moonlight flattened the scored leather bindings set in precise, alphabetical rows. Ancient botanical studies stood side by side with volumes of esoteric spiritual tracts. Most of the books had to have been first editions. One volume in particular appealed to me and I took it to a window seat where it caught the moon full strength. It seemed to be a treatise on color and sound, reminding me of Benita's books I had left unread back at the house in London. I traced the intricate gothic lettering with my eyes; from the shape of the letters I guessed they were an old form of Cyrillic, a piece of trivia gathered from my childhood museum visits.

The mottled pages were thick with engravings of glassmakers and blueprints of cathedrals in multiple stages of construction, and I decided they had something to do with the art of stained glass making. I was particularly struck by one picture that held a moon in one corner and the sun in the other. Beneath each orb incised with a cunning humanoid face of the type I couldn't abide in medieval manuscripts, was something hand-lettered in both Arabic and Hebrew. I thought of Miles's strange pronouncement before he left for Dubai: *"Letters of flame, letters of moonlight."*

I turned a few more pages when an unaddressed envelope, apparently left as a bookmark, stopped me from going any farther.

Cream paper. A fiber and sheen I had seen only twice before: when I picked up my check from Teague & Bloch, and that odd, truncated message from Miles.

I glanced out the window, my skin prickling beneath the slippery robe, the letter burning in my hand. I couldn't resist; I pulled the densely covered pages from their envelope.

*Esteemed Sir:*

*I am writing in regards to our current business. In short, I believe we are failing in our goals. As I write this I can hear you laugh and I agree it is strange that I write "our goals" after my show of reluctance to participate in your hellish search. But now, Kaminsky, I have only one desire, one I know you endorse, and that is to find the Unushka, no matter the cost. Once this is accomplished, for reasons I also know to be opposed to your own, I believe it will be possible to take the route you have laid out for us, and there will no longer be any need to return to this, or any other, life.*

*I once told you I went into geology as a means to travel, callow youth that I was. At the time I chose this field, straight out of the university, alone and without family ties except for the affections of my aunt, I was eager to begin a life that I believed would bring me adventure, wealth, and security.*

*What I never could have foreseen was our outlandish meeting in that remote and implausible setting. Sometimes I think of what my life could have been had I never attended that meeting. There is the chance I would still be searching, but my efforts would be toward more profitable aims, such as an increased salary with advancement within my stalwart company of Messrs. Teague & Bloch.*

*As it is now, I accept each new and distant assignment under a yoke of complacency, always taking the most withdrawn spots in the hope that I will encounter any word or sign of the girl. And even as I do so, a part of me is troubled not only with doubts as to the wisdom of my actions, but a horrible sense that what we are doing—what we have done—is wrong. "Evil" itself may not be too strong a word.*

*Which is not to say I will give up. If anything, my resolve to continue and succeed has never been greater. But I do so with a single hope, that when I do bring home the Unushka, you will honor your side of the bargain and allow me that freedom that can only end one way.*

*Respectfully,*

*Miles Bergsen*

The letter fell from my hands to the floor where I picked it up again, turning the pages back and forth. There was no way to know when the letter had been written or received. There were no indications of date or location, no mention of me or our marriage. The thought crossed my mind that if the letter was a recent one, Miles may have given up any interest in me and therefore wouldn't make any reference to a wife. Or worse, I may have been a diversion for him, a dalliance on his way to "bring home" the Unushka.

I re-read the contents a final time before I replaced everything back between the chapters of what seemed an ugly and sinister volume. I loosened the neck to my robe; I felt I was about to choke. First Noreen's hair and kimono, now a letter that filled me with a foreboding I was incapable of enduring a minute longer.

I returned the book to its shelf and hurried to the doorway when I remembered the sand strewn over the floor. I glanced back across the room; my footprints stood out clearly. For a moment I considered sweeping them away, then just as abruptly I changed my mind. Coming from the opposite direction was a distinct set of prints quite separate from my own. I was sure they had not been there before.

"Chèrie." Jeanne-Marie stepped from behind the shelves and I screamed. Loudly.

"What the—?" I glared as she turned on a light.

She saw my empty hands and I rammed them into my pockets. "You did not find anything nice?" she asked.

"Were you spying on me?" I passed my foot over the floor. "Is that what the sand is for?"

Jeanne-Marie pointed at me with what looked like a roll of blueprints. "You go where you should not."

I was about to say something sharp and insulting when I dropped my bluff and the only thing I wanted was the ether upstairs in my room.

"You are tired," she said, the roll of paper tight in her hands.

I nodded. For once I didn't feel embarrassed to admit I wanted nothing more than bed. What did it matter what she thought of me, anyway? It seemed decades rather than days ago that I was a rising star on the art horizon, someone with an overbooked appointment calendar and a clear passage toward a scintillating career. Now my star had fallen without so much as a bang, leaving me suspended between apathy and chaos, my life overturned by a few drops of poison I had grown to love. Without the words to explain, I turned and left, my feet scattering the grains of sand into a senseless pattern of retreat.

As soon as I returned to my room I went to the mirror, the same one Jeanne-Marie sat me in front of every night as she brushed my hair. I thought my face was different; I had changed somehow. Not *aged*, I assured myself, but I had matured in a way that seemed more sad to me than wise. I studied my chin and eyes with the same scrutiny I saved for my clients. What was it that had attracted Miles to me? I swung away from the mirror. If I could not return to Miles and the life I had planned for us, I could return to myself. But how?

I opened a drawer set into a table by my bed. Inside were yellowed sheets of paper and glass-tipped pens, their transparent barrels filled with scarlet ink. How long had it been since I had painted the panther or sketched Anton reading by the fire? I dabbed my forehead with the handkerchief I'd use to saturate with the ether and again felt my willpower slip away. Was it my weakness Miles had wanted from me? We had known each other for only hours, minutes really, when he said, "Marry me before I leave." *Before I leave.* Why? Why? If he had spoken the words back in the office, everyone would have heard them as the kind of boorish thing a man about to enter the desert says in a heavy-handed attempt to flirt.

But it hadn't been a line. I had heard the longing, the sincerity behind his words, and instead of laughter at a silly jest, I had felt ennobled and set apart, and that my life was about to come into focus, to be settled in ways I had yet to know.

I crawled to the bed, my thoughts swirling in the chronic farrago I used to excuse my bad behavior. There had to be more to his motives than pity or sex. He had married me. He had given me his bank accounts, his assets, his identity. But money had never explained the man.

Pulling the sheets aside, I buried my face in the pillows and ran through a list of possible reasons for our marriage. *He was escaping the law. Taxes. Another woman. Courtenay Claiburne.*

But remembering our final weekend together, nothing so calculated as using me seemed plausible. He had loved me; I had to believe that.

My thoughts dwindled into a remorseful sleep. Dream after dream towed me through a cold and elegant landscape. Little Gerda and the Snow Queen, dressed in white fox and ermine. Together they pushed me forward, always forward into what seemed to be a blizzard of tissue paper snowflakes, the wind whispering a word like "*ssh,*" a word like snow: *Unushka. Unushka. Unushka.*

## 21

I had to wait three days before Anton returned and Jeanne-Marie would permit me to arrange a meeting with him. I dressed carefully in a mauve silk sheath that left my arms bare and set off a simple strand of Tahitian pearls in a style I hoped Anton would countenance. For our meeting I wanted to appear subdued and thoughtful; I wanted Anton to listen to me and to respond as he usually did not: forthright and clear in his meaning.

When I appeared at the library door and entered the now cleanly swept room, I felt he was not displeased to see me, but as he lifted his gaze with reluctance from the thick wine-colored portfolios spread out upon his desk, I could see his time was money.

"Did you have a good trip?" I asked, hiding my legs under my skirt as I took the seat he offered me. As soon as I spoke, I regretted the false, over-bright tone I'd chosen. Anton and I rarely exchanged pleasantries.

"A trip is but another journey," he mused. "In between the forgeries and the commonplace, I was able to find some rather good Moghul erotica." He indicated the open portfolios, his eyebrows arched in two question marks. I glanced at the jewel-like miniatures he pushed toward me, the portrayed figures appearing more like abstract geometries than human beings. The only images that struck my curiosity were two diminutive orbs drawn into the margins. The sun and the moon, again. I sent the parchment sheets back across the table.

"I came here to ask you something," I said, wondering which I would mention first, the letter from Miles or Noreen's hair.

"A question," Anton said, "that holds, I presume, more importance than the quality of my journey." He balanced in his hand a thick magnifying glass set in a wooden frame.

I tried to keep from staring at the rays blinking from the glass. "While you were gone, I paid a visit here to the library."

Anton's expression of nonchalance shifted; a small tightening at his lips. "It was unlocked," I said needlessly; the library, as far as I knew, was always open. I lifted the pearls away from my skin and decided against mentioning the sand on the floor. "I was looking for something to read," I said. "When I opened a book on stained glass I found a letter."

"Was it addressed to you?"

"It wasn't addressed to anyone."

Anton rested the heavy circle of glass over a section of manuscript.

"It was from my husband. From Miles."

"And you would like to know why there is a letter from Miles Bergsen in my library. In a book on stained glass techniques."

I nodded.

"You are sure?"

I could barely keep my voice steady. "I am."

"What if the knowledge is terrible? Will you not blame me for telling you this thing you are so certain you want to know?"

The conversation was spiraling away from me in the manner I feared it would. I stood and walked to a shelf of books, feigning an interest in the spines. "When it comes to Miles, I want to know everything."

"All right, then," he said agreeably. "But I would prefer to see your face before we continue."

I turned back from the books. Anton took another long moment to compose his thoughts, and then said, "Miles Bergsen is not a stranger to me."

"Tell me something I don't know."

Anton played with the magnifying glass. "Such as?"

Suddenly I was angry. "Maybe you could give me some news. Or help me to contact him. Does he know I'm here? Don't you think he'd want to know that I've left his house and life? That he might never see me again?"

"No. I do not think he would want to know."

It was as if he'd hurled that heavy piece of glass right at me. The cruelty of his statement struck me as intentional, yet it came with a sense of inevitability, the sense that I knew what the words would be before they were spoken.

My shoulders tensed as I told myself not to give Anton a single sign of my unease, to not move a single muscle, because I also knew his words were the ones I had waited so long to hear, a type of spell recited in reverse with the intent of finally freeing me. Even as I wanted to escape their harshness I knew I would have heard them one day, if not in some lavish place such as this, then out on the grimy streets of an ordinary London work day. It was better like this, I reasoned; in private and from someone who did not benefit one way or the other. But my initial question remained unanswered.

"What was the letter about?"

Anton returned to his portfolios. "It is a long story, longer than we have time for today."

"I want it now."

"Sara, Sara, always the impatient one. Oh, very well," he said like my father conceding to a promised treat or outing.

He replaced the rather unexciting pornographic pictures back into their Moroccan cases, tying the silk ribbons pasted to their covers with a fussy preciseness. Again he reminded me of a world-weary parent indulging a persistent and very boring child—me. "I don't suppose Miles ever mentioned to you something called the 'Unushka'?"

*The reference in Miles's letter.*

"We were only together for a week," I said. I wanted to say that we'd had more important things to discuss, like wedding plans, but I didn't think Anton would understand. "I do know Miles had been in Siberia. The word sounds very Russian."

Anton came close to smiling again. He nodded. "Good enough," he said. "The Unushka are…women. Alluring, bewitching, women." He waited for my reaction; I bit my lip to ensure I had none.

He leaned back, his face clouded in memory. "When Miles Bergsen and I first learned of the Unushka," he said slowly, "we were in a tavern, in a forbidden area of Shanghai. The weather was hot and humid, and we were drinking, as one does. Our second bottle had just been opened when a cooley approached us, the kind the streets were rife with back then. The man was drunker than we were, raving out of his mind. When we tried to send him away, he claimed he had a story for us; one the 'English gentle-man' would want to hear. I thought he meant Miles. I also thought, from the look of him, that he had just been the victim of some nefarious ambush—for what reason, who could tell?

"The proprietor of the establishment seemed to recognize the man for the scoundrel he was. She strapped a gun to her waist and poured him a drink from the same bottle I had only just paid for. But instead of drinking, he pushed the glass to the floor, repeating a single phrase: 'The Unushka. The Powdered Unushka.'"

Once again Anton toyed with the magnifying glass. "It was clear he was not an eloquent man, but when he pronounced those three words, *The Powdered Unushka*, he could not have known that he had set in motion a catastrophe that would dictate the rest of our lives."

"What else did he say?" I asked, my voice no more than a whisper.

Anton put the glass down. "He described their clothing. He said they dressed always in shades of red: deep magentas, fiery rose. Never yellow, and most especially never white. That lack of color was kept for their faces, and the powder they used. He claimed this occult powder was mixed with crushed pearls and the essence of life itself. Their skin, he said, became like marble from using this powder, but they were not cold, and they most certainly were not dead."

The story was far-fetched, but it was more than I had heard concerning Miles in weeks, months. "Go on."

Anton seemed to debate the wisdom in continuing, but then said in a matter-of-fact tone, "He next spoke of their hair, saying it was black and woven into long ropes with golden pins. They were, he said, as exalted and as ethereal as goddesses, except for one thing. The Unushka, he declared, were evil. They were demons.

"Your husband sat by my side during this long recitation. When it was possible for him to speak, he had only one question: Where did the Unushka live?"

Again Anton paused, and I asked in spite of myself, "What did he learn?"

"That they could be found only in the hidden places, ruined temples, derelict palaces. Their taste for past glory was apparently faultless, and matched only by their insatiable greed."

Anton cleared his throat. "The man was bordering on unconsciousness, but there were still things he wanted us to know. He insisted that while the Unushka were chosen as children, even then they were capable of terrible crimes, and when they came of age, they could bleed a man dry, eat his soul, and then refuse to hear his name again.

"'Avoid the Unushka,' the man said. 'And pray you can never afford to meet one. For the hearts of the Unushka are as sharp as glass. All softness on the outside, they have spikes for souls, and their claws, when unsheathed, are those of beasts. They are demons,' he repeated. 'The demons that can never be saved.'"

Neither Anton nor I spoke. The quiet in the room muffled my courage, but I had to ask, "When did you find them?"

"The day they found me."

The silence was overwhelming. I could hear the blood pounding in my ears. "You seemed to have escaped from their clutches all right."

"Who said I escaped?" He seemed to be debating with himself, then added as an afterthought, "Only the child was saved."

Wearily, he gestured to his portfolios, the interview over. "If you will excuse me now, Sara, I must analyze this collection. Any further questions must wait for another time. I have been longer away from my work than I had intended."

I leaned across his desk. "What child?" But Anton wasn't listening. He began to write in his large flowing script onto the pages of a ledger.

I slammed my hands down over the page, smudging the ink and tearing the paper. "What child? What are you talking about?"

"I believe you have just ruined this page."

I couldn't find it in me to apologize as I reeled away, memory plunging me into some pine-filled place teeming with the howls of a hungry wolf pack.

*Kamchatka.* I shoved the memory away with a savage denial; it was a lie. The story was a lie. The Unushka. Miles searching for them. It was a ruse to distract me and I had stood there listening, hanging onto every word.

In my room, I pulled the drapes shut against the midday sun. As soon as the room took on some semblance of night I resorted to the ether without compunction and fell into a troubled sleep that worsened by the minute as I dreamed of the Unushka. Somewhere against the backdrop of their long hair and rich clothing I imagined Miles tracking them down through ice caves and along the banks of brownish, bracken-ringed forest pools. Each time I called out to him he slipped farther from me, causing me to think my stay here had been somehow pre-arranged, that Miles had delivered me to Anton as payment of some kind, and now that I was caught and bound, of no use to him any longer.

I rolled across the bed. The Unushka were singing; they were calling to me. I was being smothered in that other world, a world of lies, a world of evil. The dream ended with Miles too far away for me to reach him, and I could only call one name. The name of my missing mother. Except as soon as I uttered the syllables, they were gone from my memory, and I knew they would never come back.

## 22

The next day, before I was fully awake, Jeanne-Marie came to my room to say Anton had summoned me to meet with him on the terrace outside the library.

I had only minutes to change into a silk chemise coupled with one of my favorite cotton sarongs as colorful as a Gauguin. In my rush I left off makeup and jewelry.

Anton had his back to me when I took the short marble stairway down to where he waited. Implacable in his Panama summer suit and hat, he turned when he heard me approach.

"Jeanne-Marie said you wanted to see me." Rushing had made me breathless.

"So I did." He gave me a look that told me nothing of his mood or the reason for our meeting. Instead, he asked: "Do you believe in the concept of penance?"

"Like confession and Hail Mary and putting tacks in your shoes?" I shook my head. "I wasn't raised with religion if that's what you mean."

He shook his head and returned to his surveillance of the woods. "I thought we would walk this morning. I want to talk. Are you warm enough?"

"Depends where we're going." I followed his eyes toward the trees. The paths were heavily shaded, but my cranberry-colored chemise was made from a thickly knitted silk thread.

Anton stepped from the terrace, leading me to the graveled path away from the house and toward a leaf-strewn entrance I had yet to explore. When we passed beneath a huge natural archway of oak and elm, he took my arm in his own. The fabric of his suit was coarse but not unpleasant to my skin.

"I will tell you a story," he said as our steps fell into sync.

"About penance?" A flapping sound overhead drew my attention up through the branches; the swan from the lake. I thought back to my time at St. Anne's. Every year there had been a new clique of prayerful girls rabid to soak up the school's offering of religious discipline if it could wipe out a passel of chaste sins. Noreen and I used to laugh at them.

"A story about many things," Anton said, interrupting the memory. "But yes, penance is one of them."

We rounded a corner of tree ferns and came to a smaller version of the central fountain with a hidden cupola and curtains of morning glory. Stretched full-length on top of a bench, the panther raised its head in greeting. I gripped Anton's arm; the animal never failed to astound me. Anton ignored the beast and we continued to where the forest floor stopped at a ledge. From here we could see the greenhouses and yet another entrance, previously unknown to me, to the labyrinth. We sat down, the splash of the fountain behind us a language of its own.

"You asked Jeanne-Marie where it is I go when I leave the estate," he said.

"Was I wrong to ask?"

"No." He paused, and then said, "I have not always lived in such wealth as you find here. Once, before any of this," his glance took in the full panorama of our surroundings, "I was homeless. Friendless. An uneducated child better to have been left at birth than to undergo the life I was born into."

"No child should be left to die," I mumbled, trying to remember the day Inge claimed was the one on which she had found me. I came up blank.

"I grew up in the worst of poverty," Anton said, "and without a father. My mother, once a good Jewish girl from a decent, respectable family, had been cast off by the man who seduced her. It is an old story. With nowhere to go, despised by her family, she did the only thing she could. She sold her body by night and drank her earnings the next day to forget the night before."

I didn't know what to say when he reached over to take my hand. He stroked my fingers one by one. "Not many people know of my past. Only Miles Bergsen, and now, I find myself telling you."

"You told Miles?" The shock of hearing his name went through me with a jolt.

"He listened."

Yes, I thought, he would have listened. From the day we first met, it seemed I had done all the talking.

Anton handed me a fallen morning glory. "My mother, as I said, was a Jew. Until she left home in disgrace she had lived in a religious family. The rare times she mentioned her ancestry intrigued me. I wanted to know about this family of hers, this heritage that I could not claim, neither from her parents nor from the pious young men I would see sometimes on the street, their eyes averted as they passed me on their way to the yeshiva and through the doors of the synagogue."

Anton stared at the flower in my hand. "This was in Europe, of course, before you were born."

An electric tingle passed over me. *Before I was born.* Like something from a novel, or one of Inge's stories. But how much before? How could Anton, who appeared to be no more than in his late forties, have known a childhood that sounded like a time before the Second World War?

"I used to envy the yeshiva students," he said, unaware of the questions racing through my mind, "almost as much as I envied the *goyim* who jeered at them: blond-haired golden boys taunting the swinging coats and side curls of a people I regarded as mine even as they snubbed me. After a time, though, I grew to hate all of them." He grimaced, remembering. "That is when I knew it was up to me to make my own way in life."

Anton passed a hand over his eyes as if the memories were too much for him to recall. He stood and faced away from me, his back ramrod-straight as he continued to speak. "My mother," he said, "had a regular customer, a man named Berentz. An ugly, swinish fellow, he always gave her an extra coin as well as a full bottle of the cheap vodka they both swilled. I think he regarded her as his common-law wife, an arrangement she made no effort to change. On a day while she was without him, I made my escape."

A cloud covered the sun and Anton removed his hat before taking his story in a new direction.

"Years passed. What I did to survive is not important, but in time I worked my way toward becoming if not polished and educated, at least closer to what I thought a solid, middle class life of security and employment should be. And then I fell in love."

He cleared his throat and said, "Her name was Bella, but she was known to her husband and his social circle as Arabella di Francini Longhi. For years she had been a client of the gallery where I had been recently employed. Her husband bought the pictures we sold, but she was the one to stop by the gallery to finalize his purchases or to check on the caliber of a restoration. While in the shop, she would sometimes use her own allowance to buy the smaller goods we sold upon consignment: Dresden figurines, antique fans; trifles.

"She was, in my eyes, a ravishing woman. Titian hair, a wide and generous mouth. Her tastes were conservative: boardroom suits and men's wristwatches. Lisle stockings. Tasseled brogues. And always a pair of sapphire earrings that had belonged, she told me, to her English grandmother." Anton stopped and turned to touch my own hair, lifting it back to expose my bare earlobes.

"I was in a hurry," I said, thinking I had offended him by omitting to wear the jewels he had pressed upon me. But he only let my hair drop back into place before he said:

"You may question what she saw in me. I was fifteen years her junior, an uncouth foreigner, someone who could take her orders but never command any of my own. Yet she must have sensed in me that same passion for art and beauty that she herself fostered, making her feel there might be more than second-rate paintings and statues for sale in our somewhat eclectic gallery.

"Soon she began to request that only I escort her through the show-rooms. Next she insisted that no one other than me could supervise the wrapping and delivery of her purchases. Eventually she came to rely solely upon my judgment before she or her husband would even view a potential purchase.

"If the owner of the gallery construed any impropriety on my part, or nurtured any sense of jealousy, he never let on. He was a prudent man and did not meddle in the affairs of others so long as his customers were pleased and paid their bills on time. Obviously I was able to contribute to both of his objectives and I came to be considered one of his most important employees.

"The first time I did more than kiss the hand of Signora Longhi in my usual, perfunctory way as I did for all the ladies entering the showrooms, my employer was on a four-week buying trip through the Netherlands. I was left responsible for the daily operating of the gallery, a task I enjoyed if I also found it banal. It had been a slow start to the season. Our customers had been notified the gallery would have nothing new for a month, and now winter had arrived early. It was only October, but snow had been falling steadily from the strike of three that afternoon.

"By four, I was debating whether to light the lamps or shut the doors for the evening, when she arrived suddenly, breathless, cold, a wreath of snowflakes encircling her hat. Her trim white mink collar, more appropriate to a crisp autumn afternoon, seemed no more than a wisp of the same snow muffling the city's streets and bridges. The park across the way was already blanketed in white drifts hiding the early autumn leaves.

"As soon as she was inside the door, Bella clapped her gloved hands together and demanded coffee, brandy, anything warm and steamy. I offered her my mouth instead, which she accepted with both laughter and need.

"I remember locking the front door with one hand while fumbling with her short, unsuitable jacket with the other. We grappled like this for a bit and then made our way to the storerooms. She seemed to know the way and for one stark moment I wondered how many times she had led my predecessors to those crumbling caverns of unrestored frames and moth-eaten hangings. But she was so alive and guileless as we leaned against a bolt of rough hemp that I forgot my doubts. I grabbed her and fell into her like the starving child I had so recently been, my past much darker than I cared for anyone to know.

"We stayed there together until the snow obliterated the glow of the streetlights and she rose to say she had a dinner to attend, but could she come back tomorrow? Yes, I told her, breathing into her hair, that beautiful hair. Tomorrow and the next day and every day until the gallery owner arrived jubilant with plundered Spanish pearls and Flemish tankards. The next time, I told her, I would have the coffee and brandy waiting.

"She laughed and gathered her belongings before I replaced the little collar around her throat, my hands trembling all the while as if I were dressing one of the more decrepit *santos* we kept in sealed cases away from the public. And then she was gone.

"In the morning the papers broadcast her death. An unknown assailant behind the gallery had struck and killed her. Her white collar, it was reported, was drenched in her blood from a fatal head injury.

"I left the gallery keys with the carpet dealer next door and fled to Marseilles where I stayed for the next three days before catching a freighter for Papua New Guinea. It was, perhaps, the worst decision of my life."

A breeze stirred the leaves and I shivered; the chemise was not warm enough after all. Anton removed his suit coat and placed it around my shoulders, making me think of that white mink collar he had placed for the last time around his lover's throat. Across the image lay Daile and Laurie Granger, Benita Hansard's sons, Noreen's final minutes on some Greek highway.

Anton read none of my thoughts. "The ship never made it as far as the South Pacific," he said. "We were impounded off the coast of Africa and the crew released. I lived on the streets until I was robbed of my last franc." He brushed a hand across his chin.

"And then?" I heard the note of child-like curiosity in my voice. I didn't care; the story held me hostage and I didn't want him to stop.

He smiled. "And then one night I took shelter in the doorway of a public house. I had become weak with hunger and the beginnings of a fever. The most I remember of that pivotal night are the lurid images of seamen against a haze of smoke from the crude lanterns swinging in the wind; the smell of tar weaseling its way through the oily harbor stench, the sickening overlay of copra. My stomach heaved as visions of Bella raced through my mind, her pale fingers winding that mannish watch of hers before she left me for the last time.

"In my delirium I stumbled to the edge of the docks. A gale blew full force into my face and waves slapped the docksides with a violence I welcomed. I sank to my hands and knees and let the rain and seawater wash over my head and my clothing. And then I was in the water. I did not try to swim, I was glad my life was ending so easily. But it wasn't to be easy at all.

"Suddenly I was expelled from the harbor and plunged to the depths of some fantastic seabed of volcanic ruins. Weird turrets of stone emitted pillars of flame, boiling through the white water, rushing past my eyes like millions of scattered jewels. Schools of exotic fish swarmed past like tropical birds in frenzied flight, laughing and chattering with a sound that scrabbled in my ears as the currents continued to toss and afflict me.

"There was nothing to stop me. I was at the mercy of fate. Just when I feared I had reached the end of my life, I saw the women. They swam toward me, their arms extracting me from one danger to another as they wove their long hair around my throat like strands of kelp, pinioning me ever closer to their grasp.

"My lungs strained for air, I was certain death was close, but again, I was thrown back onto the surface of the sea, carried high and helpless by the storm that had still not abated. Gigantic waves burst and lashed around me like massive flukes as I was pulled into the air only to be submerged seconds later back beneath the water. My blood seemed to be bursting through my ears until I knew the sea had closed over me for the last time."

Anton slumped back, and I noticed the breeze had grown stronger, as if the weather had followed his unbelievable narrative. As if in agreement, the panther growled in its sleep, a dire underline to the fitful lashing of the leaves overhead. Even with Anton's suit jacket around my shoulders I was feeling the sudden cold. I pushed my arms through the sleeves when I heard a branch crack and break.

Deep in his memories, Anton ignored the weather. Instead, he continued as if nothing around us had changed. "I awoke to the scent of musk," he said. "A pair of Egyptian sheets felt smooth to my cheek. My face was shaved, my hands washed, no blood or splinters beneath my fingernails. Someone had dressed me in a clean shirt, so fresh it seemed to have been laundered that very day.

"I watched the sunlight cross the room from two west-facing windows and I guessed it was sometime late in the day. By my bedside, someone had conveniently placed a tea service. Roses and tiger lilies sat beside the silver tray.

"I lifted my head and was greeted by silence. The sea, the doorway where I had taken shelter, the shouts of the men inside the bar—gone.

"For some reason the room made me apprehensive, but I could not say why or how. And there was that divine silence that I realized was not all that it seemed. Behind it, faint, but there, the sound of—purring.

"With my eyes I followed the sound to an unlit fireplace laid with bouquets of sunflowers. And in front of it, a gleaming beast."

I nodded. So Anton had heard it first. Even now I could hear it welling within my own heart.

Anton said, "The animal was asleep, yet the sound pulled me in with an abandonment I wanted to last forever. I sat up and tested the strength in my arms and legs. I was well. No strains, sprains, bruises, or the open cuts I expected to find.

"Relieved to deduce myself whole, I closed my eyes again and entered a sleep that would last for—"

A branch the size of my arm crashed at our feet as the skies opened, drenching us through our clothing. I looked upward; wind raged and tore at the huge trees, their leaves heavy with rainwater that now poured down in torrents.

A streak of lightning cut across the sky, electrifying the panther's fur. The beast roared awake before springing away from us and diving into some secret lair amongst the trees. I spun in alarm when I heard the pillars supporting the cupola creak and groan. Anton had gone. Wildly, I struggled to stand when a heavy vine blew out and struck me across the mouth hard enough to draw blood and bring tears to my eyes. It seemed impossible for the weather to change with such fickleness until I remembered the previous shift to snow and ice and back again.

"Anton!" I called out, my voice lost in the storm. "Anton, where are you?"

A clap of thunder burst through the woods, the noise so loud I felt it in my teeth. I reached out to grab hold of the vine that had struck me but as I did so my hand passed right through the ropy stem, startling me before the entire trellis fell upon my head like a webby, sodden net.

"Anton!" I called again. I tried to push the wet leaves away only to become buried beneath their weight. Dazed and soaking, I tried harder to free myself, and when the next thunderclap exploded overhead, I felt the ground give way.

The brides, I thought, my mouth clogged with clay. My dream of the brides. Just like the dream, I felt I was falling into my own grave.

## 23

The brushes had all been moved. From where I crouched on the floor beneath my easel, my nightgown bunched uncomfortably at my hip, I took in what were subtle but disturbing changes.

A tilt to the window shade; a cord pulled from a light socket; in the open-style kitchen a plastic drink container like the ones in fast food restaurants, the kind I never used. Added together they signified either a new breakdown or a home invasion.

I groaned and rolled over onto my back only to roll over again when my body rejected the wooden flooring. Bruises from my fall sent waves of pain through me, forcing me to stand.

Finding myself back in London, not knowing what day or time it was, or how long I had been gone—if I had been gone—sent me into an adolescent anguish. The blackouts had never lasted with such intensity. The most I could hope was that I had not been found wandering the city on autopilot, annihilating what remained of my reputation. What if I had gone to the shops in my ragged nightgown? I bit the inside of my lip to keep from screaming.

Despite the pain and stiffness in my legs, I made my way to the kitchen sink and the drink container. Dead ants floated on the surface of an unappealing cola I didn't remember buying. I didn't even like cola.

The light blinking on my answering machine made me cringe; no way could I possibly respond to anyone's demand that I call back right now. Instead I went to my easel and lifted the muslin I had draped, when?

Weeks, months ago? I held my breath as I pulled the cloth away, and then exhaled slowly. Courtenay Claiburne's unfinished face stared back at me. Nothing had been touched; no slashes in the canvas, no graffiti scrawled across her forehead. I forgot the pain in my legs as gratitude gave me the strength to stay upright.

I reviewed the bones of my work, thinking at the same time about the changes in the room. Had they been made by a concerned neighbor coming in to check on me? Not everyone on the street could be as unfriendly as the woman who disliked me so. But I didn't remember leaving the doors unlocked or the windows open. The fustiness of the house could attest to that. For a second I thought: *Miles*, and then dismissed the idea of his return as wishful thinking. I let the muslin drop back over Courtenay's face. Whoever had come inside the house had left without causing any real damage.

I went to my bedroom for a change of clothes. A sudden impulse before I reached the room, however, sent me to the guest bedroom where I had stored my wedding rings. I opened a drawer and found them safely nestled in their case. It's fine, I told myself. Everything's fine. I took out an old faux crocodile handbag I had never liked, and where I had decided to keep Daile's scarf.

I unlatched the clasp and my stomach turned over as if I had just dropped several stories down an elevator shaft. The scarf was gone. In its place: a small blue vial and two monogrammed handkerchiefs I threw to the floor. The scarf wasn't with them.

I overturned the handbag again and checked it thoroughly. Zero. Only that bottle of ether; the linen handkerchiefs.

The same person who had left the ether had to have taken the scarf. Because if I had moved the scarf, or worn it in some fit of madness— where had these other items come from?

Pushing up the sleeves to my nightgown, I tore back downstairs, wincing at every step. The scarf had to be in the house somewhere. It just had to be. I searched the cupboards and side drawers like a fiend, seeking any clue of *something*.

I pulled open drawer after empty drawer, the cabinets mocking me with their spaciousness. The scarf was nowhere in sight. I prayed like I remembered the girls at St. Anne's doing: *O God, I am an idiot…* Surely I had destroyed it, burning it when I got rid of my clothes after that first series of "hallucinations."

I slammed the cabinet doors shut in one final, unproductive tour of the kitchen. The phone continued its mindless blinking. I swallowed, my throat dry as I pushed "play."

*"Hello, Sara. This is Benita. I wanted to tell you the portrait is framed. Can you come down next week? Let me know. Thank you, dear. I hope you're reading the books."* I glanced at the bare countertops, unsure if the books were even in the house.

The next voice belonged to my mother, bringing more guilt that sat miserably with the rest of my emotions. *"Sara. Sara. Are you there? If you are working we don't want to interrupt."* Inge's voice sounded strange and tinny. *"Ring us when you can,"* she said. *"We may be coming to England. A new project."* Great. After all this time my parents would arrive to find me mumbling on the floor in a fetal position.

There was a pause before the final message played a male's gruff voice. *"Sara, this is Peter at the studio. It's Tuesday. It's about that stuff you left. I've got some papers, letters or something you might have given me by mistake."* I could hear some noise on the line before he hung up.

Letters I left by mistake? And what Tuesday? I dawdled by the phone for a minute, lost in ambivalence. I thought of returning my mother's call, but a part of me drew back, not wanting to confide or explain this latest calamity. I went back upstairs to shower, anything to get my head together. Whenever I was ready to phone her, I wanted to sound sane and sensible and not like the neurotic child who pushed everyone away.

*Moder, Moder, Mamma.*

Under the shower, I couldn't stop thinking about my mother, my parents. The jets of hot water reminded me of the rain hitting the metal roof of their house in Melbourne the last afternoon we spent together, just like during monsoon season in the Far East when I was little. I hadn't known about Kamchatka, or Miles, or Anton back then. I hadn't known anything but my amah's face smiling as we splashed through the swampy streets after the rains, and the safety and camaraderie of my parents' quiet, patient work. Now they were returning to England, my father's home, and I was still playing in the mud

I stepped out of the shower and noticed the time; I had spent more than half an hour under the spray and my brain still felt steeped in fog. Which is probably the reason I then tripped over a stack of papers I'd thoughtlessly left on the floor and that sent me hurtling across the room: Twitty's manuscript, the one she made me bring home from our lunch date. My hair and back wet from the shower, I picked up the pages and laid them on top of my bed.

A Box of Golden Animals

by

Pamela Lansbury

i

Leah stormed down the stairs in the too-small high heels, the left shoe rubbing at a painful blister on her little toe. New shoes. She had to have new shoes and dresses and somewhere to live. There was so much she needed, and she wasn't getting any younger. Perhaps she should dump the kid. It was time. He was too old to see her like this, with the men, with the drink inside her to forget the men. How had it all started? She had been raised a good Jewish girl, obedient to her parents, lighting the Sabbath candles enclosed in her mother's arms until the day she could no longer hide her stomach or the baby kicking inside her. "Stop, stop!" she had inwardly begged. "Just…die." And then the shame, the guilt, the horrible racking sobs to think she wanted her own baby dead, but how could she have a baby? She was only fifteen years old! She wasn't married. Her mother had never talked about these things except for once, when her face had darkened at a neighbor mentioning some family member "being sent away" to one of those homes Leah knew were for bad girls who had let men do bad things to them. Now Leah knew all about those bad things, too, but her parents hadn't sent her to one of those homes. Instead, they had locked the door after sending her on some trivial errand. She only had the thin spring coat, the too-tight dress, and her ill-fitting underwear. Fortunately, her parents had always insisted on stout, well-made shoes no matter what fashion demanded, and the pair she had worn on that day were less than three months old. Leah remembered buying the shoes, fighting down the nausea as the young man in the shoe store lingered too long establishing her correct shoe size. Now she knew it was the baby making her feel sick, but at the time the young man's attentions were too close to the caresses of the young university student she had met by chance and then on purpose until he learned of the baby and had called her a whore and insisted the baby was not his. Leah, he said, was a loose, easy girl. Look how easily she had given in to his requests. He had seen the look on her face, enjoying it. What decent girl enjoyed that sort of thing? No, she was a bitch, a harpy, an evil seductress trying to lumber him with some other man's kid.

Her parents said the same thing when Leah banged at the back door when she returned home from her false errand. They only opened it enough to spit on her and tell her they had no daughter. She wasn't even dead because she had never been born. They had a paper from the rabbi proving it, so go away evil woman, get away from our door with your bastard and stop polluting what was once a clean, righteous neighborhood before they called the police. Go and never return.

ii

He was alone in the huge wooden tub. Water surrounded him; he felt very small. This was the tub Fleuri used for the clothes. So why was he sitting inside it? Where was his mother?

He wasn't frightened—yet, but he couldn't understand where everyone had gone. Usually Fleuri sang when she washed the clothes while the other girls in the house relaxed over the balconies in the summer, or made toast and smoked black cigarettes in the winter.

But today there was no laughter, no friendly gibes coming down the stairs, no smell of coffee and talcum powder, or the peppery, fiery smell of leftover schnapps in the tiny crystal glasses Madame Czuba kept under lock and key unless she had drunk too much of the schnapps herself. Then she would stay on her flame-colored sateen bed all day, a wet rag on her head and her dopey "new find" massaging her feet.

Today Madame Czuba was nowhere in sight, and Anton could only hear the neighbor's Pekingese barking at the jays roosting on the fence dividing the properties. Behind the barking was the added sound of a lorry, its engine idling several streets away. The sound was full of promises and packages, fresh vegetables and crates of brown bottled beer, the bottles clanking and rattling, making a noise Anton loved almost as much as the rare times he got to taste the salty beer on his lips, froth ringing his face and causing the men to snap their braces and roar with laughter until Madame Czuba put on her tsk-tsk face and sternly told him to go to bed this instant, *this instant*, do you hear me?

He sank back in the soapy water. The breeze played in his hair; the dog stopped barking. This was what heaven was like. The old wood of the tub felt spongy. He ran his fingers against the rounded planks, liking the contrast with the water and his own skin. The soap smelled good, like the geranium leaves he couldn't help but pluck no matter how he was scolded and warned and threatened. The plants had millions of leaves. They would live. He only wanted their spicy velvet between his fingers, the scent rising through his nostrils: alive, thrilling, real. Soapy geraniums. The tub was soft and slippery, making him dream of dark caverns and mountain trolls, their treasure so vast—

"Wicked, wicked girl!"

The shouting woke him; the pain was horrible; each breath hurt him, he wanted to cry. He wanted to go back to the trolls. Slaps, crying; the old doctor who checked the girls between their legs every week was now staring into his eyes, looking into his throat with a horrible white light.

Anton suddenly realized, embarrassed, that he had no clothes on. He was stark naked in front of all the girls, but they were crying too hard to notice. Madame Czuba was hitting his mother on her head with a broom—what was happening?

Sobbing, his mother grabbed him from the floor and dragged him to the room they shared under the eaves up above the kitchen. Still crying, she threw their clothes into two old suitcases. Nothing seemed to fit, and she sank to the bed crying harder than ever. Anton's chest still hurt. His ears were ringing. What was wrong?

"You," she cried. "Always I suffer for you! Because of you we are to lose the only place that gave us food and a roof to keep us dry." Her cries became unbearable.

Anton crept up beside her despite the burning in his throat and the hollow where his lungs used to be. "Mutti—" He reached out for her arm but she recoiled as if she had been scalded.

"I hate you!" she screamed. "Hate you!" She hit out with her fists, her eyes like whirls of charred sand in her bloated face. Anton ducked. He reached for a blanket to cover himself and brought the suitcases tumbling down to the rug, spilling their badly-packed contents. It was too much. Wailing her hatred of everyone and everything that had ever conspired to destroy her, his mother seized a brass hat pin from the dusty dresser, and before Anton could stop her, she had driven it into her throat. Red streams shot out of her neck, the blood spurting dark and heavy, as red as Madame Czuba's corsets.

Madame Czuba stood in the doorway, her eyes cold. "Clean up this mess," she said. "You have forty-four minutes. No more." Then she was gone, and his mother lay in a puddle of her own blood. Anton covered her with his blanket.

iii

There was nothing to eat. The cupboard held only mouse droppings and an empty sugar tin. Anton licked his finger and poked it carefully into the corners of the tin, searching fruitlessly for the mouthwatering sweetness. All he could taste on his finger was dirt mixed with a harsh metallic filth of some kind. He put the tin back on the cupboard shelf, not because he feared its change of position would be noticed, but because he had an innate need for order even in this squalid room, the curtains torn and rotten from hanging in the rain, the mattresses they called "beds" sour with age and sweat.

Anton flopped down on one of the putrid mats. He contorted his body in on itself, wrapping his arms around his chest. If he closed his eyes very tightly, he could feel full and warm. His mother had been away for a week now. Maybe she would come back flushed and happy, carrying bags of food, even clothes and extra blankets. That happened sometimes. Anton wanted this to happen again so much he squeezed his bony frame into a bar of sheer willpower. Please, please let Mutti come home happy, with food, and not like the last time, drunk and sick with her skirts torn and a bruise on her face as dark as the melons they sold on Cranachstrasse. Please let her be the happy Mutti, and not the foul-mouthed, straggling monster Mutti who hated her own flesh and blood as much as she hated the world.

Rain fell down the wall, soaking the curtain edges. Anton worried he wouldn't be strong enough to escape his mother's blows when she came home, if she did come home, that was. Maybe he should do what the other kids did: go on the streets and beg. He had never tried it but once, half-heartedly, and the fine gentleman he approached, resplendent in a beaver coat and canary-yellow waistcoat had only scowled and shouted, "Get to work, you slimy brat. Earn your bread like a hard-working German should!" The man hadn't hit him, but his loud angry words were violence enough, and Anton had crept back home, preferring hunger to another similar encounter with the big-bellied rich.

The memory still made his legs shake. He pushed the thought away and rose to his feet, draping a sheet over his head like the old men with their prayer shawls in the synagogue. It felt good, like a little tent or hood protecting him. Tentatively, he experimented with bowing and mumbling like he had seen the men do, but he knew it wasn't the same. Without the words or knowledge of what came next, it just felt like wasting the energy left to him. Despite the rain, he knew his only choice was to run down to Cranachstrasse and pick up any leavings from the market. Even a single cabbage leaf from the pavement seemed like a delicious treat. He would go. He had to.

iv

The doors to the synagogue were kept shut. Ordinary doors, they were anonymous to anyone passing by in a hurry. This was a place of old men and oldfangled ways. He had never heard his mother speak lovingly or reverently about the place. Yet he knew that somehow it belonged to him, and then again, it did not. *Jew. Jewish. Juden.* What did it mean except that he was rejected by Gentile and his own people alike? His mother was shunned by the other women because she did bad things. His father was a ghost. They lived on the fringe of the ghetto and he knew there was no acceptance for someone like him. *Bastard.* Who was his father? What had happened to him? The story, he was sure, was a bad one, like everything in his life: dirty, soiled, ugly. He was unclean.

But still he dreamed of entering those doors. The rare views he had seen of the inside, with the old men in their prayer shawls, nodding to the Hebrew liturgy, were terrifying and achingly beautiful. He longed to know what they were doing, what they were saying, but there was no one to ask. The younger brisk and bearded men who entered those doors were all business and scrupulous fealty to the law, the skirts of their black coats swinging past their stork-like legs, their studious faces alight—they were like angels as they flew down the crowded street, eyes downcast, mouths shaped to hold some holy phrase. He wished he had the courage to take one of their hands in his own and be swept up in their fervor past those heavy doors. How he would have loved to sit under a shawl, like them, and rest, just once, in the rhythm of those prayers. But the young men were too fine and saintly to approach. Their clothes, though shiny and patched, sat

on their thin bodies like princely robes. And the old men, with their fierce
frowns and fiery eyes were like the agents of some avenging goodness,
offering nothing but instant death; if he were to look directly into their eyes
he knew he would fall down dead.

So he waited, hidden in doorways, under carts, blending into the hub-
bub whenever he could just for a glimpse, a wonderful glimpse into that
world so removed from him. Sometimes he stayed until night fell, and he
would miss the baker's last call before the shops closed, forcing him to pick
the stale bread out of the trash. The bread would be wet, and his mother
would beat and slap and hurt him until his hunger and misery were nothing
compared to the torture of her calloused palms or the belts of the men
who wanted, for some reason, to please her. His mother never tried to
protect him; she never told the men to stop hitting her child, her only son,
her baby. She never yelled, "Stop! Stop!" Why couldn't she tell them to
stop? Why did she just stare, blank-faced, drunk, removed from him as the
blows fell harder and harder until there was nothing but pain and a
kernel—a cutting, sharp kernel—of hatred lodged in his throat, threatening
to grow out of his mouth and enclose him in a tough, hard shell the men
could never break.

The world was too large and angry; there was nowhere to go except
inside himself where he could hide, a place where none of them, not the
anointed yeshiva students, the stern old men, or the angels of paradise in
their terrible wrath, could reach him.

v

Rich boys. Chasing him. The cut of their clothes, their polished brown
shoes. Laughing at his rags as if it was their right, their duty to laugh and
shove and scare him away.

*"Ja! Ja!"* The streets belonged to these golden boys, and as angry as he
was, black, loam-filled angry, he knew he was angry not at the boys, but at
himself. He hated his dirty face and legs, his torn sweater, no coat, his
matted hair. Anger at himself, the world, his stupid mother—it kept him

running long after the other children had grown bored with his dirty ugliness. Their laughter goaded him forward, driving his feet through foul-smelling puddles. Bellowing rage tore through his skinny body at the old woman up ahead, doubled over, her thin, ineffective wrap pulled tight by her awkward posture. Anton saw her and her poverty, her old age, her infirmity, everything he hated most as he ran toward her, turning his body into a missile that knocked the breath out of them both as she fell, her screams a second too late to stop his running, running; God, why couldn't he be punished—now he was killing old ladies!

He ran until his feet burned and the tears that came to his eyes were as weak and as unexpected as his shove to the old woman. The anger was almost over. It happened every day. He knew he was stupid to let it matter; the smart thing would be to save it up and use it to buy his own custom-made clothes and send his own arrogant offspring into the world.

vi

He thought of all the violence directed at him: slaps, threats and insults. Survival *was* violent. You took what you could, and ran—fast. But he had no stomach for it. He would stop. Never again would he direct a blow, a belt buckle, a heartless word to anyone. There had to be a better way. Yes, he would be stern, it was the key to becoming one of the great solemn men who walked to the synagogue for torah readings, and it was the key to becoming one of the upstanding men who ran the banks and stores. Those men did not smile, but neither did they hurt. Self-reliant, powerful men who made things work and gave life its beauty and flavor. These were the good men he wanted to join. He would be one of them. He knew it. No matter how hard the others hit or starved or ignored him, he would rise up to take his place with the men of strength.

But for now he was aching and cold and struggling to regain the images that sustained and held him through the long hours of pain and loneliness. He thought of old maroon carpets hanging in shop windows; candles in milky glass holders; a woman's straw hat with a white feather as clean and as wispy as a cloud on the wide curving brim. There was so much beauty to behold, and all of it forbidden to a child such as himself. The strangeness of birth selection baffled him. How was it that he lived in the bare room of his drunk mother, he who had done nothing to anyone; how had he been assigned as the men's whipping boy after they had finished with his mother? And how did other boys fall into the easy world of wool coats and hot dinners and spending money?

vii

She was on her back as usual, legs in the air, one shoe dangling from her foot, the other kicked across the room where it lay in a pool of rainwater. Her stockings were down around her feet. The room smelled of flat beer. The man on top of her had a beefy neck the same color as the red braces flopping over his huge backside as he pumped up and down, up and down, his eyes closed as he ignored everything in the room including Anton who quailed by the side of the stove, peeking out only to see if they were finished. Finally the man groaned and rolled off his mother. She stood to wipe herself.

"Turn around," she snapped at Anton. "It's bad enough to be surrounded by pigs, but I don't have to raise one too."

Abjectly, Anton turned his back. He dreamed of the dinner his mother might buy with the change after she replenished her drink supply later tonight. Surely she would want to eat as much as she wanted to drink. Anton imagined ways he might get the whole sum away from her before she got down to the bottle store.

He looked over his shoulder. The man was buttoning his flies and whispering something into his mother's neck that made her laugh, a lewd, repugnant sound she only made with the men. The man put on his checked jacket; the good quality of the cut unable to stop the fabric from straining at the armpits. Most likely he had bought it in one of the second-hand stores that flourished now so many men were no longer alive to wear their fine suits and bowler hats.

Just before he left, the man cracked a grin at Anton and put a tiny coin in his hand. "For luck," he pronounced before he let out a roar of laughter. Whatever his mother did, it must have pleased the man enormously. Anton could hear him whistling all the way down to the street, a noise his mother refused to hear.

"Give it to me," she said, closing the front of her dress. She cupped her fingers. "Hurry up!" she demanded when she thought Anton was hanging back.

His own fingers seemed glued to the coin, but he nearly hurled the pfennig at his mother when she lunged forward with her right palm open and aiming for his face. As soon as she had the coin, she boxed his ear for good measure before wheeling back to the mattress where she hunted for a comb. "Don't think you can make money off me," she said thickly. "If you turn into the pimp your father was, I will strangle you with my bare hands. Do you understand?"

Anton nodded.

"Answer me! Don't stare like a sick cow!"

"Yes, Mutti."

"Yes, what?"

"Yes, I understand you."

"Good. I have to go out."

"For food, Mutti?"

"*For food, Mutti?*" she snarled back. "Do I not feed you?" Her face was a breath away from him.

"Yes, Mutti, you feed me," he hastily replied.

She relaxed, bored with the exchange. "See to it you don't burn the house down," she said, smirking. There hadn't been a match in the house for days.

She settled an unsightly hat shaped like a pie pan on her still abundant head of black hair; hair that had no right to be that long and full; hair that men still liked to unpin and watch cascade down her back in ripples as shiny as ravens' wings.

Anton sat on his own bed and heard the door slam. It was strange; no matter how moody and cruel and spiteful his mother seemed to him, there was no getting around the fact that his mother was a comely woman. Despite the beer and her lack of imagination, her beauty brought the men who brought the money. It made no sense to Anton why his mother, as pretty as she was, didn't work in the department stores, or on the stage as one of those gorgeous girls he had seen leaving the theaters when he went on his nightly tours looking for scraps.

Why did she just lie there on her back, legs waving in the air like some disgusting, dying bug, and then drink and yell and curse? Why didn't she just stop? Maybe she liked what the men were doing to her. That had to be it. Anton wanted to gag; the insides of his stomach closed in like an empty snare, hurting him enough to make him fall down to dream like he always did, if not of food, then to dream of the beautiful people who could afford to eat it.

viii

His mother was dragging him by the hand; he couldn't catch up with her steps: hurried, impatient, frightened. His boots were too big and they clattered noisily on the cobblestones. His mother clutched his fingers, pulling him ever forward. He wanted her to stop. He couldn't help but look back at the streets he had hated; places where he had lived for as long as he could remember.

Hurry. He had to hurry. The baby brother was dead; there was no father in the house.

A lump of mud mixed with pebbles hit his mother in the arm, then another, until she fell to the ground, blood trickling from her nose, her ear. A rock hit him in the leg. His mother grunted, *"Yud, yud, groden…groden."* What was *"groden"*? What did it mean? He couldn't think; another rock hit his back. His mother was in the middle of the street, her basket of moldy potatoes and shriveled apples overturned and smashed, her headscarf askew and bloody. Anton felt his boot slip off. He kicked free of the other one. He could run. It was his mother the crowd wanted, not him. No one saw him go. He took off, running, running, no one bothering to chase after. Running, running until the air wouldn't fit into his narrow chest anymore. Barefoot, weaker than a two-year-old, he came to a place where the street ended. He leaned against the cold wall barring his way. He was alone. Thank God.

ix

It was dark; he shivered beneath the foul-smelling cardboard he had found in the bombed-out ruins beneath what had been the Hofflerstrasse meat market. He knew the men were coming for him like they always did. They would grab him by the buttocks and pull him down from the shelf he had made for himself above the water. It was the one dry spot in the cellar. He could hear their boots splash through the water. Laughing, cursing; the men were drunk; he could hear them urinating against the walls, bragging to each other.

"The boy, the goddammed boy!" the loudest one persisted. "Bring him down. Bring him right down here, now. And that's an order." Officers. Their medals and silver bars flinty and cold. The men would maul him, kiss and stroke him. The weave of their uniforms scratched and cut at his cheeks and throat. He couldn't stop the sobs that broke out of his chest. He was sure he was dying. The men were too drunk to follow through with their game, but they went through the motions. He thought his head would explode. He wanted to die. He wished he was dead; why couldn't he die? Why had he been left behind like a rat to scour and scuttle the streets? He wasn't a rat, but he knew he was a Jew and he knew these men hated and killed Jews, but he was only a child and had no way of knowing the why of anything. The stench of curdled vomit and brackish water floated up to his shelf.

"What do we do with him?" one of the younger soldiers asked.

"Bash his head in."

"I can't see."

"You don't need to see the vermin to kill it! You can smell it."

Anton cowered against the wall. There was an opening in the bricks. If he could fit behind the bricks like the rat he was—

He hunched his shoulders, drew in his head, scooted down the opening, scraping the backs of his thighs, but he was safe, blessedly safe. The odor of raw sewage was worse in here, but he was *safe*. The men were bored and hungry, sloshing around in the water shouting for whores and sausages that didn't contain any Jew meat.

Then, silence. They were gone.

The cold was brutal; his limbs shook with what felt like fever. He had to save himself, somehow. Was there ever a time in his life without soldiers and hatred? A time when he had been a baby safe with his mother? Or had he just come into the world a terrified child, doomed to accept every morsel of contempt thrown his way?

The shivering increased. He was so thirsty, so angry. He bit his thumbnail to stop from shaking, and could taste blood. He couldn't stay awake. The dreams were worse. He stayed awake.

x

The woman hiding behind the black spotted veil stopped in front of him. Her face, what he could see of it, was the whitest white, as if her soul had died and gone away. She reached for him, then checked herself and pulled back.

Clumsily, Anton bent past her to pick up the last of the broken pastries that had fallen from his box, knocked from his arms by a gang of boys. There was no end of wild boys roaming the streets: Günters and Johanns and Tomases; all too strong and excited by their own sense of power, seizing adventure and opportunity from every chance, usually in the form of a boy like Anton.

The pastries were only two days old. They had looked so delicious, and he had wanted them so badly. A slice of strudel, a prune tart. Now they were smashed and broken and the woman in the black veil with tiny velvet violets was taking them from his hands and throwing them in the gutter.

"I will buy you new pastries," she said in a voice as fragile as the flowers floating across her face. "Don't cry, child. There, there." She was so loving and kind; she had to be an angel. Crisp paper money was pressed into his hand followed by her handkerchief, ironed into a cone and stitched with more violets. She was about to enclose him in the sweet perfumed warmth of her sparkling furs when two men, two tall and grown "golden boys," grabbed her by the elbows.

"*Mutter!* What are you doing? The child is covered in nits! Have you lost your mind? You would feed every brat in Berlin. Remember what Dr. Speight said—"

How could those men be her sons? They were leading his angel away, talking to her like she was a blockhead; how did she stand for it? She turned back to look at him, her eyes as helpless as his own while her sons whisked her away to the stores and restaurants and privileges this strange, kind woman had wanted to share with him. He had no idea why. They had mentioned someone named Dr. Speight. Maybe the woman was sick or crazy. He opened his hand. The money. A lot of it. And the beautiful handkerchief.

The cakes were on the street, but he could afford to waste nothing. He picked them up, carefully; really they were not so bad. Pedestrians behind him jostled and pushed him forward. The money! He had money. The thought scared him. Maybe this was his chance. *The* chance. He had never thought it would be like this, but it was true. It was his. But he had to think quickly. He had to plan. What to do? What to do? What had started as the need to save a broken pastry had turned into a way to change his life. Was this enough money for the train? For clothes? How did a child go to school if he had no family or address? How was anything but stealing, begging, pleading for existence done in this world? He clutched the money, becoming more frightened and more determined by the minute. It was simple— like everything in life, you just went forward. He began to eat the strudel crumbs as his feet quickened. Yes, eat, he told himself. Do not share this. Do not waste this. That woman with her velvet violets had to have seen something, something alive and strong about Anton; she had to have known he would use the money wisely. He was running now to the train station, his heart thrumming as the streets become wider and busier and his ragged appearance less common amongst the well-fed children walking hand in hand with their frowning parents. No rough boys allowed to run wild here.

Anton had to stop and bend forward to catch his breath and rub his eyes. Was it true? Could he leave this city forever? The train station was in sight. He was almost there. Like a boy in a dream he felt his feet lift from the pavement. He was flying; the sky was a huge blue bowl over his head. Flying, leaping; how open these grand boulevards were after his childhood maze of alleyways and sewer drains!

xi

A man feeding birds.

Anton approached the wide busy street: children with their nannies, wealthy businessmen striding to important meetings, a man feeding birds.

Their eyes met. Immediately Anton put his hand to the pocket with the money. Years of deprivation told him to protect what was his, like an animal. He wiped the last of the strudel crumbs from his mouth and glanced away from the bird man. He had seen the man's tenderness with the pigeons, his smooth fur collar, his large gold signet ring in the sunlight. He had noticed the man's joyful expression when the birds fed from his hands and his mock-scolding when they took more than their share. It was troubling, somehow. As Anton neared the ticket booth he wondered how some people became well-off feeders of pigeons while others like himself, were destined to starve with prostitutes for mothers and only the fumes of alcohol to fuel their dreams.

The ticket booth was in sight. A child cried noisily over a burst balloon while his mother made silly soothing sounds about buying a better and bigger one that would not break. Anton watched them with dislike. Balloons were made for breaking. What fools people could be. He felt in his pocket for the money. It would be easy to turn around and go home again, back to the basement, the only home he had.

"Yes?" the ticket master enquired impatiently. "Do you want to buy a ticket?"

Anton stood before the window, feeling stupid. The words "want" and "ticket" suddenly made no sense. What did he want? Who ever knew what they really wanted at any given time? The people in the queue behind him were beginning to mutter. *Hurry up. What's the problem?* He could feel them shoving. *Buy a ticket or piss off. Get out of our way!* All the malice he had sensed pushing and tearing at him, propelling him through his short life now hammered down upon him. These were his enemies standing behind him. He would never let them win, never.

He pulled the money from his pocket. "The sea," he decided. "I want a ticket for the sea."

Behind him the snickers were loud. The seaside? At this time of year?

"Return or one way?"

"What is the difference?"

"Return is cheaper."

Anton thought. He could save money, yes, but he was never coming back. Never, never. "One way," he said, feeling the determination rise in him like a fire, a rush of hatred and hope all at the same time.

"And one way to where?"

"The sea—"

"Pshaw. You cannot keep saying 'the sea.' You must choose."

"Choose for me."

The ticket seller opened his mouth to argue, and then changed his mind. He punched out a ticket and passed it under the grill to Anton. In return Anton passed him the money and received, incredibly, his change. Still unbelieving, he turned from the booth, the precious ticket clutched in his hand.

"Good choice," he heard someone say. The voice was low, with a foreign accent. Anton turned. The man feeding the pigeons. His hair was slicked back and his eyes were laughing.

"I too have a one-way ticket to the sea. Will you not join me?"

Anton clutched his ticket. Cold, biting anger froze his mouth into a "no." The man's face took on a wariness that told Anton not to stop.

He couldn't have placed it, but it was as if his freedom was being cut off at the root. Who was this mysterious feeder of birds, this unseemly fellow traveler? Anton had the image of the man luring the pigeons with his corn and caraway seeds, his kind words and trusting touch, and then without warning, snapping the birds' downy necks.

"No!" He shouted into the man's face before he ran down the platform, startling the matrons in their loden-green traveling suits, alarming the stout young executives puffing their stomachs out like the fat, vain pigeons. He had been the victim of too many demons to let one more enter his life. He ran to the end of the platform where his train waited, and swung himself up to the top step. Panting, he grabbed the conductor.

"That man—"

The conductor pulled away. "Where is your ticket?" he demanded.

For a second Anton imagined the ticket was lost; but no, it was firmly in his grip. He almost couldn't bear to part with it, even to give it to the conductor.

The conductor handled the stiff card with the tips of his fingers. "Humph." He clipped the corner and wordlessly handed it back, his attention already on the next—and much cleaner—passenger. Anton looked out the window. The bird man was gone.

For the first time that day, Anton allowed himself to forget his fears. He sat down on the plush seat and lightly felt the upholstery with the backs of his knuckles.

Again, he seemed to be in a dream: sunlight turning the train windows into prisms, passengers finding their berths and speaking softly to each other, newspapers rattling into position, sandwiches emerging from yawning wicker hampers. Anton sniffed. Sausage and kraut on rye bread. He was hungry, even after the strudel, but it was a good hunger, excited and certain of being filled. He was leaving. *Leaving.*

The train jolted, rolled backwards, whistles blew, bells rang, then a plaintive, cautious breath and—they were off!

The train burst into speed, rollicking down the track. He matched his own breath to the clack of the wheels. It was true. He had done it.

He was gone.

xii

Monsieur is in his Paris warehouse and atelier above the gallery and showrooms. High ceilings, arched windows, slightly dusty, alive with street sounds and summer breeze.

Downstairs, the galleries are a profusion of flocked wallpapers and Old Masters "in the school of." The second level is a warren of offices and showrooms for furniture and functional arts: ceramics, silver, houses for sale. The third floor holds Anton's flat and a workroom. The top story is for restoration and examining the new acquisitions. The canvases kept there on their rolling frames are the basis of Anton's education.

This afternoon Anton is in his shirtsleeves as he moves the paintings from one side of the room to the other. He does not wear his new waistcoat. Instead, a carpenter's bib covers his clothing.

The room is hot, but Anton favors the heat. He loves his work. Moving the canvases reminds him that after a lifetime of begging and stealing, he is a self-made man. A bastard Jew saved from the streets, he could soon be the owner of this select establishment. Moving the canvases reminds him that life is a combination of hard work and stealth.

Today he is showing the Contessa Bella di Longhi a tondo "in the school of Botticelli." But there is proof the master's hand has been on this round board, an allegory of Eve clothed. She is sitting on a rock throne while a grass snake slithers over her toes.

The trees behind her could almost be growing out of the picture, and this much is apparent: the trees are cuttings from Eden. Offshoots of the tree of knowledge of good and evil, they have grown tall, and Eve has been eating their fruit daily.

Her dress is bunched at the waist and sleeves with a cord parodying the curves of the amiable snake at her feet. The fabric is covered in a pattern of leaves like her first clothing when she and Adam realized they were naked in the sight of God. Anton is convinced the picture is a fake. And he wants the Contessa to buy it.

## xiii

"Paco!"

The child defiantly kicks the burlap sacking away; a dog barks at the Contessa.

"What are you doing, you little beast?"

"My name isn't Paco! It's Amin!"

"Amin, donkey-ass. Out of here, you wretch. Take the dog. Where are you going? What is in your pocket? Go, go, get out!"

Paco-Amin makes a face at the Contessa, who is caught as it were, with her defenses down, and he runs down the stairs, the dog at his heels. Anton is flustered and grateful. Women adore children. The image of the boy will make her lay down all her money; she will love this painting for no other reason than she loves the child.

## xiv

"Who is the boy?"

"No one. A street urchin."

"He said his name is Amin."

"I like to call him Paco. But he is not important."

"Oh, but he is. Very important. How much does he cost?"

Anton's face darkened. "He is not for sale."

"Come now. Everyone is for sale. Even me."

Anton pushed the painting to one side and mopped his face with a red kerchief, cheap and common and ordinary. He was proud of his ordinariness. But she would not have the boy.

The Contessa slapped her gloves into her left palm; once, twice, three times. "Anton."

He looked up, wishing he had a cold mug of beer in front of him. He would take one swallow to quench his desperate thirst—God, it was hot—and then he would toss the rest right into this woman's face. Traffic noise blared into the room; plaster fell from the high vaulted ceilings.

"There is no sale without the boy." The woman was insufferable.

"Then there is no deal."

The Contessa walked to the false Botticelli and Anton could see the thwarted rage behind her cool porcelained smile. "We shall see." She tapped his cheek with her hand before she extended her unvarnished nails, dragging them expertly across his cheek, deep enough to sting. His stomach roiled. He should tear off that icy suit and shove her down to the burlap sacking.

xv

He sat in the dark of the gallery, the front door locked, the heat off. Christmas. He had been away for three months. Snow fell deeply over the city, piling the streets. The shops would be closed for the next two days. The street, what he could see of it from the attic window where he sat wrapped in an old quilt, was more tranquil than it had ever been. In the early afternoon the storefronts remained unlit while their mechanical displays stood frozen in mid-air: a Father Christmas bent at the waist, removing a toy bugle from a bulging velvet sack; a marionette in grotesque abandon, left foot flung over its shoulder, wooden eyes in its wooden skull staring out onto the empty street. Dolls in satin capes sat lifeless and bored, yet there was a beauty in their ennui Anton could not help but appreciate. Like the toys, Anton felt he too could unwind and savor what was left of his freedom. He took a bite from one of the chocolate bars he had brought upstairs with him. The old pain of an untended tooth flared up for a second when the cold and sugar reached the back of his mouth. He winced and looked out onto the undisturbed blanket of snow covering the street, shroud-like and virginal. Not even the birds had left their prints. Christmas had never held any sentiment for him.

An unmarked car moved silently across the Platz. He watched its slow orbit as it picked its way past Schimmel's shoe store, pausing outside the antique carpet emporium. He wondered if the driver had seen the lecherous marionette, or the thievish Father Christmas who seemed to be stealing, rather than bringing gifts. The car crawled up the street, leaving wide tire tracks in its wake. Finally it stopped outside the door to the gallery. Anton considered leaping. Out the window, down into the courtyard; he could run if he didn't fracture his legs.

He looked out the window again. Two men in army-issue overcoats and felt hats stood in front of the door, speaking quietly. Falling snow muffled their words, their gestures; Anton had the strange sense of being underwater as he watched them consider their next move. Soundlessly, he traded the quilt for his own overcoat. He patted the pockets. The money he kept hidden was still there. Was there anything else he should take? He scanned the room. The first firm knocks sounded at the door. In seconds they would be rattling the handle, shaking panes of glass before they dispensed with legalities and broke in like the criminals they were.

He crept to the small window facing the courtyard. The gate had never been fixed; he could be down the alley and gone in less than five minutes. He knew hiding places they would never dream of. He heard the door rattle. There was no time for further indecision. He crawled onto the ledge and jumped, remembering to roll when he fell. The jump was over before he realized he had made it. The snow helped but he knew from the ache rising in his back he would pay for this act of insanity during the night. Too bad. Go, go, his brain screamed. His feet were clumsy in the snow. He could hear the crash of glass. They were inside. He ran. The gate, as he expected, split open. Bless you, Frau Schimmel. Bless your laziness, your meanness, your inattention to detail. He closed the broken slats as easily as he had shoved them apart. And then he ran toward the stinking holes of his childhood; the past—

# 24

I pulled on a pair of jeans and a cotton sweater, and then on the spur of the moment, added a pair of sunglasses and heels. Not wanting it out of my sight, I filled the frightful crocodile bag with necessities: keys, wallet, tissues. No ether. No manuscript. I needed to be with people; real people who didn't walk with magical panthers or dress like tropical birds, or lived to be a hundred years old.

The midday tube to Oxford Circus was nearly empty, giving me the space to sit undisturbed behind my sunglasses and handbag. The few passengers at the other end of the carriage talked unabashedly on their ubiquitous cell phones; cheery, demanding, petulant voices that morphed into a continuous drone. I felt invisible, unwanted and unimportant. The last few days had robbed me of personality, identity. I felt hollowed out; a nobody.

The doors to the train opened with a *whoosh* of hot air that stayed with me as I rode the escalators up to the street level. Bright, flashy posters lining the walls gave me the idea that I should go shopping for new winter clothes, but when I stepped outside into the daylight, the congested streets closing in on me, I knew I had made a mistake. I should have stayed on the train. The shop windows were caricatures dressed in black and gray. The severe clothing, dour and unadorned and worse than my own "at home" wardrobe, sent me into a renewed depression. Inside the shops it was no better. I held a functional cropped jacket with a pair of unbecoming tapered trousers up to a mirror, and could only think of the gauzy tulles and extravagant gowns I had worn with Anton. I left the fusty changing room, shoving a charcoal pantsuit into the arms of a startled customer on my way out the door.

In my hurry to escape I let myself be pushed and near-trampled with the tide of pedestrians down Regent Street. For once, I was thoroughly disenthralled by the imperial city I called home. Blindly, I walked past my favorite side streets and shop-infested lanes, their pseudo-chichi entrances too close to my memory of walking with Daile and Laurie Granger down a similar backstreet.

It was dusk when I realized I had walked all the way to the co-op studio. The evening dimness made the place appear seedier and smaller than it really was, and I wanted to reverse my steps and walk away as fast as I could. I thought of the message Peter Wilcox had left for me. I waited for a second, dismayed that I seemed to be forever walking in circles of indecision and regret. I rang the bell, my nerves strung to breaking point. A girl I didn't recognize opened the door.

"What do you want?"

"I'm Sara, Sara Bergsen. I used to have a studio here."

The girl's round face remained slack and unwelcoming.

"I'm here to see Peter Wilcox."

"Peter's out."

I stood on my toes to peer over her head. "Do you know if he's left a box for me?"

"How the hell should I know?"

I shifted the croc handbag to my other shoulder. I was about to say something about how much nicer people had been in my student days, when I saw a folder resting next to the supply kitty.

I pointed to the table. "That's it. That folder. It's mine."

The girl stomped to the table, retrieved the folder and then held onto it. She frowned at the name written on the cover.

"This says 'Sara Elliott.'"

"My maiden name."

"Maiden names went out with the ark." She thrust the folder at me before shutting the door in my face with a bang. I wondered where Rafe was finding his tenants. Jail, for starters.

I waited until I was seated on my bus home to pull apart the strip of Velcro keeping the folder closed. I hadn't the least idea what I would find but it wasn't this: several closely written sheets of paper covered in Noreen's handwriting. Like the letter from Miles I had found in Anton's library, there was no indication of where the pages had been written, but they weren't from a letter. If anything, I thought they could be excerpts from a journal of some kind.

The bus gained speed and I replaced the papers back into their folder. Despite her job as an editor surrounded by writers—writers like Twitty Lansbury, I thought with a pang—Noreen had never mentioned any desire of her own to write, or that she kept a journal.

My stomach felt queasy; I hoped it had nothing to do with the start of a dizzy spell or worse, a blackout. Food, I thought, I just need food. I was starving and there was nothing back at the house to eat. Perhaps I could get a salad somewhere. Or a drink.

The bus route ended in a part of the city filled with gaggles of office girls bunched together arm-in-arm. I watched them as I stepped down to the pavement and recalled the number of times Noreen and I had gone to lunch or dinner for no other reason than we had been friends and we relished each other's company. Best friends, I thought, until Rafe, until Anton.

My search for a restaurant became a chore; nothing I saw appealed to me. Then I remembered the Greek place Miles and I had eaten lunch together the day we met, the day he proposed.

Only a few streets away, it didn't take me long to get there, and my worry that it might have disappeared like everything else associated with Miles proved unfounded as I entered the darkened foyer. The hour was still early, and only the tables in the back were occupied, but the building was still firmly *in situ.*

"Table for—?" A Greek schoolboy helping out with the family business handed me a menu.

"Table for one. Just me." The boy's innocent, friendly face seemed so understanding it was all I could do not to break down and weep on his thin shoulder.

He showed me to a booth in the corner. "Drink?"

"Vodka. Frozen."

He left and I was tempted to pull out Noreen's journal pages while I waited, but I only managed to snag my fingernail in the Velcro before the boy returned with my drink and a plate of olives and pita bread. I thanked him with a smile, hoping he wouldn't see my hands uncontrollably shaking. Once he was out of sight again, I lifted the glass with both hands to my burning forehead and let the ice melt onto my skin while I begged my stomach to stop churning.

I sampled the vodka, then ate an olive, losing myself in the salty, earthy taste. Miles and I had sat at just such a table in the front of the restaurant, close to the windows. I remembered the way our knees had touched when our hands met over the menus. *Marry me.*

The schoolboy waiter came back to my table. "Ready to order?"

I held up my empty glass. "Another one of these." We both turned at what sounded like an argument in the kitchen amped up by the sound of breaking plates. An older version of my waiter, this time in sandals and an open shirt, burst through a swing door accompanied by a crone-like woman dressed in black.

"*Yiayia.*" The schoolboy rushed from my table to the old woman's side while the person I assumed was his brother laughed and exchanged places with him, a carpet sweeper still in his hand. Over his shoulder he shouted something in Greek to the kitchen before he turned back to me.

"You were ordering, miss?"

I started to ask for another shot of vodka when I stopped in mid-sentence. The grandmother was staring at me with what most people would think of as hatred. Black bombazine dress, mourning bonnet, face filled with condemnation, she seemed like someone from another world, intent on sending me the evil eye just because she could. Her grandson repeated his admonition to the kitchen crew, and her face took on a

wooden expression that was an ill-disguised attempt at restraint. Under-
neath her deeply carved age lines and quaint dress was a simmering mass of
emotions, fury at the top of the list. My hand collided with the dish of
olives when she shouted, "I remember you!" The fact she spoke English
was as shocking as her outburst.

"You do?" I spluttered, mopping brine with a paper serviette. I didn't
remember her in the least.

Her grandson smiled a bucket of Greek charm as unsettling to me as
his grandmother's anger. In English he said, "Don't mind Nana, she
doesn't remember anybody—not even me and I'm her favorite grandson!"

He walked back to where she stood and bent down to give the old lady
a kiss that she angrily swatted away. The young man laughed again and
began to sweep up the crumbs of honey cakes and pita bread littering the
floor beneath the tables. His grandmother glared at me. "Where is your
bracelet? Where is the gold?"

Something in my face made her grandson stop his sweeping. He ran a
hand through his uncut black hair. "Don't listen to her," he said in a more
dejected tone.

I ate another olive to cover my embarrassment. Somewhere during the
eruption we had skipped my drink order, but I didn't think it was a good
time to remind him. I glanced at the man's throat: a diamond-studded
necklace spelled out the name "Nikos."

"Do you remember the man I was with?" I asked his grandmother, my
stomach on fire.

She spat on the floor. "I remember the gold."

Nikos shrugged. "After her husband, my grandfather, was killed…"
His voice trailed off and he tapped the side of his head. He left the carpet
sweeper behind one of the booths and leaned moodily against an adjoining
table. I caught a whiff from the kitchen: fish and chips.

"How did your grandfather die?"

"He was pushed." I waited and Nikos hunched his shoulders. "From a
roof."

The grandmother scraped a chair across the tiles, nearly causing me to get up and move to another table—one in another eatery.

"Killed!" she shouted. The other diners covered their laughter by concentrating on their food.

Nikos's grandmother moved in closer. Mothballs, rancid perfume; I tried not to repulse her approach. "Murdered!" she screamed in my ear. "By that Satan! And for the gold, the wretched gold. And I saw you wearing it—you can't say no—I saw you—"

Nikos ran to her side. "It's okay, Nana. It's okay."

I picked up a pita triangle and cleared my throat, an uncomfortable ache in my stomach. "Where did it happen?"

"On an island," Nikos said, taking his grandmother's hand. "A place called Ismene. It's privately owned," he added when I couldn't stop myself from moaning.

Of course it was privately owned, I thought, watching the pair leave the dining room. Rafe never shared anything with anyone.

Hours later I sat in the dark of my kitchen, a takeaway container of dolmas and a generous serving of moussaka on the table. Nikos had sent me home with enough food to last a week. Propped next to the phone, Noreen's papers remained unread in their folder, keeping their secrets. After the encounter at the restaurant, I was undecided about the worth of any further "information." I'd already paid a high price for my insistence on going where I had been forbidden, starting with finding Noreen's hair and ending with upsetting a distraught old woman.

I peeled opened the bag of leaking paper containers. The contents had gone cold but they still smelled delicious. I tried a stuffed grape leaf and thought of Noreen eating the same food with Rafe on Ismene. I put the leaf down; the sheen of oil coupled with the tough, stringy fiber suddenly repellent.

Once there had been a time when Noreen and I had known everything about each other, but now I realized, I had known very little, especially the depth of her feelings for Rafe. To be fair, I had never told her what I had honestly thought of my former teacher, either. The day he left for good, I sat on a barstool staring miserably at a foil-wrapped chocolate Easter rabbit pushing a wheelbarrow of daffodils. I remember deriding Rafe to the bartender, seething with the thought that there was no way a chocolate rabbit was going to make up for him walking out the door with six of my filbert brushes, a novel I hadn't finished reading, and a portrait I had painted of him in art school.

My parents hadn't complained when I moved in with Rafe, but I knew Inge abhorred his work. Modern and ostentatious, it represented every barbaric nuance of the industrial, money-gulping world that she and Evan had stood against with their love of animals and the environment, that is, until their "death cries" series.

It wasn't until after the break-up that my mother had the heart to approach me. "What did you see in the man?" Inge had asked after he moved out and I thought my life was over. Good question. I had been flattered like any young, female student by his attention, but inside, I knew she was right; his work was a competent sham, more celebrity than sincerity. I supposed that's what Peter Wilcox had wanted me to know the day he showed me Rafe's painting.

I knew I should return Peter's call and thank him for Noreen's papers, but I worried that talking to him would dissuade me from ringing Rafe. I walked to my easel juggling the phone in my hands. What did I really want? The truth about Noreen? An invitation to Ismene? Or a final chance to find Miles?

It seemed I stood there in the dark with the silent phone for a lifetime, waiting with the same tension I remembered from my early days at art school for the instructors to judge our work. They would prowl the rooms to the sound of the students flipping their large sheets of newsprint over to a fresh page as the models changed positions. The sound was like a great rising wave, or the sudden whir of birds in migration lifting from the ground. I wished I could hear it now, that rush and flurry of turning pages establishing a clean new start.

I stared down at the phone, my mouth dry. By Rafe's standards the night was young. I knew he painted until midnight, and then assembled his guests and hangers-on for a dinner that could last until breakfast. When I was ousted from that jovial mob I vowed our only contact would be through the co-op. One reason I hadn't taken seriously Noreen's suggestion that I move out was because there was nothing she could warn me about Rafe that I didn't know for myself.

I pushed the numbers to his private line.

"Hemmings."

Suddenly I was unable to speak.

"Is this FedEx? Because if it is—"

"It's Sara."

"Sara." A long pause made me think he'd hung up.

"Rafe?"

"Sara. It's been a while."

"I know." For lack of anything better to say, I added, "I've moved out of the studio."

"I heard."

"The reason I'm calling—"

Rafe was momentarily distracted, talking to someone about a missing FedEx package before he came back on the phone.

"Sara, listen," he said. "It's a madhouse around here. Absolutely nuts. I'm putting together a retrospective for Belgrade. Come out and make sense of my life. What do you think?"

"I was calling to find out—"

"If I still cared for you? I've always cared about you, Sara. You know that."

I didn't know anything except Rafe was drunk and this call wasn't going the way I'd planned.

Rafe said, "Don't say no, Sara. I've missed you. It will be like old times. You know the drill. Book your flight to Athens, take the boat to that funky island with the cats, and I'll send a launch to bring you to Ismene, right to my doorstep."

I tried to cut in, but Rafe was in a hurry to go.

"Ciao, darling," he said. "Training a new assistant. You know how it is. See you when you get here." Offhandedly, he ended the call in the same breath that picked up again on his FedEx tirade. Classic Rafe.

I opened the container with the moussaka. My appetite had returned, a sign perhaps that calling Rafe had been the right thing to do. Then again, I was always hungry at the worst possible times.

I tasted a slice of roasted onion seasoned with fennel, and planned what I would take with me to Greece in the morning.

## 25

*"I'm afraid your name isn't on the signature card. There is nothing more we can do, Mrs. Bergsen. Perhaps your husband will be able to explain."*

I sat alone at a sunny bistro table, a glass of ouzo sharing space with a jet-black espresso, the bank manager's voice still nagging in my head. After the morning's debacle of learning Miles's accounts had been cleared out and closed to me, it was a miracle I had made the flight to Athens in one piece. The cheapest seat available, along with getting a cash advance, had maxed out the single credit card in my own name. Now I was not only broke and about to throw myself on the mercy of an ex-lover, but I had the added worry of Miles's depleted fortune—and it was, or had been—a whopper. There was no explanation how the money could have run out, unless my suspicions were correct about having an alter-ego, one who had gone mad at the gambling tables, or had shopped for items of such mind-boggling expense I'd squirreled them away in some "safe place" I would never find again.

The Grecian sea breeze with its scent of salty fish and crushed juniper was warm enough for me to shed the thick cardigan I'd worn buttoned to the chin since leaving London. It felt good to let the sun sink into my neck and back, its rays soaking up some of my tautness and fear. I could still hear the bank manager's scorn when I tried to tell him there had been a terrible mistake. "There are cameras," he had said when I'd thrust my hands toward him, showing him my wedding rings and elaborate gold cuffs. Too late I realized he thought I was about to assault him.

Maybe I should have, I thought as I lifted the ouzo to my lips in an effort to steady my nerves for the meeting ahead with Rafe. I glanced over my shoulder. As on my first visit to the island, I had kept my destination under wraps all day, a subterfuge that had made the bank manager even more cagey and eager to be rid of me. I shook my head and wished the boat would hurry up. Someone from Ismene would be coming to collect me during the next hour, but the wait was becoming increasingly tense and tiresome.

I drank the ouzo, and thought of the Greek restaurant in London. When Miles and I had gone there together, a girl half my age had served us, calling out the short order requests for hummus and more sauce, taramosalata and chips with an East End accent that had made us both smile. I was sure neither Nikos, his brother, nor their strange grandmother had been anywhere near the place back then.

I looked out to the sea, remembering the sound and feel of that distant afternoon with Miles, the cappuccino maker hissing away at full steam while the rain pounded the pavement outside, making the London streets as sad and lonesome as Amsterdam. Miles had toasted our future with a glass identical to the one I held now. And just like then, my hand had trembled, spilling a drop of the sweet anise liquor onto my lip.

The boat from Ismene was taking longer than Rafe had said it would. I turned to watch the other customers sitting alongside the high wall of sunwashed limestone. In the post-lunch lull, only a handful of tourists remained reading guidebooks and the kinds of paperbacks they sold at the airport. Two old men played a game of chess at the table farthest from me, while a German couple diligently wrote out what appeared to be postcards to send home. I knew for certain I wouldn't be buying any postcards, not on this trip, at any rate.

Numbly, I went over in my mind what it was I did hope to accomplish from my journey. A radio from inside the bar was tuned to some local station's version of Greek pop music, and I realized I had no definite plan in mind other than to ask Rafe outright what he knew of Noreen that she hadn't shared with me. That and some vague hope that he could help me locate Miles through Anton—Rafe had, after all, painted his house and grounds with lifelike clarity. He had to know *something*.

A solitary orange cat rubbed its head against the legs of my chair and I reached down to scratch its ears, mindful not to lose the contents of my over-full handbag. Along with Twitty's manuscript, I had jammed Noreen's journal pages, still unread, into a side pocket. Not the stuff of beach reading, but following the same inner prompt that told me to wear my jewelry, I hadn't felt comfortable leaving the pages at home.

"What do you think, kitty?" The cat let me tickle its nose, but a minute later the noisy approach of an outboard motor sent it leaping away. The launch from Ismene chugged toward the dock, stirring up a heady mix of engine oil, sea foam, and some kind of brackish weed. At the boat's arrival, the taverna owner shooed the cat inside where she followed and closed the door with a loud bang. I stared after her, hardly noticing when the German couple embraced, scattering their pens and postcards. Instead, all of my attention was focused back through the taverna window, where the owner stood, her face arrested in an expression that meant one thing in any language: out-and-out, unadulterated fear. And it seemed she had pin-pointed that fear to a single source: the man at the helm of the boat.

I gathered my luggage and walked to the launch, a smile pasted to my face. Basilides, Rafe's island mainstay when it came to anything nautical or mechanical, nodded when he saw me. Pocked and weather-beaten from a life spent outdoors, the man was as taciturn as ever, although I felt a friendly grip to my elbow as he helped me on board.

"We will be an hour before we reach Ismene," he said. "Please to sit wherever you find it most comfortable." He gestured to a trim bar area surrounded by glass.

"Thanks, Basilides. I'll do that."

The time went quickly as I found myself unexpectedly reveling in the expanse of blue sea and the clear, cloudless sky. The last fifteen minutes I stood on deck as I watched the prow speed forward to the rocky outcrop-ping that served as one of the three landing points for the island. The side of Ismene Basilides chose was bare and windswept. Except for the bleating of the goats, their bronze bells competing with the tug of the waves, it would have been easy to believe the island was deserted.

Basilides carried the larger of my bags ashore while I clutched the tote holding the manuscripts, my return air ticket, and an assortment of sketchbooks. Hidden deep within my makeup case, was the bottle of ether, as slim and as seemingly innocuous as the tubes of lipstick and eyeliner surrounding it.

An unwashed Mercedes pulled up in a cloud of ochre dust plumes. The driver could have been Basilides's twin. Apparently he spoke no English, but between us we mimed our way to placing my luggage on the back seat. After another minute conversing with Basilides, we then left him at the dock while we drove inland, the shore never far from sight. We passed more goats, as well as a "village" of whitewashed, flat-roofed dwellings. Set high atop yet another crest of tan rock was a church—more of a chapel, really; its walls painted with some of the sprightliest frescoes I had ever seen, and I looked forward to visiting them again.

One more kilometer and we were at the house. An enormous Bauhaus structure cantilevered into seven distinct platforms attached to each other by a series of steel cables and floating staircases, it was the pinnacle of Rafe's empire. Nothing had changed since I was last here except perhaps for the gardens planted with a pungent vine that wound itself over the sides of the house.

My driver carried my bags to the front door. "Is Mr. Hemmings inside?" I asked, forgetting he only spoke Greek. He shook his head, not understanding my question. I didn't try again. I knew Rafe would be where he always was at this time of day, holding court in his studio and pontificating on art theory, politics, and the downfall of British cuisine.

The thought of entering that studio suddenly made me feel schoolgirlish in my crushed shift, bare legs, and last summer's sandals. I was tempted to turn around and run back to the car, but it was too late. My driver was holding open the door that led into the immense atrium that served as both entry hall and art gallery.

My heels rang out against the tiling as I climbed the open staircase to the upstairs living areas. When I reached the first landing, I could clearly hear voices struggling to cut each other off in the middle of a vicious argument.

"You're a buffoon, Rafe. You always were and you always will be. Why I trusted you to solve any of this, I'll never know."

My hand held tight to the railing. That tony voice could only belong to one person, Monique Claiburne, and Rafe wasn't in his studio. I cringed and felt even more like running back to the car, but a teenager in a maid's uniform was hurrying toward me, all smiles and youthful enthusiasm for her job. She tucked a gold chain into the neck of her uniform.

"It's too late," I heard Rafe say. "She's already on her way here. I expect she'll be at the house in less than ten minutes. You know how Stamos drives. Besides, I've told you, we should get it over with on our own terms."

The maid curtsied with a rehearsed speech: "Please make Ismene your home away from home, madame." She then ushered me to the living room door, the argument in full force.

"You started this problem," Rafe was saying to Monique. They stopped when I appeared in the doorway, my heart thudding while I attempted a sophistication I was far from feeling.

Monique stood with her arms crossed next to a grand piano. A checkered caftan billowed out from her waist, making her look like a shapeless Harlequin. Her face remained creased in an unpleasant scowl as Rafe cinched the belt to his seersucker dressing gown and shuffled forward on rubber flip-flops to impress a kiss on my cheek.

"Sara, darling. You look all done in. Have a drink."

"I had an ouzo at the taverna."

Rafe made a face implying one drink was no reason not to have two. He moved to the cocktail cabinet while Monique uneasily plunked down into a leather sofa that seemed to swallow her whole, an action she countered by focusing her anger on me. I averted my eyes and let her stew.

Rafe shoved a Campari into her hand as she continued to center her bile on me, her eyes raking in my rings and arm cuffs with a look that made me want to sit on them. I thought of the maid pushing that gold chain into her uniform, maybe with good reason.

Monique gripped her drink and Rafe went back to the liquor cabinet. "Are you sure you won't have one?" he wheedled. "We do have ice. I remember you always liked things icy cold."

"Then you'll also remember how much I hate Campari." I couldn't stop my lip from curling. Campari had always tasted to me like something from a dental clinic. I sat on a Macintosh chair that completed the image.

Rafe closed the cabinet doors and then brought his hands together in a tepid attempt to jollify the atmosphere. "Well, Sara, darling," he said, mock-hearty, "I was just about to change and head back to work. It's wonderful that you've arrived, but I think you'll want to settle into your room and re-acquaint yourself with the premises. So I suggest Hypatia here," he paused to beckon to the maid who'd been patiently waiting by the door all this time, "take you back downstairs and then we'll meet up later for dinner. Sound good?"

Hypatia stepped forward. "Madame," she began as Rafe made a hurried and somewhat clumsy exit, "I am so sorry but your room will need a minute longer." She held her fingers apart as if lifting a tiny corner of time. "Just a minute, okay?"

I smiled. She was no more than a child, seventeen at the most. "I can wait," I assured her. She turned to leave, but then stopped when Monique said, "I hope you've cleaned up that mess the dogs made by the pool."

"Stamos is supposed to do that."

"But he isn't here, is he?"

Hypatia seemed confused, and Monique downed her drink. "Oh, don't stand there," she said. "You're like my daughter when she wants to annoy me. Go, clean, do whatever it is you do."

Hypatia ran and Monique stood, not without some effort, to pour herself another drink from the bottle on top of the cabinet.

I twisted my rings back and forth. "How is Courtenay?" I asked, nerves giving my voice a peculiar lift.

"My decision is final. The commission is cancelled." She tasted her drink and added more Campari, not letting the bottle out of her hand.

"Screw the portrait. It's your daughter's behavior that concerns me. I saw her the other day where I don't think she was meant to be."

Monique splashed more of the aperitif into her glass. "Courtenay's never where she should be." She added ice.

A thought occurred to me. "Is she here now?"

"Certainly not. What makes you think that?"

"Oh, I thought you two traveled everywhere together. Country houses. Masked balls." I crossed my legs to quell the urge to run.

Monique sniffed in contempt and returned the bottle to the back of the cabinet. Before she sat down, she carried a vase filled with sprays of rosemary to the glass coffee table. An ugly thing, I knew it was an early work of Rafe's from when he had explored ceramics and worked for a year in Japan. Around the circumference, seven misshapen faces blended and merged until each was indistinguishable from the rest. Similar vases from a set of thirty-six were usually on display whenever Rafe held a retrospective. I'd never liked any of them and the smell of rosemary was over-strong.

"Does that have to be there?"

Monique bared her teeth in unwitting imitation of the vase. I thought of smashing it at her feet.

"I didn't realize you knew Rafe," I said when she didn't reply.

She gave me a look that said she knew everybody and I remembered what Benita Hansard had said: she did. "You shouldn't have come here," she said, adjusting the vase to be closer to me.

"I don't think it's any of your business what I do." An unfinished tapestry draped the end of the piano. King Arthur. It was the same piece she'd been working on when I had gone to the house to sketch Courtenay. A basket of needles and jewel-toned threads sat beside it on the floor, giving the room an uncharacteristic femininity.

Suddenly she was in my face, close enough to make me squeeze uncomfortably against the wooden frame supporting my chair. "Go back, Sara," she said. "Go back while you still have time."

Her anger caused her to trip on the caftan, and I took the opportunity to stand, upending the basket of embroidery silks at the same time. I wasn't about to leave the island, but I had to leave the room. Where I was headed mattered little: the beach, the church; wherever I chose I knew Rafe would still be able to see me. The house and island were wired with more cameras than the Bank of England.

Remembering the morning's fiasco at my own bank together with the loss of my assets put me in a feckless mood. Let him watch, I thought. Let him see who Monique really is. That'll teach him to have eyes in the back of his head. I thought again of the ugly vase and without waiting to hear more from Monique, I hurried to the stairs, my heels sliding on the tiles in my haste. I caught myself from falling as I passed through the open doors and all but skied my way down to the ground floor. I was about to search out a path to the goats when I saw Hypatia approach from my left, her hand at the end of the chain she wore.

"Madame, your rooms are ready," she said in her soft English. "Are you all right? Shall I take you there?"

I nodded, fighting for air. "Sure. Thanks."

The guesthouse turned out to be a new addition. Hypatia opened the door for me with pride. She had unpacked my bags, hanging my summer clothes inside a simple, handcrafted wardrobe. A plain—and far more attractive—glass vase filled with cuttings from the vine outside the main house sat with my lunch tray. Cheese, bread, and a coffee carafe made up my lunch. After my run-in with Monique, it was a spa.

"Would you like anything else?"

The sight of the bed with its white coverlet made me want to get into bed and stay there. "No, this is great. Thank you."

"Very good, madame. Please ring if you need me." Hypatia pointed to a phone on the nightstand. "You can press 'nine' to reach me or the other house staff."

She left and I sat on the bed. "Nine" was the number Teague & Bloch had said to use in case of emergency. They had never answered; I doubted Rafe's staff would be any better.

I leaned against the pillows and massaged my jaws. Except for my childhood amahs, I'd never had a maid at all. Now I had two: Jeanne-Marie and Hypatia; as different from each other as night from day.

I removed my dress and underclothes, and put the idea of maids out of my mind. The draft from the open window blew the curtains into a hypnotic swell and fall, their rhythm matching the slow waves just outside my room. Within minutes I fell into an uneasy sleep, dreaming of Miles. Miles, following another, and much colder, seashore.

*The priest poured wine from a clay pitcher. Hot and spiced, the wine flowed down Miles's throat. The priest handed him a plate of black bread and the smoked herring they had brought from the beach together. The room glowed like a four-paneled icon: gilt cornices, firelight, burnished book bindings. As tired and ill as he was, Miles felt strangely alert in the priest's presence. The food had revived him, preparing him for the next stage of his journey.*

*He looked outside through the casements set into the walls. From where he sat he could see how the ocean fed the shore. Earlier there had been patches of brilliant sunlight; now swirls of fog rolled in with the tide. Somewhere off the coast a storm was birthing. He swallowed a piece of bread, savoring its taste of dried fruit and nuts. He reached for another crust, the bread midway to his mouth, when the door opened.*

*The priest turned to greet a new guest standing in the last rays of light. "Ah, Kaminsky," he said. "You have arrived just in time."*

I woke to the sound of the shudders hitting the wall, the breeze having turned to a warm night wind. After dreaming of a room bathed in light, the darkness disoriented me. I must have been asleep for hours.

Despite the wind, the sea was quiet; only the tiniest wavelets shimmered in the light of a burgeoning moon. I thought of the night I had stood with Anton at the riverbank. Had he just returned from that same cloister? From seeing Miles?

I drank some of the coffee, knowing dinner would be late. Listening to the sea, I felt a peace descend regardless of the emotional storm that had blown me to Ismene. On the wall above my bed, a crucifix made from a tree branch was nailed to the stucco. Gingerly, I reached up to touch the unpolished wood. The simplicity of the ancient symbol had permeated my school days at St. Anne's, but I had never been a believer; not then, not now.

In place of faith, a shower in the functional bathroom would have to serve as baptism and absolution all in one. While the water poured, I thought of Anton's references to the idea of penance, but I remained as ignorant of the concept as I had ever been. The best I could do was dress for dinner and put on my makeup. *Lipstick, mascara, ether.*

Out of the shower, I held the ether in my hand, knowing it was the antithesis of everything that simple cross above my bed embodied, and concentrated on my choice of dinner clothes.

Rafe would be at the head of the table where he always sat, and a piece of my vanity, a piece that embarrassed me as much as my need for the ether and my lack of belief, still wanted him to look down from that lofty place and see me. *Just to see me.*

## 26

Twenty or more strangers in various states of inebriation lolled on an open-air balcony that stretched the full upper floor of the house. I wandered self-consciously amongst their conversations and haute couture, my hair falling forward to hide my face. Even with my gold arm bands I felt like an imposter, an uninvited guest in a borrowed lace skirt and a tangerine halter I'd taken from Noreen and never returned.

I made my way to a buffet covered with hors d'ouevres and champagne buckets while upper-crust voices swirled around me like confetti:

"When I was in Budapest last year…"

"You won't remember the time we had the pools drained…"

"That dreadful man who claimed he wanted to kidnap someone…and did!"

The high-pitched, senseless posturing sounded like what I had heard at Anton's masked ball, and just as confusing. I picked at a filo pizza layered with baked tomatoes while I told myself to stay put. If I was to get anything out of Rafe, I couldn't turn tail and run. Not now. Not after coming all this way.

Hypatia and Stamos brought stainless steel catering carts from the kitchen, the signal for everyone to assemble around the main dining table. As if on cue, Rafe and Monique appeared from the wings like actors commanding the stage, Rafe assuming his customary place at the head of the table while Monique was left to find her own more ambiguous seat.

"Over here, Sara," Rafe called out, patting the chair to his right. "I want you where I and everyone else can see you." A minor shockwave passed through the party.

"This is Sara Elliott," he said as I took my place. "One of my former students." I found his choice of words interesting.

"It's actually Bergsen. Sara Bergsen," I said to the group, stretching my smile. Hypatia ladled a creamy soup into bowls Stamos placed before each guest. Sea-green capers floated to the surface, bringing a bona fide gloat to Rafe's face.

He lifted his glass. "To Sara Elliott *Bergsen* then," he stressed. "I hope you'll feel right at home."

Glasses clinked mechanically and Rafe nodded in Monique's direction. "You know Monique. And next to her we have—" He reeled off names and brief descriptions that meant nothing to me. A fashion model, a couple of art students, someone's stockbroker and his mother. From past experience I knew they were purely decorative and filled Rafe's days on the island with the illusion that he was a generous host. The truth, however, was he couldn't bear to be alone for more than twenty minutes at a time. Which would have been touching if he wasn't as equally anxious to keep the people that mattered—family, lovers, art critics—as far away as he could manage. I tasted my soup followed by a sip of wine and decided Rafe was beyond analysis; he was a force of nature.

The first course over, Hypatia cleared the soup plates as Stamos set out our salads: asparagus, baby sprouts, shredded beetroot, crumbled feta. The wine flowed freely as Rafe's guests fell back into their earlier conversations that thankfully excluded me. I had no desire to explain, if asked, what had brought me to Ismene. I looked out across the balcony and the woman next to me whispered to her neighbor:

"There was blood everywhere. It was horrible. They got everything cleared up, and when it was over you'd never know it happened, but it makes you think twice."

I pushed my fork into an asparagus spear, trying not to appear too obvious that I was listening. The girl Rafe had referred to as the model said, "Imagine bringing a panther. A real one." She tore off a piece of bread.

"The costumes were amazing, though. I wanted to take those feathered masks home with me."

The panther, the feathered masks. She had been there. I hadn't been dreaming.

"Sara, Sara," Rafe chided, noting my stunned expression. "You appear to be in the depths of despair. Smile, darling. Chin up. Tummy in. Chest out. It's a party."

Dutifully, I grinned.

Rafe set his wineglass down and cupped my chin with his hand. His fingers felt greasy. "I'm going to tell myself that you came all this way just to see me."

"Why else would I be here?" I asked, pulling away. I wiped my chin with a serviette I found under my chair.

I was desperate to find a way to ask the model what panther, what party, but instead I said to Rafe, "It's true. I did come here to see you, but maybe not for the reasons you think."

"What reasons would those be?"

I looked down the length of the table. The two women discussing the panther were now intent on a plate of broiled mullet making the rounds boarding-house style, while Monique listened to the stockbroker's mother, a glazed expression of distaste on her patrician face.

"Why is Monique here?" I asked.

Rafe sat back in his chair. "I invited her. She's a help to me. You're not jealous, are you?"

I shook my head, and he said, "In that case, sweets, don't you think this game has gone on too long? Even for you?"

"What do you mean?"

"Just that I know more than you think I do, darling. With or without the help of modern technology."

"The All Seeing One?" Rafe had given himself the title after having the cameras installed. Several of his less coherent houseguests, drunk at the time on retsina and vodka martinis, had thought it was his usual narcissism speaking, but I knew it was more than that. Rafe liked to watch.

I covered the rest of my food with the serviette. "You might know what goes on in our bedrooms," I said, "but you can't read minds."

The model, I noticed, had taken her plate to the edge of the balcony and was feeding the gulls. The sea air lifted her hair from her neck. Rafe eyeballed her for a moment and then left his chair to stand behind me, placing his chilled glass between my shoulder blades. The halter top might not have been the smartest choice.

"What are you doing?"

"Testing your reactions." He slid the glass down my back. I shivered despite my resolve to play along.

"Reactions to what?" I asked, fending off the glass. "To see how far you can go before I'm annoyed?"

He turned me around to face him. His eyes had the same cold glitter I'd felt through my skin from the wine glass.

"You aren't married, are you, Sara? Why don't you just come clean and tell me this is another of your famous 'episodes'? I won't be mad. In fact, I think it's fortuitous you've come to me for help."

I held out my left hand and looked at him as though he had been the one to lose his mind. "Wedding rings."

He examined my arm in the light. "And if I'm not mistaken, this is a new cuff. Gift from hubby?"

"Rafe—" I stopped. Monique was on her feet, coming toward us.

"Rafe," she interrupted, "if we're going to see the film we have to get started. I suggest we have coffee and dessert while it's playing." Monique indicated that Hypatia should start clearing the table.

"Coming to join us?" Rafe asked.

"I don't think so."

"Suit yourself." Rafe was about to leave when I put my hand on his sleeve.

"We have to talk," I said.

"I thought that's what we were doing now." Rafe smiled in Monique's direction.

"Tomorrow?"

Hypatia stepped forward with the coffee pot. "May I serve—?"

Rafe took Monique's arm without replying. Together they walked past Hypatia. Miffed, she held the pot out to me, her eyebrows lifted.

"No, thanks," I said, my attention on the lounge. A blue glow dappled Rafe's guests in indigo and turquoise as they took their seats around the room. Silently, Hypatia left me.

Playing against a mega-sized wall, the film I had seen in the London wine bar with Laurie Granger and Daile turned the room into an undersea grotto.

Stamos ambled toward me. "You don't join the others?" he asked, stopping to wipe down a chair covered in soup.

"That's all right, I'll just be a minute here," I said, forgetting he had never spoken English in my presence before.

I couldn't take my eyes from the screen. New scenes that hadn't played in the wine bar came into focus. The diver and the manta ray were still the primary subjects, but now I could also see a trove of statues and barnacle-encrusted amphorae tilting every which way in the water.

The diver paddled above them, swimming next to a pile of rocks where he then plummeted deeper to the seabed. When he lifted his hand, air tanks bubbling in the clear water, his excitement at the sparkle of gold was unmistakable.

The ray flapped its wings in slow motion as the film wound to a close and dissolved to a black screen. From somewhere within the audience, one of Rafe's guests passed around a bong with the baklava.

I left the table and stood at the balcony rail, trying to understand why Rafe had chosen to show that film above any other. Hypatia had come outside again and was helping Stamos stack the chairs.

"Is there anything I can get for you, madame?" she asked. The medal around her neck rested outside of her uniform; she didn't bother hiding it from me this time.

"No, I'm just tired. I think I'll go to bed. Don't work too late." I smiled and took the balcony steps down to the beach and the guesthouses.

Inside my cabin I drew the curtains and shed my now-wrinkled skirt and the poor choice of a halter top. The only thing I wanted was to read Noreen's papers and then go to sleep.

I took the folder into bed and adjusted a lamp. Noreen's handwriting had always been difficult to decipher, and the sepia ink—the ink I had used at Anton's—didn't make the task any easier.

*Informal meals are brought to me, all kinds of things, from toast to peach liqueur drenched cherries. Where these foods come from has not been explained to me. Nothing is explained to me, and I have that feeling I used to have during childhood: a sense of eternity—that time has stopped and that nothing will—or can—ever change.*

*Not that I care much. Here on the estate there are no bills to be paid, no unhappy authors complaining about the small size of their royalty checks, or asking me what I was thinking to alter their immortal words and penmanship.*

*I eat, I sleep, I walk the grounds and never give a thought to news reports of train station bombings, lowering IQ figures, or wars in countries I've never seen. Life here is an eternal summer. I cannot pretend to miss the outside world, and even if I don't understand a word of those rows and rows of books in Kaminsky's library, who cares?*

*If I could, I would want to paint all of this, to hold the colors forever.*

*I started to write "If I was like Sara," but she holds herself back. She paints only what her clients expect and regard as "safe." How can she want to be safe when there are so many shades and variations in life—constantly changing with kaleidoscopic ease? Take green for instance, the green in the panther's eyes reflecting me back to myself like some mirror trick. At times I could enter his eyes and follow that green light to someplace even deeper. I think it's the depths that Sara fears most.*

*Is this madness? Or the residue of a prepared hallucinogen I am digesting with those simple meals? But nothing seems as disconnected as I would think insanity or drug use would be. If anything, I am exceedingly clear-headed. I am totally, ultimately alive. I am reborn. The air is finer to my touch; my sight and hearing are so much more vivid than in the past.*

*It's as if everything I had known before was only a walking death and now I am entering my first real experience of life, of myself. And if I am to believe Kaminsky, it's because of Sara and that bangle of hers. Kaminsky wants it. But this is from the man who asked if I would mind giving him the hair I had cut last week. Talk about crazy. I*

*told him to ask Rafe and he hasn't mentioned it again since. Which doesn't mean
anything other than—I have to stop writing; somebody's coming—*

I couldn't read the rest; the lines were lost beneath the splatters from
an ink spill. No matter; I had read enough to know that Noreen had indeed
been on Anton's estate. And I'd also read enough to know that every word
she wrote about me was true: I did hold back, I was afraid to live, and I
couldn't keep blaming my past.

With or without the ether, I relied too much on outside forces to support and carry me. Miles, for instance. Left to my own devices, I was in
shambles. I turned out the light and wondered if it was the "depths I
feared" that made me unable to throw the blue vial away.

As soon as day broke, I showered and dressed in a pair of capris
topped with a cotton shirt and my jewelry. I then set off for the church
without waiting for Hypatia to bring my breakfast.

My walk up the hill was haunted by disjointed thoughts of last night's
dinner and Noreen's journal entry. Remembered fragments of the evening
threatened to trip me worse than the rocks underfoot: the women talking
about what had to be the ball I attended with Anton...the odds of that
underwater film appearing here on Ismene...Rafe saying I was mad,
hallucinating, prone to the hysteria that had broken us up as a couple and
still kept me from dealing with my parents...Noreen believing I was a
stick-in-the-mud loser. Something was wrong with me, I couldn't deny it.
But I refused to doubt my marriage to Miles. If I wasn't married, how had I
purchased the house? How had I met Daile and Laurie Granger? Where
did I get my wedding rings?

I stopped beside a lavender hedge, the flower heads so top-heavy the
stems bent to the ground, and gathered an armful with the thought of
decorating the church. The sharp herbal scent of the flowers mixed with
the dry salty air, clearing my head. *This,* I thought, *this is real.* I had to
believe I was sane. I had to believe I was well and healthy and able to keep
living. I took as much of the lavender as I could carry and then continued
on, emptying my mind of everything but the beauty of the island.

I reached the church feeling almost light-hearted. On some level I thought my profane thoughts from last night had been heard; the church wanted me here. I pushed open the doors. Other than a new coat of paint on the windowsills, everything was just as I remembered it. The quiet of the sanctuary was as peaceful as that grotto in Rafe's strange film, and I drank it in like water.

After a minute I sat on one of the benches lining the walls and held the lavender loosely on my lap. Despite the intrusion of Rafe's cameras that I supposed had tracked me to the front door, my overwhelming sensation was one of safety and solace. I lifted my eyes and noted with pleasure the frescoes I had come to see, scenes of the disciples hauling their fish-filled nets onto improbable nursery-sized boats. One corner of the ceiling still made me smile with its depiction of the Blessed Virgin negotiating the price of sardines.

Beneath the frescoes, red votives flickered against rows of solitary tin arms and legs, the dismembered limbs interspersed with fading photographs of boats and mustachioed men in shorts and singlets, their smiles as wide as the bay itself. I wished I had some photos of Miles and Noreen to place alongside and keep them company. I tried to think of a prayer, not sure what good it would do, when a wail followed by a sob broke through the silence. The sound seemed to come from outside.

I left my bench to peer out the door. A woman crouched against a retaining wall marking off the courtyard. She held her hand to her mouth as if to hold back her sobbing and to communicate something to me at the same time. I was sure I recognized her from Rafe's dinner last night; she still wore the same vintage dress, the kind I'd seen in old magazines: draped fabric covered in printed poppies bright as bloodspots.

"Can I help?"

Her face darkened as she silently appraised my jewelry.

"Did you want to go inside the church?"

"Never!"

Puzzled, I stood still, trying not to frighten her any further.

From her demeanor it appeared my efforts were of no use; she stooped deeper into a squat, and then sank to her haunches, her eyes drawn uneasily to my face. I was the frightened one now. I remembered the panther striking out at the masked ball, and the tension between us became unbearable until suddenly she was on all fours, scuttling along the base of the wall like a crab or a large spider.

"I'm not going to hurt you," I called after her. "I don't even know who you are."

She skidded to a halt and twisted her face over her shoulder. Her eyes flashed. "Your jewelry," she growled. "You should not wear the gold!"

I looked at the cuffs on each of my wrists. Before I could ask more she spat out: "He will take it from you. He will kill you for it, but he will not give it to me. No, he never gives it to me! Only to her, the English bitch." Her Greek accented vowels sounded like the long pull of a steel knife grating through a sharpener.

"Who? Who will kill me?" I faltered.

She jutted her chin down the hill toward the house. "Him," she said. The way she said it, the word came out like "heem."

My skin crawled. The woman's tone was eerily close to that of the Greek grandmother back in London. I wanted to ask if she was referring to Rafe, but the question died on my lips when she stood and sprinted away to the open hillside. I watched her go in the direction of the village until all I could see was the powdery dust raised by her bare feet, blocking her from sight.

Thoroughly bewildered, I went back inside the church to reclaim my bundle of lavender. I had to leave, now, and I decided to take the longest and least convenient path to the house, a trail secreted behind an embankment of cypress and juniper.

I could feel the plant stems wilting in my damp palms as I hurried down the rocky walkway. I couldn't rid my thoughts of the woman and the madness in her eyes, and I crushed the flowers as if trying to crush out the sound of her voice.

A resinous oil covered my hands, and instead of the refreshing scent I had loved only minutes ago, the smell of the lavender buds sickened me, reminding me of the ether, and I fought against the impulse to find—and use—the stuff as soon as I returned to my guesthouse.

Rafe and his "friends" had done something to that woman, something that had scared her witless. I turned to the ditch running alongside me, and tossed the lavender as far away as it would go.

## 27

"Madame Bergsen?" Hypatia wheeled her bicycle over to where I stood beside the ditch. "Are you okay?"

I jumped. I wanted to ask what she was doing out here by herself so early in the day, but all I could do was take a shallow breath and weakly gesture toward the hilltop. "There was a woman at the church. She—she frightened me."

Hypatia scanned the road, balancing the bike with both hands. "I did not see anyone," she said. "Are you sure?"

"Of course I'm sure," I replied more sharply than I intended. Hypatia flinched, and I said, "I'm sorry. She was just so odd. I think she's a guest of Mr. Hemmings."

The morning sunlight made Hypatia look young and pretty in a frilly blouse worn loose over a short denim skirt. Her black patent leather sandals were an exact match to a pair I'd noticed Monique wearing at dinner.

"Do you live in the village?" I asked attempting to fill what had turned into an uncomfortable silence.

"No. But my mother does." She smiled. "She would be honored if you would visit her."

I hesitated and Hypatia said, "Please. Come and have something to eat. You have not had breakfast yet."

The sparkling white houses below us huddled on the hillside leading down to the sea. My morning plans hadn't included socializing. All I had wanted was to see the frescoes and take a break from the undertones that always followed Rafe wherever he went, home or abroad. But Hypatia was waiting for my answer, a pleading expression in her velvety brown eyes.

"All right," I agreed, thinking it was a pity I didn't have a sketchbook with me. "But I don't want your mother to go to any trouble. Promise?"

"Promise." We walked the short distance down the hill, Hypatia steering her bicycle toward her family's small single-story house projecting over the bay. A steep, twisting staircase led straight down to the water, while at the top of the stairs the front door was already open to welcome us. The surname "Palakis" was painted above the doorframe surrounded by laurel leaves.

"Mama," Hypatia called out. "I have brought Mrs. Bergsen."

Hypatia's mother came to meet us wearing the prosaic black worn by all the island's married women, with the addition of a red gingham apron. Her hair was knotted into a bun she kept secured with a gold and coral comb. After she had kissed and greeted me with an exuberance I attributed to her living so far away from Rafe's enclave, she saw me checking out the ornament.

"It's beautiful, no?" she asked, pulling it loose. Long brunette hair tumbled around her shoulders. Hypatia laughed and kissed her mother's cheek.

"Mama, you should always wear your hair down like that. You are still young, you know."

Hypatia's mother clicked her tongue. "Don't be such a child. I am simply showing Mrs. Bergsen what your father gave me for our betrothal." She handed me the comb.

Finely carved and inlaid with star-shaped pieces of bright coral, it was obviously very old and worth a great deal of money. It was also uncannily similar to my own armbands. Mrs. Palakis placed it in my hand.

"For you."

"Oh, no, I couldn't."

"A gift. Besides," she added, "it goes with your dowry."

"Dowry? These are just—" What were they? "These are just family pieces, from my mother," I concluded, dissatisfied with my answer.

"Now you have another 'family piece.'"

The subject closed, she then showed me to a table loaded with honey-soaked breads, pistachios and dried fruit, making me believe Hypatia's invitation wasn't quite as spontaneous as she'd made me think.

"Sit, sit," Mrs. Palakis said, radiating hospitality.

Hypatia poured thick Turkish coffee into tiny cups followed by glasses of her mother's homemade "herbal liqueur." When her two older brothers came inside, hot and freely sweating from their morning's work in the olive groves, I was ready to fall asleep. The constant chatter accompanying a pictorial saga of wedding albums, snapshots of distant relatives in New York and Iowa, and incongruously, a series of store-bought photographs featuring movie stars and pop idols from the 1960s came to an end when I asked to use the bathroom.

"This way," Hypatia said rising to her feet and swatting away her brother's hand when he reached for the last pastry. "That's for Mrs. Bergsen. Our *guest*."

"No, please, I couldn't eat another thing," I protested as Hypatia took me through her mother's bedroom to a tiled room facing the ocean and filled with conch shells.

Hypatia joined me at the window. She reached across and straightened the comb in my hair. "It is right that this is yours now," she said. "It is like my mother knew it belonged to you." Before I could reply she laid a clean towel over the basin rim and left me alone.

I used the old pull-chain toilet, and after washing my hands with a bar of pumice soap, I placed my damp towel on top of a hamper, sending one last, appreciative gaze out to the ocean. The sight made me wish I could recapture the innocence of my childhood travels; the freedom and luxury of journeys that required nothing more from me than my good and quiet behavior. Regretfully, I polished the stones on my rings with the edge of my shirt and thought it was time I returned to my hostesses.

On my way back through the bedroom I noticed the door had been closed to give me, I supposed, an added element of privacy. The spotless room with its tinted photographs of fat babies and old married couples presiding over the lace curtains and crocheted bedspread reminded me of my grandmother's room. I was thinking how much Gran would have liked the hand hewn furniture when my attention was seized by a wooden chair draped with a colorful piece of silk. Except when I looked more closely, the silk was acetate, and I thought I would be sick.

As gaudy as the first time I'd seen it back in London, Daile's Eiffel Tower scarf was now in the bedroom of a housemaid's mother on an island in Greece. Even before I saw the pearlescent lipstick smear gracing the top of Paris's most famous landmark, I knew it was the one Daile had left behind. In less than a minute I had it under my shirt and tied around my waist, the ends tucked into the front of my pants.

I returned to the combined kitchen and living room where Hypatia's mother was preparing yet another plate of halva, and tried to appear apologetic. "It's been a fantastic visit," I said, "but I do need to get going. Mr. Hemmings is expecting me." Hypatia agreed with my lie and said it was time to head back.

"Yes, Mama, we have to go."

We said our goodbyes and Hypatia retrieved her bicycle. I thanked her mother again for the hair ornament while the stolen scarf burned its way into my waist like a brand. I couldn't imagine how Mrs. Palakis didn't feel the heat of it as she hugged me in an excess of affection I was certain I had done nothing to merit.

Once we were out the door, my legs were noodles. When Hypatia bumped the bike over the stones dividing her house from the road, I lost my footing, threatening to send us both down to the water below.

"Be careful," Hypatia warned. I didn't need to be told twice.

I helped her carry the bicycle back onto the road and we started the trek back to Rafe's. Hypatia pushed the bike in silence. Away from her family's exuberant company, she had reverted back to the shy, self-contained girl that came to my room only to clean, or deliver food. For my part, all I could think of was the scarf around my waist.

"Have you always lived on the island?" I asked somewhat woefully.

Hypatia's face lit up. "Oh, no. None of the villagers are from here." She laughed. "We are all imports." She slowed her gait to explain. "Before Mr. Hemmings, the island was deserted. Ismene was not even called 'Ismene.' It had a name that is hard to translate, but it meant the meeting of the sun and the moon."

There they were again: sun and moon and a million questions in between. "Do you mean an eclipse?" I asked, thinking of the fuss the TV and radio, and even Twitty Lansbury, had made about what was apparently the next "big one."

"An eclipse?" Hypatia frowned. "That is a close meaning, but it is also more about the power of the two together. Do you understand?" She lowered her voice. "However you say it, the island was somewhere people did not go to." She brought her bicycle to a stop. "Mr. Hemmings had to pay a lot of money to get his workers to move here."

"But what about the church? Surely someone lived here before Mr. Hemmings."

"They say a group of monks was here at one time. But nobody can remember when."

We started walking again, the bicycle wheels churning the dust. "There is a place even older than the church," she said, casting me a sideways glance. "A labyrinth cut into the ground."

A labyrinth. That made me pay attention, but Hypatia drifted back into her earlier silence as we climbed the dusty road intersecting the vineyards on one side and the sea on the other. Halfway up the incline Hypatia decided to walk the rest of the way barefoot. Even wheeling the heavy bicycle, she scampered over the ground like one of the goats.

The wind rustled through the grass as I followed behind her, the air full of late summer hints of the autumn to come: *Ismene, Ismene.* I wondered what village life was like when Rafe left the island to strut through his galleries and television circuits.

"Do you get lonely out here?"

"How could I? Mr. Hemmings has so many dramatic and creative guests." She smiled. "Like you."

I didn't know whether to feel lauded or admonished. "How long have you worked for Mr. Hemmings?"

She counted the time on her fingers. "Maybe six months? I do remember the day I started was the day Mrs. Claiburne crashed the car."

"An accident?"

She nodded. "At the time I thought it was a bad sign to start working on such a day, but everything has turned out fine." She raised her voice, the wheels of her bicycle squeaking over the stones. "It was terrible for that poor girl, no?"

"What girl?"

"I can't remember her name," she said, "but she was taken to the hospital by boat. Everyone said she was going to be okay. But an accident is no good. I felt bad for her."

Somehow I kept walking; Noreen had been in a car accident, in Greece. Except she hadn't been okay. I wanted to ask more, much more, but we had reached the end of the path. Monique Claiburne stood waiting for us beside the stuccoed pillars marking the entrance to the house.

Hypatia visibly stiffened at the same time I felt my stomach muscles constrict. Even from where we stood I could see the angry set of Monique's mouth, a hardened gash of deep rust red. I held the bicycle upright while Hypatia stepped back into her shoes.

Hypatia bent over to tighten a strap when Monique pounced on us. She shot me a look of undiluted venom before turning her irritation on Hypatia. "I didn't give you those shoes to traipse about in the dirt and dust," she said. Immediately Hypatia turned a shade close to Monique's own flaming cheeks. Monique whirled to face me. "And I would ask you not to waste the servants' time."

"But it is my morning off," Hypatia said.

"It's twelve-thirty. You were needed in the kitchen an hour ago."

Hypatia scurried away, and all I could think of was Monique being involved in Noreen's death; maybe she'd done something to Laurie Granger and Daile, too. Adrenaline surged through me; I felt like pulling the scarf from around my waist and throttling her with it. In a voice that didn't feel anything like my own, I said through my teeth, "It's my fault Hypatia is late for work."

"Yes, it is," Monique replied. She looked at my hair. The comb was still in place. "Where did you get that?"

"None of your business." Just as I was thinking I should try to run, she grabbed the comb from my hair, hurting me. She then made a move for my left hand, and I gasped as a sharp sting burst up from the base of my fingers. Horrified, I twisted out of her grasp, blood welling inside my fist.

"Jesus, Monique."

She brandished a pair of cruelly pointed embroidery scissors, the tips tinged with blood. My blood. I choked back my shock; the wound was superficial but painful, bleeding faster than I would have thought possible.

"You're mad," I said, holding my hand away from my clothes. I tried to stalk past her with my dignity intact, thinking I was an idiot to have baited her. I needed to get off the island, contact the authorities, and tell them everything I knew.

She stopped me by gripping the front of my shirt. "Next time it will be more than your hand."

I shook free of her. "I suppose you'll say it's my face after that." She didn't contradict and I was about to aim for her shins with my foot when I saw Rafe on the balcony. From this distance I couldn't tell how long he'd been there; it could have been seconds or hours.

Rafe waved to us. I supposed from his vantage point it might have looked as if Monique and I were having a friendly tête-à-tête. He waved again, this time with more vigor. "Sara! Phone. I think it's your mother."

## 28

Rafe left me with the phone and a paper towel in a windowless gallery the size of a closet and featuring his pencil sketches for a Covent Garden production of *Agamemnon*. Severed heads and gore-heavy swords loomed down at me as I perched on the edge of a gallery bench, the towel wrapped around my fingers. I sighed in frustration; Rafe had been far more worried about his furniture than the fact I had just been attacked by a second madwoman masquerading as a houseguest.

I hunched forward, the phone to my ear while I rearranged Daile's scarf with my free hand.

"Sara," my mother said. "We've been trying to reach you for days."

"I'm sorry. How did you get this number?"

My mother made a noise that registered somewhere between pique and solicitude. Instantly I regretted my question.

"It was the number you left us for emergencies," she said. "When we didn't hear from you I thought I should use it." Her voice softened. "Are you in trouble? Where are you?"

"Greece." I wanted to cry. I'd forgotten to tell her to throw the number out.

"You are on holiday?"

"No. Please, listen, I can't talk right now—"

"If there is a problem then let Pappa and me help you. Is it Miles? Your husband?"

"Moder, listen, I have to go. I'll ring you when I get home."

"When will that be? Sara, talk to me now."

"I can't."

Inge spluttered something in Swedish and I put the phone down. I felt horrible, a complete failure as a daughter, but I couldn't let her know my desolation or the danger I was facing. I just couldn't.

I found Rafe with a drink and a sketchpad in the living room. I set the phone next to the hideous multi-faced vase now holding a bouquet of Siberian iris. Down by the pool, the model was flirting loudly with the stockbroker, her giggles making my head ache.

"You can take some of those flowers if you like," Rafe said without looking up from his sketch.

"I don't want flowers," I said.

Rafe glanced up. "And what does take your fancy these days, Sara? Still painting debutantes and poodles?"

"They were dachshunds."

"What?"

"Nothing." I thought of the painting Peter Wilcox had shown me back at the studio. If what I had seen was any indication of Rafe's new style, he was verging close to poodles and debutantes himself.

Rafe tore his drawing off the pad. "I thought I made myself clear about keeping your visit here private," he said in an acerbic change of subject. He stared at my hand. "Don't drip on the tiles."

I tightened the pressure on the paper towel. "My mother *is* private. Or she used to be."

"How is your mother?"

"Worried. I'm sorry she called. It won't happen again." I wadded up the towel; the cut stung like hell. "I have to go clean this up."

"Let me see."

I held out my hand. Rafe clucked like an old mother hen, lightly fingering my wedding rings.

"Any chance of Monique visiting a psychiatrist before I head home?"

"She's angry," he said. "I'll speak to her."

"Speak to her? The woman's deranged. Like all your guests."

"Courtenay's dumped her boyfriend. Again. Weren't you painting her wedding portrait?"

"The wedding's off?" So she could go after other people's husbands?

We both turned when Hypatia entered the room. She had changed the black sandals for a pair of sky-blue sneakers. My hand raked through my hair, feeling for the missing comb. More than ever I felt like kicking Monique, hard.

"Madame Bergsen," Hypatia said. "I went to neaten your room, but it is locked."

"Never mind. I'll look after it."

She bobbed her head and left the room as quietly as she had entered. I stood to follow her when Rafe said, "Change of plans for tonight. We won't be having our usual dinner *al fresco*. Hope you don't mind a tray in your room."

"A tray is fine. It will give me a chance to get some work done." The sight of Rafe sketching made me want to start a drawing of my own.

"Good." Rafe scratched the side of his nose with his pencil, an old sign that our conversation was over.

I left him without any attempt to hide my irritation and returned to my guesthouse, grateful that I had managed my way downstairs and outside without encountering Monique again. Fresh sheets and towels were piled outside my door. I carried them inside and then removed the scarf from around my waist before stuffing it into the bottom of my suitcase. That done, I thoroughly washed the cut on my hand, and then stretched out on the unmade bed, sedated by the heat. Sketching would have to wait; the only thing I wanted was to sleep. I kept my eyes closed and didn't make a single effort to move.

The waves breaking against the sand woke me, their steady roll as strong as a heartbeat. I sat up; outside my window the wet shoreline glistened in the moonlight. My stomach grumbled; I was starving. For some reason, Hypatia hadn't delivered the promised dinner tray. Just as I was about to check outside my door, I saw a shawl that didn't belong to me resting beside a pillow at the foot of the bed. A paisley shawl. A shawl that I did not bring with me. The shawl from the upstairs room of my London house.

The open window had made the room cold. I wrapped the shawl across my shoulders and gave up any attempt to understand how it had landed on my bed. The facts were: I was cold, I was hungry, and if I wanted to eat I would have to find Rafe's kitchen.

Once again I followed the sandy slope leading up to the house. The lights were off, making it difficult to see in the dark. I stood quietly to listen for a moment; the house appeared vacant, not a single houseguest or staff member to be seen or heard. But I could hear something in the distance, something stronger than just the crash of the waves. It sounded like chanting, a hum so distinct I thought it had to be more than the wind passing over the rocks.

The cameras were surely monitoring me, but I decided to go after the source of the noise anyway. I veered from my usual route, the sound pulling me forward over the rise and past the sleeping goats. The moon was so low I felt I could reach out and touch it. The hum became more distinct, fluctuating with an insistence that chilled, yet compelled me to listen. I climbed up through a gap in the stones until I came to an overhang dropping into a ravine. From where I stood, I could see there was nothing natural about the stones aligned into their regimented patterns; they had to be part of the labyrinth Hypatia had mentioned earlier in the day. I studied the complicated circle. Except for the stones taking the place of box hedges, the layout below me was a good replica of the one I had seen on Anton's estate.

I peered into the blackness. Voices carried toward me from several places, an undeniable beauty to their tone and harmonies. My mother would have been beside herself listening to the many nuances, the call and response of the words floating through the air.

A flash of yellow burst across the sky at the same time the voices grew louder. I positioned myself behind the rocks, crouching on my knees so that I could continue watching whatever was happening in the hollow.

What I saw next nearly made me laugh aloud. My amazement turned to revulsion when I saw Monique, dressed in a weird monk-like robe, conducting a pack of Rafe's motley guests down the opposite hillside. The woman in the poppy-covered dress cavorted after the group, acting as berserk as she had been in the churchyard—as if she'd been force-fed Spanish Fly for the last twenty-four hours and then left to pick up the pieces of her mind as a party game.

I'd heard of secret societies before: cabals of bankers, judges, and out-of-work reality stars; but the sight of all those po-faced modern-day British subjects, each carrying a lighted candle and wrapped in their dressing gowns, was even more cockeyed than anything in the tabloids. No wonder Rafe kept Ismene so hush-hush if this was the swanky idiocy that went on. It made the people at the masked ball with Anton look like vanilla pudding. Then I remembered; some of those people were here right now, including Monique.

Strands of moonbeams wove their way over the scraggy goat paths, lighting the way for the procession to enter an inner circle harboring a raised slab of black stone. Hand in hand, the individual members gathered around the stone as the chanting died down to a sigh. In the void I could hear the sea, and then the sound of something, or someone, being dragged along the ground.

At a shouted command, the group parted to make way for a hooded, bound figure roughly hauled into the center by two thugs posing as sentries. One of the men I thought could be Stamos, but the other man was a stranger to me. I was certain it wasn't Basilides; the figure was far too squat. Amidst some shuffling of places and a short-lived struggle from their chosen victim, the group then mumbled a unison phrase before the hooded figure was pushed face down onto the slab.

I leaned farther out from my hiding place. Idiots. I was about to crawl down to the next level of rock, when I had a strategic change of plan.

"Don't you dare," Rafe whispered. He clamped a hand over my breast, his fingers digging in.

"Let go, you moron."

Rafe chuckled as he pushed back the hood to his own robe. "I'll never let you go, Sara." He grabbed hold of my wrist just above the golden cuff, the pressure abnormally strong—for Rafe—and reminding me too much of my run-in with Monique. I wondered if he had an evil pair of scissors up his sleeve, too.

"You're hurting me," I whispered as loud as I could.

He jerked our joined hands behind my back. "He told you to come here, didn't he?"

I twisted my arm to no avail. "What the hell are you talking about?"

"Kaminsky." Rafe bent my fingers into a knot. "He sent you to get the sun and the moon. Sorry, darling, they're not for sale and you're certainly not leaving here with them stashed in your suitcase." He pulled me into the shadows. "In fact, Sara, you're never leaving here again."

"In that case you can answer a simple question. Did you know Anton before or after you killed Noreen?"

"Before."

I was about to mention police and prison, but a shout cut through the air, ringing off the hilltops and giving me the chance to slide closer toward the labyrinth, dragging Rafe along with me.

"Sara! Sara!" The cry came from the site of the black stone.

I tore away from Rafe with a wrench that sent us both to the ground. Without a second thought I was back on my feet and hurtling down the rockface.

"Sara!"

I ran toward the circle. I would know that voice from anywhere, even in my dreams.

## 29

Rafe had me by the hair. "Open your mouth and it's the last time you'll speak," he hissed.

The gully spun in a dizzying flash of light, making my eyes throb and my ears pound, the images below dancing crazily through my mind. If I was on the verge of a blackout, it couldn't have come at a worse time. Miles was down there with those people in their weird robes while Rafe tried to scalp me. I groaned and Rafe hooked his hand over my mouth before pushing me hard against the rocks.

I clawed his hand away and rolled over onto my back. "How long has he been here?"

Rafe kept his eyes on the group below. "Shut it."

"What are they doing to him?"

Rafe made me stand up. "Get going," he said. He pulled me forward across the ledge and I felt the ground give way.

"I can't walk. I'm too dizzy." I tried to sit, but Rafe refused to let go of me. "Just for a minute," I begged.

He shoved me ahead of him. "You can nap when we're inside," he said. The chanting had started up again, but this time the sound was caustic and violent, containing none of the music I had heard only moments ago.

Rafe half-walked, half-dragged me down the hillside toward what appeared to be a series of openings or doorways between the rocks. "Do what I say and—" He stopped when a scream shot out through the night.

We both strained to listen, but the sound wasn't repeated and Rafe got busy pushing me into the caves. "Bend your neck before you break it."

He shoved me through a low-ceilinged space cut from the rock, similar to the tombs I had visited with my parents in the Valley of the Kings. I hadn't liked the claustrophobia then, and I didn't like it any better now. A sharp blast of cold air reminded me that I had left the paisley shawl outside on the ledge.

Rafe's cavalier concern for my well-being as we blundered down the slippery surface reminded me of the one time we'd tried ice skating; I would slide forward while Rafe hung on to my arm for dear life and told me to go faster. I thought of collapsing and letting him carry me the rest of the way to wherever he insisted I go, but before I dared try anything, we arrived at the end of the tunnel.

My vision was so bleary all I could detect was the barest ooze of dripping water on the walls. Rafe let go of me and this time I did collapse, too ill to care where I landed. The floor was solid and if I closed my eyes it didn't move. A small mercy, but enough to give me the strength to plan my next move: play dead.

"Get up," Rafe said.

"Why? If you're going to kill me you can do it on the floor."

"Always the drama queen," he complained. He nudged me with his toe. Below the hem of his robe he was wearing dress socks with his sandals. I wanted to laugh; Rafe and his perennial clothing faux pas. Then I remembered what he'd done to Noreen.

Rafe turned away from me at the sound of a commotion somewhere, the noise coming through the sides and roof of the pit-like room. "They're here," he said.

"Yippee."

Rafe shook his head and stood at the back of the cell. Whether the cramped quarters had once been cut from the rock for the solitary monks who had built the church, or to imprison ancient Greek criminals, Rafe apparently now had his own uses for the place.

Bypassing my feeble attempts to keep from vomiting, he stepped out of the cell and pulled a grate across the entrance; the metal scraping the floor set my teeth on edge. He then fastened the hasp with a modern combination lock.

The chanting continued to reverberate through the walls. "Why are you doing this?" I asked, the vertigo about to demolish me. "Rafe, please. Talk to me. What do you want?"

"I want you to behave," he said before he turned and walked away.

This isn't happening, I thought, waves of sickness washing through me. I needed to think of some way to get out before Rafe returned for me—assuming he would return. To calm myself, I listed the sundry places Evan and Inge had taken me, from chic urban high-rises to the most primitive of forest campgrounds. *Brazil, Majorca, Finland.* I had got to my grandmother's house in England when my mind fell blank and I went with the sense-defying darkness.

*Warily, Miles observed Anton standing in the arched doorway. How the hell had the man found his way here? The sea wind howled under the eaves, rattling loose tiles. The priest noticed nothing amiss and Miles resumed eating, watching from the corner of his eye as the priest pulled out a chair for his new guest and then passed him the plate of bread and fish.*

*"The miracle of the loaves and fishes, Father?" Anton quipped, tasting the thin wine the priest poured into a brass cup for him.*

*"If there is a miracle," the priest said mildly, "it is that I should have not one, but two guests at my table. I cannot remember the last time the monastery was so full."*

*The priest turned to Miles. "Forgive my lack of manners. May I introduce my visitor? Anton Kaminsky."*

*"We are acquainted," Miles said shortly.*

*The priest appeared astounded and crossed himself. "But this is remarkable. Another miracle!"*

*"The only miracle, Father," Anton said, spearing a piece of the salted herring with his knife, "is the fact that as a child I would have wept at the sight of this food, this room." He waved a hand toward the bookshelves. "And now the food is mine. The books, if I so desire, are mine. This very monastery is my personal treasure house—if I were to give the word."*

The priest tilted his bird-like head and looked from one man to the next. "Then you are indeed blessed."

Anton interrupted. "I am not a religious man, Father."

"The Wandering Jew." The priest's brief laughter sounded grim in the silence. "The sea has washed many strange things to my door," he said, "but never anyone of such legendary magnitude."

Miles drank more of the wine, his eyes never leaving Anton's face. Despite the close scrutiny, Anton continued to eat and talk. "Some people have thought of me as a wanderer, it is true," he said, "but the real story behind my wandering is much stranger than any story or legend could invent."

"And that is?"

"Quite simply, I and the gentleman who sits across from me have both lost our souls."

The priest frowned. "A soul can never be taken without one's consent, unless," he stopped to cross himself again, "you have entered into some unholy pact that should not be discussed outside of the confessional."

"Don't bother with your rituals, Father," Anton said harshly. "My sins—" He lifted his chin toward Miles. "Our sins are beyond discussion."

Miles had not spoken since Anton had entered the room. The fire in his eyes belied his icy tone: "What Kaminsky is trying to say is that we are both beyond redemption." He swallowed the rest of his wine. "And it is not religion we seek, but a woman."

"You won't find her here," the priest replied with his earlier good humor.

"No, I suppose we won't," Anton said. "The woman we are looking for is a whore."

The priest blanched at the word, while Miles looked as if he would rise from the table and choke the life out of Anton's smiling, cynical face.

"Oh, she's no common slut," Anton said. "Her morals, what she has of them, are above reproach. As for her beauty, she is the rival of any painted Madonna."

The priest shot Anton a look filled with reproach. "It is ungenerous of you to speak in such a way."

Anton cut a fillet of herring and placed it in his mouth. "My intention was not to offend. But because you sense some slur in my words, I will apologize. But let me ask you this: Do you not agree that the most beautiful representations of the Holy Mother, the *woman your church claims gave birth to your Savior, are based and modeled on real, actual women?"*

*"It is rumored of some pictures," the priest replied testily. "But God has directed the artist's hand and skill to depict these women with all the sanctity of the Queen of Heaven. They were blessed to offer their beauty to the Mother of God."*

*"It is the same for the woman of whom I speak."*

*The priest appeared unconvinced and Miles said, "What he says is true, Father. From the day this particular woman entered the world she was trained toward one aim only: ecstasy. Some of the greatest men known to history have destroyed themselves, their families, even their nations in their desire to spend but one night with her. Some have succeeded; most others have failed abysmally."*

*His eyes locked with Anton's. A curtain of rage and ancient resentment shrouded the room. The storm had not yet reached land, but its lowering threat had already infected the men. Anton's eyes were the color of slate.*

*"This is not the usual talk of this place," the priest said. "Forgive me if I ask you not to speak of these subjects again, for it is precisely to avoid such wanton talk and influence that the brothers and I have come to this far-off coast. We seek only solitude and God's blessings."*

*He turned back to Miles. "I beseech you, my son, give up this idle quest that can only end in tragedy, and make your journey one for God."*

*Miles set his knife beside his plate. "I cannot," he said. "The woman I seek is more than Kaminsky can understand. She is a member of a select and elite clan. To bring her to safety, alive, unharmed, and unbroken—that is worth more than my soul to me. She is my passage from hell."*

Hell. I had gone to hell. My skin tingled with more than the cold. When a hand grazed my sleeve I couldn't stifle the half-scream that escaped my throat.

The hand passed over my face. "Sara?"

I crammed myself against the damp wall, my eyes searching out every impenetrable corner.

"Sara, please, it's me, Courtenay."

"Courtenay? Courtenay!"

"Ssh, please, Sara, we don't have a lot of time. He's here."

My back became even more rigid, as if I could somehow meld with the rocks. "Rafe?" I whispered.

She made a dismissive noise. "Not Rafe. *Miles.* Your husband."

"Listen, Courtenay, I don't know what you're doing here or why you're talking about my husband, but something is—" My teeth chattered. "Something is definitely very wrong," I managed to say.

"You're right," she said. "And I want to help you."

The cold was growing worse, increasing my shivering fit that had begun from sheer emotional chaos. Before I could stop her, Courtenay snuggled up to me like a kitten. My first instinct was to push her away, but I couldn't resist the extra body warmth.

"W-w-why would you want to help me?" I asked when I could get a full sentence out.

"Because my mother is dangerous and I have to stop her."

I shook my head and moved so I could face her. "I have to tell you something. I saw you. I saw you with Miles when he was supposed to be somewhere in the Middle East working on, oh, I don't know, old pipelines. He lied to me. And you lied to me when you asked me all those silly questions while you hid that sketch! You and your mother have been gaslighting me from the day we met."

"I had nothing to do with that sketch. I don't know where it went."

I stood up; my head was killing me. "The point is—" I stopped. What was the point? I just wanted out of the dark, the cold, and the feeling that I was losing my mind. "How did you get in here, anyway?" I asked.

"Elementary, Watson. I'm not supposed to be on the island but my mother's not very good at covering her, uh, *peccadilloes*. It was easy to figure out where she'd gone."

Apparently nobody was ever where they were supposed to be. Courtenay reached for my sleeve again and I could smell her perfume—my perfume: Bal à Versailles. "You have to believe I'm trying to help you," she said.

"Why?"

"Look, I found out about Miles being in London the same way I got here, eavesdropping on my mother. It all started with Rafe. My mother's been collecting his work for years, and then she had this big opportunity to meet him at some gala dinner, and after that they started meeting secretly. My father's never home, and Rafe and my mother were hardly what you'd call discreet."

I knew what she meant; Rafe did have an innate need to show off.

Courtenay got to her feet and jogged in place for a minute to warm up before she continued speaking. "One morning I overheard them talking," she said, "about a 'Sara Elliott' who could paint my wedding portrait and how she, you, that is, had been Rafe's ex-girlfriend, which made my mother totally jealous. They argued until Rafe convinced her there was nothing between the two of you, and that he was only trying to help your career. Your credentials were sterling, he said, only you could paint the portrait.

"But then after you got the commission, you got married, and this seemed to infuriate both of them, which made absolutely no sense."

"No, it doesn't," I agreed, horrified that I had perked up a degree when Courtenay said that Rafe had recommended me.

Courtenay took hold of my wrists and examined the golden cuffs with her fingers. "I think it has something to do with these bracelets of yours," she said. "Rafe likes them. So does my mother."

"Any artist would like them."

"Especially one with a desire for power."

I wanted to ask more but the chanting had recommenced. "Can you hear that?" I whispered.

Courtenay held open the barred gate. The combination lock swung from one of the bars.

"How did you open the lock?"

"They're coming closer," she replied, sidestepping my question. "We have to go."

The chanting was giving me an ear ache.

"Hurry," she urged.

I hobbled to the corridor, the strident chanting drilling into my head like a piece of broken machinery. The noise didn't seem to bother Courtenay; she directed me down one rocky junction after another as if we were on a holiday expedition.

"This doesn't seem right," I said, my bearings gone haywire. I was certain Rafe had shoved me only a few meters into the narrow crevice before he had thrown me into that cage.

"Wait," I said. "Slow down." The air was too thin. "I think we're lost."

Just then she stopped, causing me to slide into her back.

I regained my footing, my head spinning with the pain of a migraine. "You don't know where we're going, do you?"

"Yes, I do," she said when a pair of arms reached out to catch and steady me.

## 30

*Miles.* All the months of doubt and waiting, all the months of self-recrimination, and now at last we were together and it couldn't have felt worse. I didn't know what to say, but words would have been pointless when he bent down and silenced them with his mouth. I thought the tears would never stop.

"Where have you been?" I gasped. "Why didn't you let me know where you were? Or what happened to you?"

"Sara, Sara, don't—"

"Don't what? Don't care that I've been trying to forget you even existed? Don't care that I saw you just a couple of weeks ago and you never told me you were home? Or that, what? An hour ago you were in the middle of some insane coven—"

Miles kissed me again, just like when we had first met, and my angry thoughts and words melted away.

"I just don't understand," I said. I glanced behind me when I thought I heard a noise. "Courtenay? Is that you?"

Miles gathered me back into his arms. "Courtenay's gone," he said. "It's you I'm worried about."

"Me too." I let myself be held, blocking out any further questions. Miles was here, I was here. I wanted nothing more than for things to stay that way. I felt his clothing: thick shirt and trousers, similar to what I had seen him wearing with Courtenay and in my dreams. The sleeves felt like leather. "What are you wearing?" It was too dark to see.

"We only have a few minutes," he said without answering me. "There's too much to explain in such a short time. But know this, believe this—everything I have done has been for you, Sara. For you."

"I thought I'd lost you," I said into his chest. "It's been terrible. I'm a wreck. I've been seeing things, dreaming things—"

He gripped my shoulders. "Sara, please listen. This is important. You are special. You're the last of—" He paused as if to find the right description. "A lineage. A people. And there are other people who want to make sure it stays that way."

I clung to him. "What are you talking about?"

Impatiently he seized my wrist and held it to a miniscule beam of light streaming from the ceiling. For a second I was able to see our surroundings. The rock walls had been smoothed to a satiny finish revealing a series of murals and frescoes like those in the church. Miles moved my wrist back and forth, catching the light with my first cuff while the look in his eyes was pure anguish.

"When I saw you," he said, "with this bracelet on your arm, I knew I had to be with you. Nothing else in my life meant anything to me; only that I protect you."

"Protect me from what?"

"From Anton Kaminsky," he said, the anger in his words making his voice shake. "And then when I learned you knew Rafe and Monique, there was only one way to save you." He dropped my wrist and pulled me yet closer against him with a fierceness matched only by my desire to regain every minute we had lost.

"But if I go with them," he said, "you'll be free, free to do what you love, to paint, to grow, to be who you were meant to be. You're young, Sara. You'll marry again, someone more worthy of you."

"Miles, you're not making any sense whatsoever. What we really have to do is find a way out of here." I turned, still in his arms. "Where did Courtenay go?"

"Don't worry about Courtenay. I promised them my life."

"You don't know what you're saying. They've drugged you, or used voodoo on you; maybe it's the ether. They gave it to me, too."

Miles wouldn't be appeased. "I'm talking about you being able to fulfill your destiny, your heritage. I thought that by marrying you we could stay together, but it wasn't the answer. I should have known that."

He pulled me to the floor and I felt him breathing into my face, my lips. "You have never heard of the Unushka—"

"But I have," I interrupted him.

"From Kaminsky." He shook his head and began to speak as if he had to fit an epic into a few short sentences. "You can't know what the Unushka stood for, why they existed."

"I don't want to know."

"You have to hear this. They were the guardians of sound and color, the keepers of the creative forces that make life what it is. When they were given this task—what year, what century—the answer is lost.

"Some say they took it for themselves. But there was a time when they ruled the earth. They were known by their symbols of sun and moon."

I nodded, a chill of recognition creeping down my arms. "The sun and the moon. You told me to remember them."

He kissed me again, then said, "Two thousand years ago, the Unushka's knowledge was lost in a battle beyond comprehension.

"Everything was destroyed: the accounts and genealogies, the secrets, the legends, the truth. The truth, Sara. All from the flame of a single arrow that still burns today—the flame of alchemy.

"It's up to you to bring the Unushka back. You have to recover that knowledge. And you have to do this alone, without me."

I couldn't listen anymore and pushed him away. "You're no better than Anton!" I cried, my voice raspy. It hurt to speak, but I said, "These stories are hogwash. All I want is for us to go back home to the house I bought for us, the one you told me to buy. I don't care about the sun and the moon. I don't want to change the world; I just want us to go home!"

"The Unushka have no home." The look he gave me stopped my next words before they were out of my mouth, and I almost believed him.

"Let me get help," I said. "I could steal a boat, or start a fire. What I won't do is stand by and watch these lunatics kill you during the second round of their sing-along."

"That 'sing-along' may be the very method they're using to keep us here. You can't go anywhere. I can't go anywhere. I have to do what they say. There isn't any other choice."

"But why you?" I sobbed into his chest. "I don't want to live without you. I don't want to do anything without you. I can't. Without you I'm— I'm anchorless. I get dizzy. I walk into walls. I drink too much. I yell at people. I do bad things, Miles. Dangerous things."

He lifted my chin and held my face. Softly, he kissed the tears spilling down my face. It felt so trivial to cry. I thought of all my wasted tears in the past: a leaky pen; a party I was not allowed to attend; thinking Miles had been unfaithful with Courtenay Claiburne of all people. Stupid, stupid tears I had cried as if the worst thing in life was a mediocre school report or a misplaced mitten. Now I was being shown what genuine grief truly was, and I had only seconds left to lay my head on my husband's chest and listen to the terror in both our hearts.

Miles stroked my hair. "If there is any possible way out of this, I will find you. I promise."

I held him tightly, wanting to believe him, but knowing I couldn't. Not because of the Unushka, a story I could only listen to with a skeptical ear, but because Rafe and Monique were killers.

"Miles," I asked, barely able to choke out the words. "Who are you, really?"

He shook his head. "There's one last thing," he said.

I waited.

"Stay away from Kaminsky."

I woke, as I feared I would, on the dusty hillside, the sun burning my face and neck. No caverns, no metal bars, *no Miles*. I tried standing and was only fractionally relieved to find my nausea and dizziness had evaporated along with the improbabilities of the night before. My clothes were a mess; dirt and leaves clung to my knees and elbows. When I shook them away I made things worse; there was nothing I could do to improve my appearance without bathing and changing.

I wasn't too far from my guesthouse when Hypatia spotted me trying to sneak back unnoticed. "Madame Bergsen!" she cried out. "We have been looking everywhere for you!" She eyed my clothing with dismay. "We have been so worried," she said, taking my hand and propelling me up to the main house. I tried to extricate myself, but she was emphatic. "There is some food left from breakfast," she said. "You must eat."

I was too late to meet up with the rest of the household, but the balcony serving table still held a selection of rolls and coffee. Next to the table, draped over a chair, Monique's tapestry glinted in the sunlight. With a twinge of my earlier nausea I noticed she had filled in more of the design; the images were decidedly more gruesome than the last time I'd seen them. Embroidered blood spurted from some hapless knight's crewelwork visor.

Hypatia handed me a plate and I turned my back on Monique's attempt at arts and crafts while I put a hasty meal together. A pair of fishing boats skirted the coastline; I watched them bring in their catch.

Hypatia pushed a deck chair toward me. "Sit."

"I need to head back to my room," I said, holding out my crushed skirt and indicating the mud on my knees.

"And miss this incredible view?" I jumped when Rafe snuck up behind me, a bottle of whiskey in one hand and a glass in the other. "That will be all, Hypatia. Thank you." He waved his glass in my direction. "Mind if I join you?" The monk's robe had been replaced with a T-shirt and a Speedo.

"Where's the rest of the cabal?"

Rafe made a vague gesture toward the sea. "Fishing. You didn't think those boats came here uninvited, did you?"

"Is Miles with them?"

"Miles?" He took a swig of the whiskey.

"My husband." I set my coffee cup down. "I know he's here. I saw him. I talked to him." I was about to include Courtenay and then had a better idea. "Why don't we go look at your videos? You must have everything recorded." *Me leaving my room; Monique tormenting Miles; Rafe trying to kill me.*

Rafe clapped the bottle beneath his arm and repositioned his Speedo. "I think you're delusional, darling."

"Show me the recordings," I demanded.

He took another swallow of his drink, and then said matter-of-factly, "All right. Let's go."

We didn't have far to travel. A nondescript security booth was tucked invisibly into a corner of the balcony. Sitting before a bank of computer monitors, Stamos grunted some guttural greeting while he remained glued to a view of Hypatia entering a guest cottage, her arms piled with towels and her skirt too short.

Rafe tousled his henchman's hair, and then turned to a screen where he scrolled through the indistinct images. I didn't know how much longer I could stand the fetid room with its low buzz of computer equipment, but after a minute Rafe found what he was looking for. "Here we are," he said, clicking a series of shots frame by frame while Stamos kept his eyes on Hypatia.

The now-in-focus section of tape showed me leaving my room without closing the door behind me. I then walked up to the deserted house, waited, listened, and when I found myself alone I continued walking up the hillside. In the grainy monotone footage I looked like one of the undead, blankly inattentive to my surroundings. The next few frames showed me drop the shawl beside a rock, stagger a few more steps, then seesaw to the ground like a sick animal. After that I slept. And slept. No Miles. No Courtenay. No chanting, no Rafe, no underground cells. Like my wedding photos, the pictures were only of me, alone.

"So you've doctored them," I said, knowing he had done no such thing.

Rafe closed down the computer before he gave a quick perusal to the other screens. Satisfied the island wasn't being invaded by journalists or tomb robbers, he pointed me back outside. The sun was blinding. I wished I'd had my sunglasses.

"Why don't you believe me, Sara?"

"Why should I?"

From the other side of the balcony, stepping into the glare, Monique walked over to collect her tapestry.

"Because he's telling the truth," she said. "And I think it's time you were put away."

Monique chose a seat facing Rafe. "I thought you could help. But you're no more useful than that harebrained friend of yours. What was her name? Nora? Nellie?"

I turned to Rafe in desperation, but his face was an empty canvas refusing to help me out. Fear and anger pulsed through me as my eyes darted back to Monique. Before I could stop myself, I said, "Is that why you killed her? Because she wasn't 'useful' to you?"

"She was playing with dangerous toys; she knew the risks involved."

"You mean she got in the way and you had to get rid of her. Just one more messy job to accomplish before you put on the drapes and played high priestess with my husband."

Rafe slapped me across my face so hard my knees buckled and I knew what it meant to see stars.

"Don't mock what you don't understand," he barked.

I laughed in spite of the pain as a myriad of angry retorts sprang to mind, but none of them seemed worth the effort of delivery.

"Besides," Rafe added in a more affable tone, "you can't be married. The Unushka can never marry."

I looked up, startled, but just then Stamos appeared with a plastic bucket, ready to clear the breakfast table.

"What would you know about the Unushka?"

A smell like bleach came from Stamos's bucket. Laconically, Rafe pointed to me. "Take her away."

Stamos reached for me, but before he could get a hold I slipped past him, my cheek still feeling the imprint of Rafe's slap. I ran to the stairs and was halfway down to the beach, Stamos following like a bad-tempered mastiff, when Rafe shouted over the balcony, "I'll win!"

I didn't look back.

Hypatia was waiting nervously for me inside my guesthouse, earbuds to some musical contraption in place while she drummed the window ledge with her fingertips.

When she saw me approach, "escorted" by Stamos, she removed the plugs from her ears and rushed to the door.

"Please, Madame Bergsen," she said, her voice hard as if she hated the words leaving her mouth. "You must drink this." She held up a cloudy tumbler filled with what looked like ouzo.

"Early, isn't it?"

Hypatia blushed and looked close to breaking down. "The master," she said. "He has ordered this."

"I can assure you, Rafe is no 'master.' Not of anything." My bravado failed to convince either of us. I looked at the window. It was closed, probably locked. Stamos stood guard at the door, his back to us. I glanced over to Hypatia, the glass trembling in her hands.

"Please," she said. "You must drink."

I started to argue, and then gave it up. Without Miles I'd lost everything worth living for anyway.

"In for a penny, in for a pound." The aphorism appeared to confuse Hypatia but I wasn't about to enlighten her. I took the glass and downed the licorice-flavored liquid in one baleful gulp. When I was finished, I slammed it down on the dresser. "Now what?"

"The drink will make you sleepy, but I will stay with you. I can sing if you like," she offered shyly, back to her old self.

"I didn't know you sang," I mumbled, feeling the drug stampede through my veins with an effect not dissimilar to the ether. Where had I put that last bottle?

Hypatia helped me to the bed and I tried to remember what I had come to the island for. Something about wanting to find Miles, or Noreen. It was all the same. Hypatia removed my shoes and I was a child again, falling asleep in a foreign hotel room while strangers' voices entered my dreams like birdsong, or the waft of trade winds.

After closing the shutters and then covering me with a sheet, Hypatia began to sing. I picked at a loose thread. "Were you there last night? In the labyrinth?" I asked over the melody.

Hypatia didn't stop singing. Her voice was unskilled but lovely, causing tears to gather that I was too weak to wipe away. The words to her song were unintelligible, but they swayed back and forth like the boats I had watched casting their nets offshore. I knew the song had to be about the sea and the women who dwelt in its depths, perhaps the ones who had come to Anton's rescue once upon a time. The tidal pull of each verse and refrain felt like the loss of love, a breach that could never be healed. Perhaps, I thought, the song was about me. Or Hypatia. Just before I fell asleep, I realized her own tears were falling on my face.

Basilides placed a hot cup of tea into my hands. It took me a full minute to understand I was on the deck of his launch, resting on a pile of fluffy sheepskins, wearing clean clothes.

I sent a breath across the top of my cup. *Chamomile. Sea spray.* "Where are we going?" I asked, feeling suddenly unsteady.

"Easy there," Basilides cautioned. "We are headed for Athens."

Right away I was up, in search of my bags, but he motioned for me to sit. "Your luggage is below," he said. You are safe. No problem."

"What about Rafe? Monique?"

He smiled. "No problem."

I hoped he was right. The sea opened before us like a glassy highway painted with a child's watercolor set; the colors running together until they formed a single shade of blue, *Rafe's blue. Like that film with the diver and ray.*

In the past I had thought Rafe kept his Greek island home a secret to ensure his work could continue undeterred by gallery owners, avaricious collectors, and would-be disciples. Now I knew nothing could be further from the truth. Rafe maintained the enigma for one reason only: a pretense at power fed by myths and dreams, smoke and mirrors. Monique's role was to keep those dreams alive by recreating a primeval cult of moon and sun worshippers so jaded with life they'd try anything—even murder.

I finished my tea but kept the lukewarm cup in my hands. "Psychopath" would have been an overly-generous term for either of them.

I thought back to everything Hypatia had said about the island being deserted before Rafe arrived to build his private playground. If there had been a cache of gold, Scythian gold, it would explain much of his rise to wealth and his reluctance to share it. What it didn't explain was how I had been found as a small child with a piece of that gold, unless I wanted to believe what Miles had said, that it was my rightful heritage as a member of the Unushka.

For one instant I had a clear vision of my birth mother fleeing through the Kamchatka woods. What had she done? Who was she? The picture began to fade and I tried to recall the villagers finding me with the wild animals and nothing but lichen and berries to eat, but the vision was gone before it truly started.

Twilight gave way to night. The lights of a marina and the adjoining clubs gave the sea a strobe effect as Basilides brought the launch toward land; bright neon signs and flashing buoys guiding us forward.

"Next stop is Athens," he said, bringing me my shoes and bags. He helped me to stand. I reached into my handbag and found my air ticket neatly placed in a side pocket along with the hair ornament Hypatia's mother had given me. My wedding rings and the two armbands were wrapped in the Eiffel Tower scarf. And there was also an envelope. A heavy, unaddressed, cream envelope.

I closed my fingers over the crisp rectangle, my heart scudding, hard. I would open it later, much later. I ducked my head to hide my excitement and took out the hair ornament as if it had been what I was looking for. I held it in my palm for Basilides to see. "She found it," I said. "She found everything."

Basilides gave me a thumbs-up and nodded to a taxi ramp. "God go with you," he said, lifting me onto the pier. He handed me the paisley shawl with a wink.

I wondered how long it would take Rafe and Monique to discover I wasn't on the island. "What about Hypatia—will she be all right?"

Already Basilides had put the boat in reverse, away from the docks. "She is with me!" he called out. "I will look after her. No problem!" He waved once in farewell and navigated his way around a yacht the size of a cruise ship. I watched as the stern left a trail of foam in its wake.

"Taxi, Mrs. Bergsen?"

I turned. Hypatia's youngest brother held the cab door open for me, his eyes as warm and as gentle as hers.

"Yes," I said. "Oh, yes. The airport, please. And hurry."

## 31

The locks had all been changed. Signs from an unknown estate agent covered the windows, advertising an auction to be held on the fourteenth of next month, a Sunday.

I carried my bags around to the back of the house; in my absence someone had pulled the weeds and swept the patio, sprucing up what was apparently no longer my home.

I put my face against the glass of the solarium dining room: dustsheets covered the gray and white sofa, the matching wing chairs, my teak dining table. On my easel, instead of Courtenay's wedding portrait, my painting of the panther glowed like a beacon. The gilt border—the one I never managed to finish—framed the piece like a ribbon of Spanish lace, nearly stealing what sanity I had left.

The only way to get inside was to break a window. I should have been scared. Or guilty. In just a few short days I'd lost my husband—twice, gone through his money, and now I'd vandalized his house. I couldn't even begin to think of what I'd done to Laurie Granger and Daile, maybe Courtenay, too.

Once inside, however, I was too worn out to worry about any of it. I listened to the empty rooms and realized the only sound I could hear was the hum of the refrigerator, still plugged into the wall. That wonderful, engaging purr was gone. I didn't know whether to be glad or sorry; glad because it meant my mental health was improving, sorry because I missed the panther. Whether he was real or not was beside the point; he had given me the painting shining out at me from my easel. In many ways it was the finest work I'd ever done. So what if my bank accounts were closed and my house repossessed; I had never felt more at peace. It was time to open that final envelope.

*To Sara, my wife:*

*In your dream, I was the icehouse, the first melt of spring snow. I was the white birch tree, and black leaves in moonlight. I was the rabbit running across your deep winter fields. I was the sound of thaw and crack, an icicle breaking off the roof of an old barn, full of the smells of warm straw and last summer's births. I was the moon shining over winding winter roads, the banks of the river empty and silent, a world without voice, a world asleep.*

*All night I heard you breathing. The sound of sheets moving damply in the humid night air, the rustle of your turning, the slide of your arm shifting position. Your breathing.*

*In my dream you were wearing a silver dress of stars and memory. A patchwork of your forgotten childhood incidents: stealing a peach from a neighbor's tree, a plastic ring with a secret decoder, a doll with a missing leg. You wore a crown of forgetfulness, beautiful in its disarray, meaningful to those who can see and in seeing find their own truths. I watched you and I found that truth.*

*Later, we dreamed together. In our dream we flew with the migrating birds, snow-birds that sought out the ice caps, the reindeer, the steam off the frozen lakes toward the sun. The wind was beneath our feet. We saw beyond the trees, the endless forests and distant prairies. We could see forever. And then you became afraid.*

*I never wanted to make you think you had to fly, or that I would fly so far away I could never come back. I was hiding in my own thoughts, I was planning my future and I wanted to have it right before I showed it to you.*

*But now the future is our past, and we are leaving the ice. We are going to the hills, to the dry, dusty sage-covered hills. Out of the ice, into the sand. We will test our strength together, turning ice into glass, exchanging icicles for sun-baked dunes and the chance to walk free. We will leave furs and parkas, sealskin boots and reindeer rattles in the gullies between snow-laden pines. It will grow warmer and we will leave our possessions and the tools and trappings of survival behind.*

*We will walk forward into the sun, collecting trinkets for your ears and ankles. We will sell hides for gauze and muslin, we will let the sun reach deep into our skin. Our feet will be alive against the sandy earth; we will run toward the sun, the drying lavender, the wide expanse of sky and sea. We will run and run, flight behind us, knowing only the fullness of our bodies against the earth.*

The sound of the bell startled me. The estate agents, I thought. I scrambled to my feet and shoved the letter back into the envelope. For a second I considered not answering, but the noise was relentless. By the third shrill *brrrng* I ran to the front door.

On the doorstep, a tatty canvas bag slung over her shoulder and a new suitcase with collapsible wheels at her side, Inge was just about to push the bell for a fourth time.

"Moder?" My father was right behind her. "Pappa?"

My mother didn't wait for explanations. Instead, she drew me into a hug and said, "Sara, Sara. My God, what has happened to you?"

"Do I look that bad?"

My father bent forward, his face creased with worry that quickly relaxed into relief. Awkwardly, he joined my mother and me in an embrace that nearly knocked us all off our feet. Encompassed by my parents' concern, the words I had wanted to say but had kept bottled up while we'd been apart fell out before I could stop them. "I'm sorry, so sorry," I said, switching to the Swedish, "*Ursäkta mig.*"

Inge let go of me long enough to blow her nose and squint over my shoulder to the draped interior of the house. "You are moving?" she asked, her eyes widening in disbelief.

I held my hand out for a tissue. "It appears that way."

We walked into the dining room where my father made a beeline for the panther painting. "Oh, this is very nice, Sara," he said. "I've always found animals a much more likeable lot than my fellow human beings." My mother looked like she needed to sit down and I rushed to pull the sheet from the couch.

"Why a panther?" my father asked, dismissing four years of separation in his old way that had always perplexed and amused me as a child.

I brought my mother a glass of water. Like the fridge, the rest of the utilities still seemed to be working. "He belongs to a friend," I said, reluctant to elaborate.

"Really?"

My mother signaled to him, trying to catch his eye; they weren't here to discuss art.

Inge tipped the glass into a houseplant. "The pipes haven't been used for awhile," I said.

She shook her head. "The water's fine. It's this house that is not right. Forgive me; I know this is your new home. But there is a very bad resonance here. Like a tremor."

She glanced toward my bags still packed from Greece. "Pappa and I are on the way to our hotel. Bring your things and come with us." Her tone let me know there would be no arguing. Torn between memories of our last unhappy meeting and gratitude that they wanted to be with me, I collected my luggage to follow wherever they led. Once again I was the dutiful daughter I had always been in my parents' company, subdued into compliance with the promise of an Orangina and a new comic book if I would only wait ten more minutes for the tape to finish or the phone call to end. Except this time it was bliss to have them take charge. Just before we left, my father propped one of the agent's signs over the broken window.

An hour later we were comfortably settled in my parents' hotel room with a pot of tea and a plate of chocolate biscuits. The bed-and-breakfast they'd chosen was a high-end boutique hotel not far from the Claiburne villa. No more windy tents or sandy bivouacs for the Elliotts, I thought.

"So you're here for a new project?" I asked when my father gave me another biscuit, this time with fondant in the middle.

"Yes, for the eclipse. You've heard it's coming? A film crew wants to document it and edit in animal cries."

"You're kidding."

"Don't worry—they'll be happy animals. No teeth or claws." He aped a scary animal face for me like he used to do when I was a youngster. "Your panther will be safely out of sight."

"Very funny." I took off my shoes and then for no reason put them back on.

"Sara, love, you seem so skittish. We explained years ago about those tapes you hated so much. Can't you just let them go?"

"It's nothing to do with that. It's travel jitters. I just got off a plane."

"You were always a good little traveler," he said, exchanging looks with my mother. "Everyone used to comment on your behavior. So patient and grown-up."

Me? Patient? Grown-up? What had happened?

"Tell me about your new work," I said.

My father went to his suitcase. "We do have a rough cut you might like on tape here." He found what he was looking for and switched on the hotel room's VCR.

"Pappa did all the filming himself," my mother said proudly.

On the tape, my father zoomed in with the viewfinder to the mother bird, a roadrunner. A thin metal ring attached to the bird's leg sparked steel blue, a series of ID numbers just visible in the cold sunlight.

"Where was this taken?" I asked.

"New Mexico." My father explained that this part of the video was for his own records and wouldn't be used in the final product. "We should have taken more film like this when you were a child," he said. "I miss not having any movies of us together as a family." The tape fogged for a second before the next shot of Inge, laughing. Behind her, Maxfield Parrish mountains dominated a sky so wide and clear it made me want to paint it.

I could read my mother's lips: "Stop playing." She laughed into the camera. "Watch the bird." The smile on her face turned the reproof into an endearment. I had never seen my parents so at ease.

"You look like you're having a good time," I said as the camera returned to a nest of fledglings.

"New Mexico was spectacular," my father agreed, fast-forwarding through what appeared to be accidental shots of tree roots. In his haste he jammed the tape. "Damn." He fiddled with the buttons. For someone who'd spent most of his life operating technology, the uncomplicated hotel machine had him stumped.

"We never went much to the States together, did we?" I asked.

My father hit the remote against his leg until Inge took it away from him. "Pappa, enough." She pushed some buttons he hadn't seen, and the tape started rolling again. She sighed and gave him back the device, but not before my father had seized and kissed her hand.

While the tape rolled, Inge turned and busied herself with the clasps to her suitcase. "No," she said.

I looked away from the television. "No what?"

"No, we never took you into the States more than we could help it."

"Because of my passport?"

"Because the Americans always ask too many questions. They mean to be polite, I know, but it's intrusive." She shook her head, her Swedish reserve backing away from the thought of American spontaneity.

"You were afraid the authorities might have been looking for me."

Inge opened the suitcase, forcing me off the bed.

I went to my father's side and took the remote from him. I lowered the sound. "What if they were looking for me?" I asked. "What if they wanted to take me back to wherever I came from?"

"Trust me, you wouldn't want to be there," my father said.

"How do you know?"

"We don't," Inge said, exasperated. "But at the time we did what we thought was right because we believed it was. And that was because we wanted you."

She turned from the suitcase. "We wanted you," she repeated, and for a moment I understood. At the same time I couldn't help but hear her number one phrase when I was a child begging for yet another indulgence: *"Just because you want something, doesn't make it right."*

My father left his chair and put his arm around my mother. "We had to act fast," he said. "Who knows what the Soviets would have done? If we hadn't come along, you would have been placed in an orphanage, no questions asked." At his words, my mother's face fell.

I wanted to memorize the way they stood together, united, leaning into each other for support. They'd been married for over forty years. I hadn't been with Miles more than seven days, but when we were in that cell on Ismene, I'd felt that same sense of belonging to someone. House or no house, money or an empty account, we would have each other again one day, if only I could find a way to turn the world upside down.

"But you bought me."

"We didn't 'buy' you," Inge said sharply. "We paid the villagers for having looked after you—for dressing and feeding you." She moved away from my father and took me by the shoulders. She gave them a little shake.

"You had a good life, no?"

I couldn't argue. She and Evan had shared the world with me. Never had they once begrudged or criticized; only cherished me. My madcap life through college and afterward was regarded with patience and tolerance. It was I who had criticized them and those animal sob stories, and the ingratitude of my earlier anger seemed horribly unjustified. But I still had troubling questions that even the happiest childhood couldn't erase.

"Tell me about my bracelet."

Inge placed my father's shirts onto wooden hangers. "You were holding it when the villagers found you," she said. "And you wouldn't let it go." She paused when she saw a loose button.

"But that doesn't explain the 'how' or the 'why.' It's worse than those fairy tales you used to tell me." The frustration in my voice made her turn.

"The villagers said the bangle protected you. They said the night they took you in, a giant panther had been seen prowling the woods, but it left you unharmed." She held up a pair of cargo pants. "And that, to them, was a sign of benediction—not a fairy tale." She closed the suitcase. "They were a very superstitious people," she said. "I never could make much sense of their beliefs."

"Yet you interviewed shamans and holy men whenever you could," I pointed out.

"For knowledge," she said. "To verify anything that might lead me to understand you." She gazed into my face. "You were different than other children. A good child. A sweet child. But sometimes you seemed, unearthly." She turned to my father. "That's a word, yes?"

My father picked up the laminated instruction manual attached to the television by a plastic cord. He pored over the stiff pages printed in no less than twelve languages as if one of them could unlock the secrets of my birth once and for all.

"It's a word," he said, not looking at us.

Inge hugged me, nearly knocking me off balance again. So much affection was new to me. As a family, our isolation in the field had made us close, but my parents had always been proscribed when it came to expressing their emotions. Even on our rare visits home to England they didn't let go of their professional image: shopping for new equipment, splicing and editing, lunches with filmmakers and agents, catching up with long distance colleagues and employers. During those sojourns to the real world it was up to Evan's parents to treat me like a normal child with Mars bars and Monopoly while he and Inge secluded themselves in their rented studios.

"It's past suppertime," Inge said, patting my head as if to make up for all those missed opportunities. "Let's go eat, and then I want to talk."

Something in her tone warned me she had things to say I might not want to hear.

## 32

My father declined dinner, saying he was too tired, but I knew he thought Inge and I should spend some much-needed time alone. We chose an Indian restaurant at the end of the street, and after my first plate of pilau rice and saag paneer I told her the full story about how I met Miles, his instructions that I buy a house followed by our wedding and his departure for Dubai. Reciting the facts aloud made them sound more authentic somehow. But when I got to the part about Anton and the panther, not to mention the events on Ismene, I veered away and instead brought the conversation to the upcoming auction advertised on my front windows.

"It's a mess," I admitted. "I don't know how I'll get the house back— if it was even mine to lose."

Inge patted my hand. "In the morning we will call the estate agent. There must be some mistake. It will turn out fine, you'll see."

I stirred my rice with my fork. "The thing is, I'm not sure I want it to. Turn out fine, I mean."

"You don't mean that."

A waiter came to our table with a second plate of chapattis. I took one and dipped it in chutney and yogurt. "I do. The house is—was—too much for me. Decorating, planning, keeping up with the Joneses. It did things to me."

"Blackouts?"

I nodded and helped myself to the dhal. When my plate was full, I asked, "Have you heard of someone named Anton Kaminsky?"

"Kaminsky?" she repeated. She glanced over to the other diners, small groups of locals too busy with their food to hear us. Satisfied no one was listening, she whispered: "Why?"

"You met so many people over the years. He's involved with art. Museums, too, I suppose. And then I—I read a manuscript. Or part of one. It was written by Twitty Lansbury. Remember her? Pearls? Headbands?"

"I remember Pamela. She's a writer?"

"She thinks she is." I refrained from describing our disastrous lunch together. My mother disliked bad manners.

"But what has this to do with, what is his name? Kaminsky?"

I poked at my food. "He's the subject of her book."

"That could not be."

"Why? Twitty always was a swot. Writing suits her." It did, now that I'd grown used to the idea.

Inge paused, her hands rearranging a selection of condiments. "When we took you out of Russia," she said after a minute, "everything went like clockwork. It was almost too easy. Pappa kept saying I worried too much, but I was terrified we would be stopped and that you would be taken away. We had entered the country illegally—"

"But you said—"

She waved away my interruption. "Sometimes we had to bend the rules. Anyway, our plan was to leave as we had entered, on a Japanese trawler headed for Alaska. When we boarded the boat, there was another passenger. He introduced himself as Anton Kaminsky."

The overheated, Bollywood-inspired room suddenly seemed too small a space to contain us both. "You make it sound like 'Kaminsky' wasn't his real name," I said.

"It might not have been. Think about it—we had just left Kamchatka. Kam-insky?" She shook her head. "We'd met people like him before. He claimed to be an art collector, and that he was traveling through Russia in search of icons. When he saw you holding the gold cuff, he tried to get you to show it to him. You refused." Inge gave me a proud smile. "You hit him on the nose with it," she said, spooning more yogurt onto my plate.

"For the next three days I tried to keep you away from him," Inge said while I tried to imagine Anton with a bloody nose, "but he kept asking questions: Why did we allow our child to play with such an apparently valuable piece of jewelry? Where were you born? Did you always travel with us to such remote locations? Why didn't you speak either English or Swedish?

"Pappa kept telling him the bangle was a toy, a cheap piece of costume jewelry, and that you were smart enough to never speak in any language to strangers. But Kaminsky remained suspicious. He never left us alone.

"I stayed with you in our cabin to keep away from him. When we arrived in the Aleutians, we changed our plans and left the boat. I couldn't bear to be with Kaminsky a minute longer. The last we saw of him, he was on the deck of the trawler, staring at us, at you. His desire for the bracelet made my skin turn to goose nubbles."

"Bumps. Goosebumps."

"What?"

"So you never saw Kaminsky again?"

"No." She stacked our empty plates just like she did after all our meals. "It's been over thirty years, but hardly a day has passed that I haven't looked over my shoulder, expecting him to turn up somewhere. Sometimes I think—" She faltered, and then said, "Sometimes I think he was the man your real mother was running from."

My face reddened at the word "real." "What makes you think she was running from anyone?"

"The villagers thought so." She added the chapattis to the stack of plates and signaled to the waiter to bring our bill. "It was such a confusing time, Sara. So many versions of the same story. Like telling me about the panther, for one. Some said it was huge, some said it was made out of fire and could fly. Others in the village kept saying that your mother was dressed in eccentric clothing. That she had been chased down like a deer. That she died from a wound to her heart."

"Did you see her body?"

"No. The villagers had buried her before we arrived. But they showed us how they had built a kurgan over her grave and decorated it with their fetishes, scraps of ribbon and bone hanging from a magnificent pair of antlers. I told you they were a superstitious, primitive people, but their faith in an afterlife was profound." She grew quiet, and then she said, "In its own strange way, the grave was fit for a queen."

Our waiter brought the bill and Inge put down her credit card. I went for my purse; I had a few Euros left from my cash advance, but she stopped me, saying, "One thing that has always been with me from that time was the word they kept using for your mother: 'Unushka.' I looked it up when we got back to England and took you to your grandparents, but I could never find it anywhere. In hindsight I think it was a phrase of their own. A lifetime working with sound has taught me that not everything can be translated."

"It's a word," I said, thinking of my father's confirmation to her of that other word, "unearthly."

"How do you know?"

"Miles told me it was."

We decided to stay for coffee while this time I gave my mother the unedited version of what had happened on Ismene, and how to the best of my knowledge it was Miles who insisted I was the last member of the Unushka. I looked at my clothing as I spoke. My not-very-clean top and wrinkled skirt weren't quite the brilliant clothes the Unushka were famed for wearing. But even in pajamas a lot of things made sense. Miles's proposal; Anton's pursuit of me; Rafe and Monique's crazy role-playing games; Laurie Granger and Daile sideswiped before they knew what hit them. Now, after hearing my mother's account of meeting Anton, I was convinced he had been searching me out for most of my life. Rafe and Monique, Laurie and Daile—they were the self-deluded victims of a chimera. It was Anton who knew the truth about me—and Miles.

Inge and I walked back to the hotel, the air crisp and autumnal, the moon almost full. Using her key card, Inge let us into the room, her lips rounded into that careful, oh-so-familiar, "Ssh." My father had fallen asleep on his side of the bed, his feet crossed at the ankles.

"We should get you a room for the night," she whispered. "That or a cot for in here."

I smiled. "I'm not five years old," I said with a laugh. "It's a kind offer, but I want to go back to the house."

"Not tonight."

"Yes, tonight," I said, thinking of the upstairs room. I had to see Anton one last time.

Inge turned on a wall heater, her hand trembling in the cold. "How long will you be?"

I couldn't bring myself to answer.

Inge nodded and reset the thermostat. I went over to Evan and kissed him on the forehead without waking him.

"Say good-bye for me, okay?"

In reply, Inge fetched my bags, but she didn't hand them over right away. "You're going to that man. To Kaminsky."

"Please, Mamma." I didn't know what else to say. "I can't explain, but I have to do this."

The pain in her eyes told me that as much as she didn't want to agree with me, she understood.

I hugged her. "Remember how you wouldn't let me pick flowers when we were in the field? Or interfere with the animals? You said we had to just observe and record them from a distance."

She nodded again, her head against my shoulder.

"It's time for me to break that rule."

Inge sniffed and gave me my luggage.

"Good-bye, Moder," I said. I held her close one more time. "Good-bye, Mamma." I felt like I was being crushed by weights of grief and doubt combined, but I had to go. The pull to find my identity and why it involved Miles was greater than I could resist. Inge sensed it too.

She brushed my hair from my face and kissed me. "You are my daughter. Raising you was my life. It still is."

I stayed in her embrace until she said, "Go before it's too late." Both of us crying, I started for the elevator while she watched from the open door. Behind her I could hear my father turning over in his sleep. Just as I pushed the "down" button I thought of something.

"Mamma," I said, running back.

"Always."

"Did I have a name when you found me?"

She didn't hesitate. "Surya. Your name was Surya. We changed it to 'Sara' so Kaminsky wouldn't—"

"It's okay. I understand. Thank you for telling me." I gave her a last kiss on her forehead, and then hurried back to the elevator where the doors were just creaking open. Surya, I thought. Sunlight.

I stepped out of the elevator and into the hotel lobby when another thought occurred to me. I approached the night clerk.

"Do you have a padded mailer?" I asked. I held my hands apart to show him the size I needed.

The clerk reached under the desk and brought out a self-sealing envelope. "Will this do?"

"Just what I wanted. Thanks." I put the mailer inside my luggage. As I did so, I removed a cardigan from my bag before I began the long walk home. It was cold out there.

A few streets later, cocooned in the sweater's warmth, I stopped on the corner across from the Claiburne villa. A single light shone from an upstairs window: Courtenay's room. I saw her come to the window, pull her curtains aside, and look out across the deserted square. She didn't see me, and I didn't know whether to call out or draw attention to myself in some way. Had she been on Ismene? A part of me thought not, but I could see even from where I hid in the shelter of the neighboring houses that she had cut her hair. I hoped it wasn't for Anton. I hoped it wasn't for me. I hoped I could find some answers.

## 33

I let myself in through the broken back window for the second time that day, wondering if I had told my mother the truth: Was the house too much for me? Now that I was about to leave, I was in two minds.

I carried the padded mailer to my dining table. Using a felt tip marker, I addressed it to Benita Hansard. Her books were where I had left them in my bedroom and I fitted them inside the mailer. I then added Noreen's journal pages, along with the letter from Miles, Twitty's manuscript, and Daile's Eiffel Tower scarf. I thought of including the bottle of ether, but then changed my mind; the ether could be a necessary key to help me find Anton. In its place I scribbled a note describing the enclosed items as "evidence" and sealed it with packing tape. I took the Euros from my purse, wrote out another note explaining they were for postage, and set everything in the middle of the table. There was nothing more I could do; it was time to go upstairs.

My heart beat so loudly I couldn't think straight. Be calm, I told myself, taking each step one by one. Soon this would be nothing more than the memory of a "dream within a dream" as I had once heard a teacher at St. Anne's read from Poe.

I paused on the landing and remembered that same teacher telling us to look at our feet whenever we found ourselves lost for inspiration in the art room, the paint dripping aimlessly from our brushes. At the time we had laughed at her, Noreen in particular, her skills as a mimic never greater. But the trick had always worked for me. I looked at my shoes, the sandals I had bought the summer before meeting Miles. *Before meeting Miles.* Had there ever been such a time? If there had been, I no longer wanted to remember it.

The sandals made me wonder if there was anything else I should take with me. Besides the ether in my hand, all I had was what I stood in: my jewelry, light blue skirt and top, cardigan, sandals. Too summery for the beginning of autumn, perhaps, but I had clothing at Anton's, clothes that could never match anything from my own closet.

I climbed the final set of stairs that led to the attic. The door stood ajar from my last visit. I had no guarantee this would even work. What if I couldn't reach Anton? And if I did manage to return, would he welcome me back? Would Miles understand why I had to go against his request: "Stay away from Kaminsky"?

I chewed my lip, nervous energy fueling me as I recalled the regrets, doubts, and anger of these past months. I thought of ancestral Chinese women with their tightly bound feet, or the blindfolded courtesans in the shuttered rooms of Spanish grandees. Cretonne dresses stretched over wire frames clinching them in at the waist. The dark, silent fall of a velvet veil over my face. The Unushka and their bartered stores of Scythian gold.

Memories? Or my overactive imagination at work? Whatever they were, I knew the only place they belonged was in Anton's covert and enticing world, and with any luck they would hopefully lead me to Miles. I pushed open the door and entered the room, the bottle of ether warming in my hand.

Let me go back, I breathed; make this work. Ad hoc promises with God and the universe played across my mind like the credits at the end of a film I was impatient to leave: I'd never drink again; never sleep late; I'd be nice to my creepy neighbor.

The divan was gone.

In its place, set into the wall, was another door. So simple. The ether dropped from my hand and rolled across the floor. Its clatter was the last thing I heard as I crossed the threshold.

*The wild swans flew overhead, their wings slicing through the sky like fan blades, the kind in those cafés from my childhood: whirr, whirr, whirr. I spread out upon the grass inside the labyrinth, remembering the child I had once been, listening to that noise, sipping ice water through a paper straw, my parents discussing their day's work, or resting in silence, content with their private thoughts. Such a long time ago.*

I gazed into the sky to watch the birds, the turbulent parts of my heart reaching for them as they flew toward another day. The solitary swan had been joined by a new flock. They circled above the trees, their long necks articulating their resolution to reach home, wherever that was. I thought they were majestic, and watching them I was in awe of every experience life had given me. Unabridged and mine alone, it *was* a life worth remembering.

# 34

Anton was in the library. He took one look at the contrast between my disheveled appearance and the gold armbands, and then carefully shut the book he was reading. "Jeanne-Marie will help you change into something more suitable," he said.

"There isn't time." He lifted an eyebrow but said nothing. "I want to know about my mother," I said. "My birth mother. After that you can tell me about Miles. And Noreen. Oh, and Twitty. How on earth did you get involved with her?"

Anton spoke without expression: "She's a writer."

"What's that got to do with anything?"

"It gave her the ambition to follow Noreen and to find me."

"Twitty was here?" I looked around, expecting to find an angora twin set lying on a chair.

"Miss Lansbury and I met in town. She favored lunch at the Carlton. Eggs Benedict."

I took a ragged breath and realized it was me, not the floor, shaking. "Maybe I don't really want to know about Twitty," I said. "But what I'm beginning to understand is that you're the center of the labyrinth. Everything leads back to you. Miles searching for the Unushka. You searching for my mother—my real mother. You may even be the reason she died."

From the way he drew his brows together I knew my words had struck a chord. He went to a tall cabinet where he retrieved a bound portfolio similar to those he used for his prime etchings and prints.

"Sit down," he said, laying the portfolio on his desk and opening it. "I cannot promise this is what you are looking for, but it may be of some assistance."

Inside was another casing, a white damask sleeve he untied and opened to reveal an enameled portrait of a girl in peach and crimson robes, her black hair wreathed around the comb Hypatia's mother had given me. Anton rotated the portrait so that I could see it better.

"Who is she?" I asked, knowing the answer.

"Someone who did a good job of keeping you away from me." He flicked away a speck of dust. "I have never blamed her."

I pored over her face and clothing. It was difficult for me to associate the dignity and nobility of her profile captured there in lacquer and porcelain with my own broken nails, unkempt hair, and baggy sweater. I looked at her hands; they fondled the hilt of a delicate dagger she wore curved against a pearl-encrusted sash. When I looked more closely I could pick out the pattern embossed on the sheath: a panther ready to spring in a downward dive.

"It was the symbol of her clan," Anton said. I lifted my eyes. "And yes," he answered although I did not ask; "she preferred to fall on her dagger rather than spend her life with me." His voice grew cold. "My great misfortune is that I confused the myth with the reality, leaving me with only a fraction of the power, and none of her understanding or wisdom."

"And my father?"

Anton shook his head. "Whoever he was, he, too, she kept secret." He reached for the portrait and gently flipped it over. Tucked into the frame was a folded piece of thin parchment, so worn along the creases it had nearly cracked apart. He removed it from the frame.

"I don't know when it was written," he said. "But later, when I returned to the village where it was reported the woman and her child had last been seen, it was left on her grave."

He gave me the page, the sides crimped and rounding as if it still held the body of the animal whose skin it once had been. Cautiously, I flattened it against the desk, the columns of arcane glyphs reminding me of Evan's pastime of painting on reindeer skins. When I had the sheet spread to its full size, another document fell from the center, this one on fine paper and handwritten in English, the bold script sloping across the page.

"It took years to translate," Anton said. "The language of the original is unique, I believe, combining so many elements that it is a virtual Babel of incomprehension. Hebrew, Arabic, Sanskrit, Sumerian, Greek, and a cipher of her own invention. It's a map of contradictions. A riddle. Just as she was herself."

He went to the windows and leaned into the night. "Read it, and when you are finished you will know where to find me." Soundlessly, he walked from the room.

*Dearest Child,*

*Our domain is finished. We are relics, fossils from a bygone age that once believed we mattered, that once believed we could, indeed, rule the world. You've known this from the day you were born. And afterwards, from the time you could crawl the polished floors, running your small hands along pine grooves and oak tongues, speaking a language of dust and footprints, sitting in the dark and hush of history, you knew your current existence—our way of life—was coming to an end.*

*You were born to a father lost in the clang of swords and breastplates and helmets; helmets with hawks' and foxes' tails, herons' claws; so many helmets and warriors marching side by side. Your father left us for the empty halls of war and pageantry, our lives tied with strings of diplomacy and the intrigue of one thousand nights at court.*

*It began with a memory. You were not two years old, but already you recognized the white powdered faces of the painted Unushka, their legacy of sun and moon.*

*No one saw you remembering. They thought you were only sitting on the floor, unable to walk. In reality, you were unable to speak. There was nothing in your vocabulary to express what it was to be born into the Unushka, a forbidden child in a forbidden time to a forbidden people. Forgive me, and may you live as I cannot. May you live.*

"Anton." I met him walking to the center of the labyrinth, the sun shining into his face. In his arms he carried the silver glass globe, the "mortgage ball," close to his chest. Miniature clouds soared across its surface and I realized it wasn't glass at all; it was a giant ball of mercury. I looked at his hands as they worked to steady the thing; I was certain they had aged in the time since I had read my mother's final statement to me. Night had become day, and Anton had changed in the same way I saw the boxwood hedges had aged and toppled over to expose great swathes of rotted wood and blighted boughs. It was as if some accelerated process of decay had struck while I had been reading my mother's words. Had they contained a spell or incantation of some kind? The document had answered none of my questions; I was no closer to knowing who I was or where I had come from than I had been while staying on Ismene, or in my parents' hotel room.

Anton held the wobbling sphere in both his hands. "Shall I throw it down, Surya? Throw it and break it like the ogre she claimed I am?"

I hated to see the ball reflect and mock Anton's carefully constructed world like something in a funhouse. In one section of a curve I could see myself, a tiny doll-like image trapped in a mirrored universe repeating itself endlessly.

"I read the parchment," I said. "Or I should say I read your translation. And I want the rest of the story. I want you tell me about Miles." The sphere held me fixed in place. What would happen if Anton did toss it down?

Anton spun the sphere in his hands and I backed away in fear. Miles had wanted me to live. My mother had wanted me to live. I had to take that desire and turn it into something meaningful, something worthy of both of them. "I want the end of the story," I said again.

Still holding onto the globe, Anton walked nearer to the center of the labyrinth. He contemplated the moving surface, and then set the ball down upon the grass. Miraculously, it stayed together.

"You, Surya," Anton said. "You are the end of the story." He patted his pockets in search of a cigar or a cigarette. His hands came away empty. He seemed agitated, and without his usual air of confidence.

I sat on the grass next to the quivering mortgage ball. "A story needs a hero," I said. "The heroine can't rescue herself."

"You had Miles."

"Not for long." I pulled at the grass. "Is he real?"

"Oh, he's real. His upbringing may be somewhat atypical: an abandoned orphan first raised by affluent, upper class parents, a series of nannies before he went to a snobbish prep school. His 'Aunt Winifred,' the woman who took him in when his parents were killed, was in actuality his mother's aunt."

As intriguing as I found this information, it wasn't what I was looking for. I pretty much knew the story, having heard it from both Aunt Winifred and Laurie Granger. Anton sensed my impatience. He switched his narrative to a description of his first meeting with Miles.

"I was on my way to Yemen, a routine search for antiquities," he said. "On the way out, my plane was diverted to Ethiopia. The stopover was to be for twelve hours, and I went to the bar to wait it out. There was another man on the plane, and he joined me for a drink. We spoke, as one tends to do, and drank yet more. When he mentioned oil exploration, the profession fit; he impressed me as a man to be counted on in a crisis. I gave him my card. I told him that if he wanted a change in employment to contact me through my agent in Paris. One never knows what new leads can come about through chance, and I had worked too long alone. I needed, I thought, a confidant. A friend."

Anton stared into the distance, his hands hanging loosely by his sides. He is old, I thought. He is an old man. Why did I never see this before?

He spoke again: "Months later we were both, quite by accident, in the same part of Asia, close to the Gobi. When I heard of the coincidence, I took the liberty of inviting Miles Bergsen to dinner.

"I believe he was as much taken by the invitation as he was by the locale. I had arranged for a tent to be erected in the desert and Miles to be my only guest. It was then, over a roasting lamb carcass that I had the idea of telling Miles Bergsen about the lost child I had seen in Kamchatka, and how I believed she was someone special, from another world, another race, and the last of her extraordinary kind.

"At first he thought that I was drunk, that the facts of the case had been grossly exaggerated. But when I alluded to the adventure and the salary I would pay him for his assistance in the matter of locating her, he agreed to the arrangement.

"I often ask why he consented to my plan so easily. It has occurred to me that his own early losses made him sympathetic to the plight of another orphaned child. Then again, he may have simply wanted her—a woman—for himself." As he spoke, I felt his gaze upon me. I looked away, anywhere but his eyes.

"Whatever the reason," Anton said, "Miles Bergsen and I worked well together. As I grew to respect and trust him, I told him much of what you know from having lived on the estate yourself. About how I came to live with a magical beast and how through my misadventures as a young man time has stopped for me. I told him how the estate is a place where dimensions intersect, as if events and lives can overlap and reform into ever new contingencies. And I told him how it was a woman who had provided me with this strange world of mine.

"As before, he had trouble believing me. That is, until Shanghai and the story of the powdered Unushka. I had never used that term myself, but once it was spoken aloud, everything changed and Miles submitted to the search with a passion that surpassed my own." He stopped, exhausted by the flow of words. With an effort he said, "The search grew in scope until it drove us asunder, sworn enemies to the death. If only such a thing could come to me." He picked up the mercury again, frightening me.

"Don't, Anton. Please, just leave it."

"I'm sorry, Surya. It's the only way." He tossed the ball into the air where it traveled higher and higher and then stalled, as if deciding whether to continue flying, or to return to earth, when suddenly it came crashing back down to the ground with what sounded like a terrible scream, splintering into a million mirrored raindrops upon the smooth white stones.

I don't know what I'd expected after that; for the hedges to catch fire, or the trees to bend and break in a mindless hurricane of the worst misfortune. For a minute I thought we were safe, that the ball was no more than a garden folly, the trophy of a dilettante. But when the high keening whistle broke through the sky, scattering the birds and sending a crash of rain, neither of us laughed.

*Miles watched his former friend leave the monastery, and thought of everything they had gone through together: birch bark and ice, sand and dust, faith and doubt, one dead end after the other. He knew why Anton was deserting him: for Sara, for the vanquished Unushka, for a chance to regain the power he had lost.*

*He tried to walk. Sea birds shrieked as they wheeled overhead, forcing his ears and eyes to an unwanted attention. If only he could see Sara again, see her and explain what he had given for her sake.*

*The memory of Anton's face was gone; he could no longer feel the cold. Forgiveness meant nothing by now. He could not forgive himself for losing her, so why ask it from others? The surf hit the shore. He thought of her voice, her laughter, her trust in him. If she was to be saved from Kaminsky, he had to live one more day. Just one.*

The groans cracking and thundering from the mansion signaled the start of what I knew were its death throes. When I turned to call for Anton, he had already gone, his bones fired to ash and ferried by the wind before being pummeled and dispersed by the rain.

The wind gathered speed as I tore my way through the ruined hedges. I could hear the glasshouses crashing in upon themselves, the sound of sheet after broken sheet of glass howling over everything else. Across the treetops I saw the flames from their ruins rise into the sky, too dense to be doused by the rain. I ran out from the labyrinth onto the sodden, muddy lawns.

"Jeanne-Marie!" I shouted over the wind. "Grégoire!"

From where I stood I watched in horror as a portion of the mansion's roof caved in; what was left of the structure a blazing mass of orange and scarlet. I thought of my beautiful clothing burning along with the manuscripts, the paintings, the tapestries and the jewels.

Up ahead, through the trees: black fur. Dripping rain and mud, the panther waited for me, eyes pointing to the river.

Blocks from the mangled structures shot into the sky, fiery missiles falling back upon the debris and scorched gardens. Again and again they clashed with the noise of the rain, the blast of yet more bricks propelled into the night, the destruction of century after century collapsing around me. I thought I would never survive this final testing ground.

By the time I reached the panther's side, my feet slipping in the mire, my nerves frayed beyond feeling, I knew it was too late to save anything. The walls bursting apart sent me to my knees as the swollen river rushed past us, the water rising over the banks.

The panther nudged me with its head, insisting, demanding, until I had the courage to look up through the rain and across to the other side of the water. There, in his sealskins and bloodied pelts, was my husband. Miles had kept his word. He was, as Anton had said, my hero.

# Epilogue

*The man, the hawk, and the panther. A Roman road; fertile dust. The heat of the sun, the smell of crushed thyme, pressed sage. The hawk weighs down the man's arm; the panther glides by his side.*

*I am greeted by all three. My dress is a sheer slip of fabric; my skin is a rich bronze. My hair is much longer, fuller, it curls past my shoulders. On my arms are the golden armbands, in my hair the matching comb. My rings are made of moonlight; I have new earrings and anklets that glisten in the sun.*

*The panther lies at my feet; the man presents me with the hawk, his gift to me.*

*"Miles," I whisper, when he kisses me.*

*The hawk rustles, preens, its eyes turned to the sky.*

*The panther is languid as we sink to the ground. My dress is so thin against the hard leather breastplates, the leather kilt. I am in his arms. I am the sun, the moon; my jewelry is made from their light.*

*The man touches my neck, my lips, and the hawk rises into the sky. We lean into the dark side of the panther, crushing the sage and juniper, the rocks beneath our legs. I welcome the sharpness of the stones, a reminder of what we have endured to be together.*

*The sky broods, the eclipse approaches. A boat, he tells me, is waiting. I fit myself more securely into his arms. We are going, Miles says as the light leaves the sky, we are going to Kamchatka. We are going home. All I need to do is believe.*

*Of course I believe him.*

*I've always believed in fairy tales. I've always believed in love.*

# About the Author

Valerie Storey is the author of eight books including *Better Than Perfect,* a young adult novel set in New Zealand, and *The Great Scarab Scam,* an Egyptian mystery for young readers. Her how-to book, *The Essential Guide for New Writers, From Idea to Finished Manuscript* is based on her series of writers' workshops. When she isn't writing, Valerie enjoys working with hand-built pottery as well as collage, drawing, and watercolors. Valerie currently lives in the Southwestern United States and has also lived in both New Zealand and England.

For more information about Valerie Storey and her other books, please visit www.valeriestorey.com.